DELIVERING DEATH

DELIVERING DEATH

A NOVEL

JULIE KRAMER

EMILY BESTLER BOOKS
—
ATRIA

New York   London   Toronto   Sydney   New Delhi

ATRIA PAPERBACK
An Imprint of Simon & Schuster, Inc.
1230 Avenue of the Americas
New York, NY 10020

First Emily Bestler Books /Atria Paperback edition September 2016

EMILY BESTLER BOOKS / ATRIA PAPERBACK and colophons are trademarks of Simon & Schuster, Inc.

For information about special discounts for bulk purchases, please contact Simon & Schuster Special Sales at 1-866-506-1949 or business@simonandschuster.com.

The Simon & Schuster Speakers Bureau can bring authors to your live event. For more information, or to book an event, contact the Simon & Schuster Speakers Bureau at 1-866-248-3049 or visit our website at www.simonspeakers.com.

ISBN 978-1-4516-6466-9
ISBN 978-1-5011-5510-9 (pbk)
ISBN 978-1-4516-6468-3 (ebook)

To Alex and Andrew, who make me proud

DELIVERING DEATH

CHAPTER 1

A guard checked a number against the ID bracelet on the man's wrist while marking his name off a clipboard as he stood in line.

Another chained the man's cuffs to his waist and shackled his feet together, so he had to shuffle to board the prison bus behind other stumbling inmates in orange jumpsuits. He heard some snickering among the jailers about something called "diesel therapy." The term puzzled him, but amid the scuffling and stern faces, he had no time or nerve for questions.

His answer came thousands of miles later via a road trip through highway hell during which he had to constantly remind himself that he was Jack Clemens and he used to be rich.

After the first day, he had learned not to eat the baloney sandwiches offered for lunch. Not only did they taste like shit, but bathroom breaks were stretched hundreds of miles apart and by the time the bus finally stopped for gas, he'd soiled his pants.

"Idiot. Asshole." The guy in the next seat swore at him, looking as tough as his talk with cornrows, tattoos, and scars.

"Sorry." Those who knew him on the outside would have been surprised by such a quick apology. Atonement had never come as naturally to him as blaming others. During his court sentencing, Jack had been given a chance to speak, but instead of expressing regret for his crimes—as his attorney had urged—he insisted that he'd been unfairly persecuted. All that blather did was piss off the judge and land him ten years in the slammer.

Now, seven hours into this excursion, the entire bus reeked.

This wasn't the deal Inmate 16780-59 had envisioned. After all, he wasn't a violent felon. Or a repeat offender. Maybe some of the outlaws on the bus deserved transport torture, but not him. Sure, he had tried to game the penal system and that arrogance had cost him his comfy bunk at a country club prison camp in northern Minnesota . . . but what did they expect? He was a white-collar criminal.

Until his crime made headlines, his wealth wasn't the kind that made Jack Clemens a household name. He didn't own a professional sports team, or appear in television commercials, or invent a product that changed the world. He simply moved money around various financial accounts, and thus could walk down the streets of Minneapolis without being recognized. With brown hair and blue eyes, medium height and weight, this middle-aged man was average in every way but income.

That night, after six hundred miles crammed in narrow plastic seats with stiffening legs and sore arms, the chained gang left the bus to be housed at another prison overnight. The inmates were given fresh uniforms and a chance to shower. But he was afraid of the showers and cleaned himself with water from the toilet.

He had no idea where he was, where he was going, or when the journey would end. He'd stopped trying to calculate what direction they were headed in, knowing only that he didn't belong on this bus with these animals. The guards ignored him when he tried explaining that a mistake had been made. He waited for the attorney to fix things, but days turned into nights and the wheels on the bus kept rolling.

CHAPTER 2

From the postmark date, I could tell that the letter had probably been sitting in my newsroom mail slot for a couple days. Unopened.

Most of the correspondence I care about comes by email or text. My paychecks are direct deposit. My bills are electronic. Checking snail mail isn't a high priority for me—even at work.

The first thing that caught my attention about the manila envelope was the lack of a return address. Sometimes sources send letters to journalists without wanting the contents traced back to them. They get deniability and anonymity: I get a scoop. I reveled in the possibilities for its contents as I carried the letter back to my office and shut the door.

The second thing I noticed was the package's bumpy texture. It made me suspect Bubble Wrap might be shielding something fragile—something important. Maybe a compact disc or thumb drive with valuable computer files. The prospect of ratings gold made me smile and take care opening the envelope.

The third oddity hit me as I immediately smelled a foul odor when I opened the envelope. Reluctantly, I looked inside.

Someone had mailed me a bunch of teeth.

The blood was dried; the stench fresh. Some of the roots were long and pointed. Some twisted. Others broken and jagged. I quickly shut the flap but the stink and the sight stayed with me.

I'm Riley Spartz, an investigative reporter for Channel 3 in Minneapolis. Why anyone would send me such a ghoulish package was a mystery within a mystery. More important: Were the teeth animal or human?

CHAPTER 3

I stood at the waiting-room counter while the receptionist double-checked her computer screen before insisting that I did *not* have an appointment. "Although I left you several messages over the last two months about coming in for a cleaning," she snapped, sounding disapproving of both my dental hygiene and manners.

I mumbled something about being busy lately, then explained again, "I'd like to see Dr. Mendes anyway, on a professional matter."

"He's with a patient."

I offered to wait. "It will only take a minute. I have to show him something."

I texted Malik to bring his camera inside. He used the time we lingered in my dentist's office to complain about having to shoot the teeth. Malik fancied himself an artist as well as a news photographer and to him, the fangs seemed more crass than creative. At this point, without any obvious news value, he would have rather been assigned to shoot weather video of interesting clouds over urban sprawl.

I had gotten his initial cooperation by reminding him that vampires were hot these days and perhaps the teeth might lead to a story about real-life urban bloodsuckers, which might lead to a movie deal. It was quite a stretch, I had to admit, but the pitch hooked him. Still, he remained grouchy.

"This may not be as bad as the time I had to video that puppy mill," he said, "but it ranks right up there."

"We need to document each step." I tried to hush him by motioning toward a patient sitting on the other side of the room. She was pretending to read a magazine, but I could tell our conversation, and the Channel 3 camera on the floor, interested her more than diet tips or fashion advice.

I wasn't about to confess that I carried a purse full of extracted teeth, but did confirm that, yes, she might have seen me on the news, when Dr. Charles Mendes stuck his head through the door.

"Riley Spartz. About time you showed up. You're overdue." He waved me in, and I whispered for Malik to wait behind for a few minutes to give me time to land the interview.

Dr. Mendes directed me toward the chair in one of the exam rooms. Obediently I sat down and he leaned it backward. "Open wide." He flipped an overhead light. "Now what is it you want to show me?"

"Not my mouth." I pulled out the envelope from my black bag. "This."

The smell didn't seem to unnerve him when he peeked inside. He gave an appreciative whistle and raised an eyebrow. "Where did you get all these?" He pushed the dental instruments to one side and dumped the teeth out over a piece of paper on the tray. Under this light, and up close, I could see that the roots looked more yellow than the crown. Two-tone teeth.

"Are they human?" I asked.

He used a sharp probe to roll them around. "Most definitely." He pointed out several fillings. "But I see that you still have your pearly whites intact, so who are these from? The tooth fairy?"

I explained all I knew, which wasn't much. "I was hoping you might be able to give me some clues."

"Well, I can tell you that these are not senior citizen teeth. They did not fall out from natural causes. They put up a fight."

Dr. Mendes put on plastic gloves to examine the teeth and estimated the age of the owner to be between twenty and thirty years old. Then he indicated scratch marks on the enamel where they had been gripped prior to being yanked. "I would also venture this person was a smoker." He noted places where one tooth had a silver filling and another had signs of early decay. "But certainly not to the degree they needed to be removed."

"Male or female?" I asked.

"That, I can't tell you. You'd need a forensic dentist to determine the subject's sex. But DNA can be found in tooth pulp tissue, and that should reveal the answer."

He looked inside the envelope once again and counted the teeth out loud until he reached the number twenty-seven. "Are you sure that's all? We seem to be missing a few."

"What do you mean?"

"The human mouth has thirty-two adult teeth. You are short five. Of course, some might have been removed earlier for cosmetic or dental purposes."

By then Malik was standing in the hallway, holding his camera and listening to the details unfold about molars, incisors, and bicuspids. He seemed more interested in the assignment upon learning that every tooth has a story. Especially the rotten ones.

"Would you mind talking about this on camera, Dr. Mendes?" I asked. "Just in case I end up needing it? I'm not sure where I'm going with this."

"Maybe you should go to the police," he said. "I can't think of any good reason why these teeth shouldn't still be in someone's mouth instead of the mail."

I had been wondering the same thing ever since he declared the teeth *human*. But journalists like covering news, not making it. And I could imagine the headlines after some cop leaked my report to the other media. The newspapers would have fun playing with lines about me sinking my teeth into the investigation, taking a bite out of crime, and of course, my own big mouth.

"I need to discuss my next move with my boss first, but in the meantime, how about that interview?"

"Certainly, Riley." My dentist glanced down at a file folder, apparently containing my dental chart. "As long as you make an appointment to come in next week for a cleaning and bite wing X-rays. You're overdue."

Dr. Mendes packed up the teeth after our interview, handing over the envelope and giving Malik and me each a new toothbrush and floss. On the way out, I observed the woman from the waiting room leaning back in a chair in another examination room with a dental hygienist looming over her mouth. Still, she noticed us leaving and interrupted her polishing procedure to ask what day this story would be on TV.

CHAPTER 4

Technically, I'd done my dental research over lunch. That's where I had told Ozzie, the assignment editor, Malik and I were going, and I even bought him a Reuben sandwich to go at Cecil's Deli on the way back to the station to keep our story straight.

Minneapolis–St. Paul is the fifteenth-largest television market in the United States. More people watch local news here than almost anywhere else in the country, which leads to intense competition between stations. Channel 3 was typically battling for the number two spot against Channel 8, having seemingly given up the fight for number one.

Commotion was coming from inside the production studio. When I ducked my head inside, I saw a crowd of my colleagues assembled around news director, Bryce Griffin.

The room was the size of a school gymnasium, formerly used for filming television commercials for automobiles or vacation getaways. I waited in the back. Bryce and the general manager had just commanded the staff to join in a noisy team-building countdown: ten . . . nine . . . eight . . . the chant grew until reaching the apparently magic number of three.

"That's right," Bryce shouted. "Let's hear it for Channel 3!"

Amid some lackluster applause, a spatter of blue confetti fell from the ceiling like an underfunded political rally or overproduced prom. I didn't know how to react to the scene and apparently neither did the other employees. So we remained quiet, rather than risk saying the wrong thing and being admonished for not being team players.

"In these difficult economic times," Bryce said, "television stations need to move forward. To stay static is to stay behind. So, in the name of progress, Channel 3 is getting a new studio set."

He pointed to his boss, the general manager, who dramatically yanked a piece of cloth from an easel, unveiling a framed sketch that resembled something from a science-fiction movie, perhaps the deck of a spaceship.

"This is the future of Channel 3," the GM said. "This is what the viewers will see when they tune in to watch our talent bring them the news."

"Are there any questions?" Bryce asked.

I had plenty of questions, like why not put money into covering actual stories or hiring more street reporters rather than a superficial gesture like changing the look of the anchors' desk and chairs? Our travel budget had been slashed. Overtime was virtually nil. Yet news executives always seem to feel cosmetic changes like a revamped set or flashy on-air jackets with station logos will create buzz and attract viewers.

But I stayed silent because Bryce and I were going through a phase where we weren't speaking to each other.

The new boss didn't like me. I didn't like him. We each had ample reason to distrust the other. I considered him a lecher and he regarded me as an extortionist. We each had valid reasons for our opinions.

True, I had played a role in blackmailing him. Shortly after arriving on the job, Bryce had used his power, private office, and lewd texts to sexually harass Nicole Wilson, a rookie reporter. I'd taught her the mechanics of hidden cameras to document his misbehavior. While I had urged her to go public with a lawsuit, Nicole had worried that exposing Bryce exposing himself might mean the end of her TV news career if she were branded a troublemaker. She decided to handle the situation more discreetly, and put him on notice that we were watching—in effect, putting our boss on probationary status.

Rather than blame himself for the tawdry situation, Bryce blamed me. So we confined our conversations to the news huddle, where the day's story coverage was discussed and debated among managers and staff. As some point, our feud would have to end, but for now, I figured I could outlast this young hotshot. The average tenure for a television news director is only eighteen months, and he'd already been here four.

The producer for the late news—our showcase newscast—broke the dead air to ask a critical question about when the new set would be completed. "Will it ready be in time for the February sweeps?"

"That's when we'll debut it," Bryce replied. "But we'll promote it ahead of time to build suspense."

The station had recently hired a new anchor, Scott Ramus, and he beamed enthusiastically at the announcement. "I just want to say how thrilled I am to be the first anchor who'll deliver the news from the new set, and how proud I am to be part of the Channel 3 family."

I understood his eagerness. After all, much of his workday would be spent sitting there, on his throne, smiling into the camera while his subjects watched from their living rooms. But personal experience told me that no TV ratings month was ever won on the back of a new set. Anchor desks did not build viewer loyalty. Viewers might click in once to see what all the fuss was about, but exclusive stories and great reporting are what keeps them from switching channels. Not fancy chairs or slick big-screen wall designs, but news content they can't get anywhere else.

That's my job. Stories that make a difference.

As Bryce was praising Scott and explaining some of the logistics of the new set, I kept my mouth shut and my head down as I slipped out the door to the newsroom. The area was empty except for Ozzie, still manning the assignment desk in case a big story broke. He was engaged in an animated conversation on the telephone with an irate viewer, upset that the snow we'd forecasted hadn't materialized.

He held the phone up toward me so I could hear the yelling on the other end. "First, your station botched Christmas, and now your meteorologist ruined our ski vacation!" I tuned them out, as Ozzie encouraged the caller to "take it up with Mother Nature." I was thankful that he handled most of the cranks.

Then I remembered I still had the tainted teeth. Rather than taking a risk and showing them off to the entire newsroom, I decided to bring the envelope upstairs to Channel 3's attorney and get his advice.

Pulling the package from my purse, I shook the envelope. "You have the right to remain silent." Even though I knew it was childish, I teased the teeth in a dramatic cop-actor voice. "Anything you say can and will be held against you." Just then, I turned around a blind hallway corner and crashed into Bryce.

"I'll talk if I want to talk," he said, "because I'm the boss. Your job description includes listening to me, following orders, and not threatening me to keep silent. That's a slam dunk for insubordination."

I tried explaining that I wasn't actually speaking to him, but he gestured around the empty hallway. "Then who?"

"These." I gestured to the envelope, and tried to keep my tone neutral. "I was looking for you, Bryce. I have something to show you."

He seemed suspicious, then curious, then excited. Bryce had an expressive face that made it easy to discern his emotional state. "Will we be able to air them if we blur body parts or add black boxes?" I realized he was hoping the envelope contained compromising photos of a state politician or some other local celebrity.

I was frustrated that our first face-to-face conversation in weeks had turned to smut within thirty seconds. "No, it's nothing like that." Not wanting to be alone with him in the dim corridor, I suggested we move to his office. The glass windows of his headquarters looked out on the rest of the newsroom, so I felt comfortable in knowing that witnesses could observe our meeting, but not hear our actual words. The transparent/no-walls look was part of the terms Nicole and I had settled with Bryce.

Once the door was shut, I dumped the teeth on the center of his desk calendar. The stench caught him off guard and he glared at me before wheeling his leather chair backward to escape a pearly white ricochetting toward him.

"They're teeth."

Forgetting they might be evidence, I quickly reached out the palm of my hand to block the enamel runaway from falling off the desk. The roots didn't freak me out so much anymore now that my dentist had explained that they'd had a mysterious life, cut short. I had empathy for their demise, besides curiosity, and wanted to tell their story.

"Oh. Just teeth?" That seemed to calm my boss, but he couldn't hide the disappointment in his tone.

"Not *just* teeth. *Human* teeth."

"Why do *you* have human teeth?"

I rolled my eyes. "No matter what you'd like to think, Bryce, I'm not a news robot. I am human."

"You know what I mean, Riley. We're not talking about your on-air smile, although you might consider some whitening work right here." He tapped his finger against his front teeth, but I ignored the put-down, figuring it was his way of trying to remind me who was in charge.

"So where did you get these?" he asked.

"Someone mailed them to me here at the station. Anonymously."

I pushed the envelope toward him. The postmark was from

across the Mississippi River in St. Paul. My name—RILEY SPARTZ—was carefully penciled in block letters.

He wrinkled his nose, but began to perk up. The smell of a ratings spike overrode the odor of decay. I knew the scent of money was also on his mind because Bryce held a degree in business rather than journalism and appreciated stories that were cheap to produce. Under his watch, decreased costs were just as good as increased ratings. No worries about that here. These teeth were definitely past the point of needing root canals or other pricey dental treatments.

Boldly, Bryce reached for a tooth, but I slapped his hand back. "No touching."

"Fine," he said. "But what do you think? Are they a threat, or a tip? What's their message?"

"Sorry, boss. They're not talking."

But if they could, they might have warned us of what lay ahead. Then I would have thrown them in the trash instead of going to the police—story be damned.

CHAPTER 5

Inmate 16780-59 had been settled far from home in a tougher penitentiary in New Jersey, where the name Jack Clemens impressed nobody. With a double razor-wire fence patrolled by armed guards, this was no Camp Cupcake. For the first time since high school, he would have traded brains for muscles, and charm for a scary tattoo.

During intake, he was finally allowed to call his attorney, who warned him that their telephone conversation might be monitored.

"You got to get me out of here." He tried to make his words sound more like a command than a plea, like the Jack Clemens whom everybody used to take orders from. But no luck: his voice cracked and came across as thin and nervous.

"Nothing I can do, Jack," his lawyer said. "You belong to the Bureau of Prisons now. You messed with BOP and now they're messing with you."

He'd had the misfortune of being housed in a prison bunk room when a cell phone was discovered, hidden behind a toilet. Cell phones were taboo behind bars because of fears they could be used to intimidate witnesses, run drug gangs, or organize escapes.

He wasn't plotting any of those misdeeds and few people

would have taken his calls, but because the guards couldn't pin the smuggle on anyone, they blamed everyone. But then a search of his bed revealed a cache of pain pills. No doctor's prescription appeared under Jack Clemens's records, so the medicine was considered contraband and confiscated.

The pills, like many bootleg objects in the prison system, were presumed to have come from a corrupt employee or a prisoner with stash to spare. But just as reporters protect their sources, so do inmates. Maybe even more so.

Instead of putting a disciplinary note in Jack Clemens's file and pushing back his release date, the warden put him on the bus—glad to be rid of the scrutiny that comes from housing a high-profile inmate. Since his incarceration, the local news media remained interested in documenting his downfall and his name had become a punch line in Minnesota comedy clubs.

"This is about them teaching you a lesson, Jack," his attorney continued. "I can't change this. I'm sorry."

Those words rattled him. He had expected deliverance from the current dilemma. After all, the same attorney had made a convincing argument that the court should grant him "self-surrender" status, meaning he could remain free on bail while awaiting his incarceration date. Yet a month later, when he was dropped off outside the federal penitentiary in Duluth to be processed into the prison population, his identity formally changed to inmate number 16780-59.

"Remember, Jack, I warned you that the two most important things you could do after you turned yourself in was to be smart and behave. You screwed up and you're on your own."

He figured his banishment had less to do with rule-breaking than with the feds' determination to break him down. He knew better than to raise that theory just then, but he was convinced the whole brutal transfer business was a ruse to make him talk and spill secrets about money . . . and more.

Truth was, he was sitting on a whopper.

The lawyer was blind to that fact. His final remark was to inform his client that their legal relationship was over. So when his connection to the outside ended with a click and a dial tone, Inmate 16780-59 began to seriously sweat.

CHAPTER 6

The as-yet unidentified teeth were now in the hands of Minneapolis Police detective John Delmonico. He was more puzzled than repulsed as he peered at the contents inside my envelope, unlike the others I'd confided in about the grisly delivery. After all, the teeth were tame by most crime-scene standards.

We sat in a conference room down the hall from his office because he didn't like visitors—especially journalists—near his desk. He once mentioned worrying we'd use reporter tricks like reading documents upside down to gain confidential information. His fear was not unfounded; I'd used that technique occasionally to gain exclusives. If you could see it, you could confirm it. If you could confirm it, you could report it. The first media outlet to break any big story won bragging rights—and hopefully, a growing audience of viewers or readers.

From my experience, sources sometimes leave paperwork in plain sight because they want to leak something, but don't want to be held responsible. But whenever gleaning such a lead, I always double-check to make sure my scoop wasn't really a red herring.

Still, I contemplated informing Delmonico that desk spying was passé and had been replaced by hacking email accounts, but he kept our discussion focused on the teeth.

"You got these in the mail?" He went over my story with me again, this time making notes. "Any idea who sent them?"

"No." I pointed to the outside corner of the package, over-loaded with about three bucks' worth of postage. "Too bad about the peel-and-stick stamps. Otherwise we might have gotten the sender's DNA from their saliva."

"I know about forensics. It's my job." He ignored my efforts to be helpful, making it clear that we were not a crime-fighting team like Holmes and Watson.

I was giving a statement; he was taking down my report. I'd interviewed him before, in the field, for news stories and found him to be a by-the-book cop. He might not do me any favors, but neither would he screw me over by giving my teeth tip to media competitors.

Still, his manner seemed off today. No chitchat. No grous-ing about the media. I guessed nameless loose teeth might be enough to make anyone want to protect their own gums by re-maining tight-lipped.

"I didn't know what else to do with them," I said. "My den-tist suggested I bring the teeth here, and my boss agreed that it wasn't really a story until we learned more. If they're simply a means to harass me, we're not sure we want to give the sender any publicity."

"So how many people have actually touched these teeth?" he asked.

I had been dreading this question, and tried to be contrite with my answer. "My dentist was careful to avoid direct con-tact, and I made my boss keep his hands to himself, but there's a chance my handprint might be on one of them."

Delmonico's demeanor didn't change at my mention of the possibility of contaminated evidence, but that might have been what was eating him. Clearly there was trouble he wasn't willing to share.

"The teeth might be nothing," I continued, "but they might be something." And if they were something, I tried extracting a promise that he'd let me know by reminding him that Channel 3 had video of the teeth that we could air at any time. "But we decided to hold off for now until we had better context."

He made me sign a statement affirming my story about how I came into possession of the teeth. "I'll stay in touch," he told me.

"So will I." I knew better than to take him at his word. He was a cop and I was a reporter. Sometimes our goals meshed, but often, not.

"Are you being cynical?" he asked.

I shrugged off his criticism. "That's such an ugly word." As journalists we sometimes claim we're not jaded, but merely critical thinkers in a messed-up world. Other times we use cynicism as a way to keep our emotions in check during harrowing experiences like knocking on the door of a family who has lost a child. "I'm being realistic."

That seemed fair, considering we all have hidden motives on the job and off. I wasn't yet at the point where I knew the purpose of the package wasn't just mailing teeth: it was delivering death.

CHAPTER 7

I called my mom from my cell phone as I walked from the cop shop toward the station via the skyway to avoid the brisk January wind. I'd trained her not to call during newscasts when I might be live on the air, but she sometimes forgot. Reaching out to her when it was convenient gave me leeway to duck her calls when it wasn't.

She immediately tried persuading me to attend my fifteen-year high school class reunion, about a hundred miles south of the station. "It would be a nice way for you to keep in touch with your old friends."

I'd received an email urging me to attend because if enough alums showed up, the bar would give us a free keg. Turnout had been on the decline for previous reunions, so the organizers thought they'd try moving the gathering to winter when farmers—who made up much of the class—weren't so busy.

I'd deleted the invite, but Mom had seen the event mentioned in the *Monitor Review*, my hometown's weekly newspaper. "It says your classmates are even touring the Spam Museum."

"Mom, I've spent a lifetime trying to escape jokes about Spam."

I'd grown up on a family farm in southern Minnesota where Hormel was legendary. My folks and our neighbors all sold cattle and hogs to the Fortune 500 meatpacking company. Funny thing was, I've never actually tasted Spam. We'd butchered our own beef and pork on the farm, so it was cheaper to eat it off the hoof than from a tin.

But without a doubt, Hormel had put money in my family's pockets, so my mom started lecturing me about how canned meat had won World War II for America and our allies. "Without Spam, we might be living under communism."

"I can't hear you, Mom. You're breaking up. Must be all the tall buildings downtown. Sorry."

Then I hit end on my cell phone just as I reached the parking ramp where I'd left my car. I knew Bryce would be preoccupied with the evening newscasts, so I left him a message that the police had custody of the teeth, and that we had no story—yet.

"This may be one of those that takes weeks to chase down evidence and even run forensic tests," I explained.

Chatting with my mom made me think of my childhood priest, Father Mountain, who was currently assigned to a church in St. Paul. I decided to stop by the rectory before heading home for the evening. As he welcomed me, the smell of cinnamon drew my attention to a still warm apple pie on the kitchen counter.

He noted my interest. "Mrs. Houle just made that pie." His parishioners were always dropping off homemade treats to remain in his good graces. He demonstrated his generosity by serving me a hefty slice oozing with apples.

"This must be the best part of being a priest," I said. "Warm pie on a chilly day."

"No." He shook his head. "The best part is saving souls."

"When are you going to save mine?" I asked, digging in.

"Only you know that answer, Riley. You can't be saved until you want to be saved."

I regretted teasing him about his calling. Eternal salvation was not a discussion I wanted to have just then, so instead, I told him about my incognito package. "At least people don't send you creepy things in the mail, Father."

"Instead, they tell me creepy things in person and I hold their guilty secrets forever in my heart."

That was more theatrics than I usually heard from him; typically he used humor to make a theological point. "Is that a hint I'm due for confession, Father?" My priest. My dentist. My boss. I was surrounded by people with a claim on my time.

He responded with only a demure smile, hinting perhaps at being the keeper of some of my secrets. I diverted an uncomfortable conversation by sharing details about the teeth. "The cops just grilled me on how I ended up with them, and frankly, I'm still baffled about what to do next."

I shrugged, as if the whole episode were no different than any of the hundreds of news tips I'd received during my career. But the plain truth—I was a little spooked, hence my eagerness to hand the teeth over to the cops. Nobody mails a letter like that to a TV station without a mission. To seek glory for a crime? To scare me silent? If the former, I was supposed to broadcast something. If the latter, I was supposed to keep something quiet. I had no idea which, but a wrong guess might upset the sender and bring us face-to-face in the dim alley behind the station.

"You seem uneasy." Father Mountain startled me from my internal debate. "Perhaps you should pray to St. Apollonia for guidance."

"Saint who?" I routinely say a prayer to St. Anthony whenever I lose something. Sometimes my prayers are even answered. But for grace to work, the item has to be tangible. After all, once a television sweeps month is lost, not even God can change viewer demographics.

"St. Apollonia," he repeated.

"Apollonia?" I recalled the rock movie *Purple Rain*, part of Minneapolis's music and film culture. "Wasn't Apollonia Prince's hot love interest? I know creative geniuses can be a challenge to work with, but that shouldn't qualify her for sainthood anymore than me having to work for a bozo."

"The Apollonia I'm referring to is the patron saint of toothaches."

Father Mountain pulled a leather-bound Catholic Encyclopedia from a shelf and turned to a painting of a beautiful woman holding a set of pincers against her chest. Her story: Apollonia was a virgin martyr whose teeth were pulled from her mouth during an uprising against Christians in the year 249. Afterward, when her attackers gave her the choice of renouncing her God or being thrown into a fire . . . she leaped into the flames.

"Wow. That's a pretty disturbing tale," I said. "But how did she become a saint? I thought the Catholic Church disapproved of suicide."

"Apollonia was making a statement," he said. "Dying for a cause is quite different than dying for one's own sake. One is noble; the other, selfish."

This was another topic I regretted raising because once, in a closed garage with a running engine, I considered leaving this world behind. Nothing as dramatic as St. Apollonia's exit, but Father Mountain never missed an opportunity to confer with me about my nearly fatal error. That spell of despair was the selfishness he had alluded to. He didn't want a repeat performance and regularly claimed his priestly prerogative to probe my state of mind and ensure I was keeping a healthy distance from the dark abyss that had once tormented me.

My husband had died a hero's death in the line of duty while our marriage was barely past the newlywed stage. Grief and guilt messed me up for a while. Not in a mood to watch reruns of that part of my life just then, I thanked Father Mountain for his hospitality and left to brush a light coating of snow off the windshield of my car. On the drive home, I worried about slipping from cynical to bitter.

Flossing that night, my gums bled. I envisioned horrific scenarios involving my own teeth as I spit blood into the sink. Later, I buried my face in my pillow but couldn't shake the bad omen. I prayed to Apollonia for distraction.

Too haunted to sleep and too cowardly to lay awake, I got out of bed to search online religious history websites on my computer to ponder what might be a suitable cause for me to aspire for sainthood. My curiosity did not pay off; the good causes were already taken. St. Francis de Sales had become the patron of journalists because, back in the sixteenth century, he wrote the first religious tracts. I had no problem with him receiving that honor: being first is what journalism is all about.

But I was unconvinced that St. Clare of Assisi deserved sainthood. She was named patron of television because, bedridden with illness, she apparently heard and saw Mass on the wall of her room—even though the service was happening miles away. Was her experience a thirteenth-century miracle or a mere hallucination?

And while I felt that I could make a persuasive case to be deemed patron of lost causes, St. Jude had already locked that one down.

All this may have been for the best. The downside to being a patron saint was that you had to be dead.

I turned off my computer and crawled back between heavy flannel sheets; the fuzzy bedding was to fabric the equivalent of what mashed potatoes are to food—ultimate comfort. All that religious exercise checking out saints had proved worthwhile; by then I felt drained and ready to rest—albeit fitfully.

CHAPTER 8

It was a slow news day in the Twin Cities, and Bryce wanted fresh ideas at the huddle. Neither of us mentioned the teeth. We had an understanding to keep our mouths shut about *that* story.

Ozzie spoke up. "A viewer called, mad about the Mall of America's curfew. Says they only enforce it against minority kids."

"The mall has a curfew?" Bryce asked.

"They like to call it a 'parental escort policy,'" I said. "Anyone under sixteen must be accompanied by an adult after four o'clock on Fridays and Saturdays."

Bryce looked puzzled by the rule. "Isn't that bad for business? After all, they have an amusement park in the middle of that giant mall. Who do they think is going to flock there if not teens?"

"They used to have a gang problem," I said. "Shoppers were feeling unsafe, or so the mall claimed."

"But that was at least a decade ago," Ozzie added. "Once they started the curfew, things calmed down. Except for that one fight with all those kids throwing chairs in the food court that went viral off someone's cell-phone camera over Christmas break. Now they're expanding the curfew to school holidays."

Bryce seemed to be mulling over this information. "We've been doing some focus group research."

After those words, I zoned him out by pretending I'd received an important text message. TV stations like to hire research companies to help them figure out how better to appeal to viewers between the ages of 25–54, the most coveted age bracket for advertisers. To me, that seemed like media hocus-pocus. All I cared about was doing the best reporting I could, and trusting that the ratings would follow.

"The Mall of America tests well with our key demographics," he continued. "Maybe we should investigate this curfew idea." He turned to look at me and smiled as he said the word *investigate*. "Riley, what would it take to nail this?"

I would have been elated to chase the story, except for one thing—location, location, location.

I didn't want to set foot in the Mall of America. My former betrothed, Nick Garnett, was director of security. Things had been said during our breakup that would have been better left unspoken. I had since vowed to do my shopping online rather than cross his turf.

"Riley?" Bryce was sounding exasperated. "What would it take to air this?"

"Sorry." I stopped daydreaming about lost love and focused on how to convince Bryce to steer clear of the Mall of America. "Trying to document this story would demand a lot of time with no guarantee we'd be able to prove any discrimination. It's a long shot."

"That's for me to decide," Bryce said. "What would it take?"

"Well, we'd have to set up some surveillance and watch which teens got kicked out," I said. "Maybe even use some undercover kids. Might be best to have someone hang out there casually some weekend to see what they could observe before bringing in a full team with hidden cameras."

Ozzie interrupted to point out that the mall required news cameras to register with the media relations office before videotaping on-site.

"They'll never give us approval to shoot this," he said, "and it's not worth being shut out of future stories because we antagonized them by using hidden cameras."

"Ozzie is right," I said, thinking fast. "We should just forgot this angle. That ice castle the mall built outside is still attracting plenty of attention. And it's visual. How about an update?"

Bryce disagreed and ordered me to conduct the pre-surveillance at the Mall of America this weekend and report back to him.

"You mean tomorrow? I can't. I have plans."

There was no way I could tell him I was boycotting the mall for personal reasons relating to my love life. He was the only one in the huddle who didn't know about my broken engagement. I glanced at the other reporters around the table, hoping nobody would bring up that juicy detail in front of Bryce or suggest that might be the real reason for me shirking the mall assignment.

"Perhaps someone else might enjoy working on the story." I finally asked, bluntly, looking straight at Nicole.

I knew she liked to shop. Nicole wore sleeveless sheath dresses, even in the winter, to show off her toned arms. No cleavage, just bare arms that communicated a smart-sexy look on the air. The trend was a way for women journalists to show skin on television without seeming slutty. Just the other day, Nicole had talked of giving my wardrobe of colorful blazers a similar makeover.

I shot her a save-me look, but before she could express interest in the curfew assignment, Bryce nixed any volunteers.

"Nope." He shook his head, while pointing at me. "Riley, you claim to be our investigative reporter. When it comes to news, we all have to make sacrifices for our job. You'll just have to change your plans."

I played my ace. "I'm sorry, Bryce. But I'm going to my high school reunion. Many of my old classmates are Channel 3 viewers. I can't disappoint them."

CHAPTER 9

Parking was the worst.

CLOSED signs flashed at each of the lower levels in the Mall of America ramp. Waiting in bumper-to-bumper traffic, I cursed my news director.

I lost both ends of my fight with Bryce, and was going to have to go to two places I would rather have avoided: the mall *and* my reunion. He decided there was time for both, that I could case the mall starting midafternoon Friday and drive to my hometown on Saturday. I had been using my reunion as a bluff, but now he was insisting I post a picture of myself with my classmates on Channel 3's Facebook page and tag their names to their pages.

"It will be a great 'relatable,'" Bryce said. "That's the key to social media promotion. People have to relate to you by feeling you share common interests or experiences outside your job. Kids. Pets. A class reunion. Those all work."

I was tempted to add bad bosses to his list of relatables, but knew better than to push him too far.

Finally, I found a parking space at the mall and took a picture of the nearest numbered pillar with my cell phone to help me find my vehicle later. I don't like wandering around the ramp alone at night when it's easy to become disorientated in the vast space and—in my case—spooked by the shadows.

Yet, I'm always wowed when I walk inside the Mall of America, sort of like Dorothy was when finally entering the Emerald City before clashing with winged monkeys and a wicked witch.

MOA is an enclosed city, with more than 100,000 people passing through many days. Shopaholics surrounded me, eager for a buy, but not necessarily a bargain. Surveys estimate nearly half of all the mall visitors are tourists—some traveling from around the world to browse specialty stores under one roof. And they're willing to pay top dollar for the experience, especially since Minnesota has no sales tax on clothing.

I walked a lap of about half a mile and when four o'clock hit, started looking for teenage curfew breakers. I kept my distance, taking notes and pictures reflecting their numbers, sex, race, and whether or not security guards escorted anyone off the property. At some of the mall doors, other guards were quizzing teens trying to enter.

"So how old are you guys?"

I overheard one exchange, and saw a couple boys being carded. Because it was so easy, I took photos of the rotunda with my phone, pretending to be a tourist enamored with Legoland rather than a reporter chasing a potentially controversial story.

"Do you mind showing me some ID?"

Similar scenes played out during the next hour. But the teens being asked to leave the mall seemed just as likely to be white as black or Asian. My impression was that proving racial bias in curfew enforcement might be difficult. I wasn't looking forward to breaking that news to my boss.

As I stepped off an escalator on the third floor, a figure abruptly moved in behind me. I instinctively clutched my purse close to my body and stepped up my pace.

"Relax, I'm not after your bag," a man said. "I just want to talk."

It was Nick Garnett's voice, but I kept walking toward the parking ramp without even turning around. "How long have you been following me?" I figured a curfew officer must have complained about me, but I was wrong.

"One of the guards monitoring the security cameras alerted me to a suspicious patron," he said.

I'd been in the underbelly of the Mall of America's security headquarters when Garnett and I'd been on better terms. The team had an impressive wall of surveillance cameras in their security center—resembling the news control booth of a TV station—all the better to track miscreants through the millions of square feet of open space.

"Your threshold for 'suspicious' must be pretty low to focus on me," I said.

Garnett cut in front of me, so I had no choice but to look him in the eye, then casually up and down. His hair had a touch of gray, but not enough to age him. He wore a well-cut suit, and could have passed as a business executive, except for the small print of a gun under his jacket.

We stood near the Chapel of Love—the scene of thousands of weddings at the Mall of America. He didn't seem to notice the irony.

"You met the criteria, Riley. Alone. No apparent shopping pattern. No purchases. You were observed taking photos."

Suddenly I realized I wasn't suspected of being a common criminal, but something much more dangerous. "You think I'm a terrorist?"

He had the decency to be embarrassed. "If anyone thought you were a terrorist, one of our security team would have questioned you by now. I decided to take care of the situation myself."

"So now I'm a 'situation'?" That was a far cry from once being a fiancée.

"Certainly not," he said. "I just was surprised to see you on the surveillance screen and wondered what you were doing here."

"I wasn't looking for you, Nick, if that's what you mean."

"I deserve that. I'm sorry for how things ended between us, Riley."

"Which time?"

I'd broken up with him once. He'd broken up with me twice. That meant he was leading in our game of love and war. Looking back on our long romance, I concluded neither of us were at fault for the early rifts. Our relationship became a casualty of evil, when those around us were destroyed in dual waves of bloodshed. We had each killed killers, pulling the trigger on psychopaths. That shared experience should have bonded us for life, but we were too racked with guilt to find comfort in love. Yet, on some level, we both were desperate for another outcome . . . willing to try again.

Garnett still hadn't answered my question, so I tried another. "Why did you move back?" He had returned to Minnesota from Washington, DC, after our broken engagement without even telling me.

"I wanted this job."

His answer was cold. The job meant more to him than me. I remembered a time when those priorities were reversed and was tempted to get into the kind of pointless squabble one gets in with a frustrating ex, but controlled the urge. I suspected the security guards in the dispatch center were monitoring us on surveillance cameras and taking bets on how long before I slugged him.

Or kissed him.

That sudden romantic fantasy startled me, and I pushed it away, but once you've shared passion and danger with someone it's hard to stand close and not remember the heat.

Our third and final split was different from the others. He considered it a trust-breaker, while I saw it as a misunderstanding. I'd kissed another man while Garnett and I were broken up. It had meant so little to me, I thought nothing of telling him. It had meant so much to him, he couldn't bear to hear it. And thus ended our courtship.

Meanwhile, a young woman in a floor-length, strapless white gown almost crashed into us as she danced by in wedded bliss. Following on her heels were tuxedoed men, bridesmaids in shimmery dresses, and flower girls in puffy skirts. The bridal party all wore broad smiles, except for a white-haired lady who dabbed the corner of one eye with a pink hanky. Nick blushed as he finally realized we were standing outside the wedding chapel.

Bad juxtaposition.

He took me by the elbow, out of the way of the celebratory nuptials, but I yanked free from him. "You're not allowed to touch me anymore."

"Not so fast," he replied. "I'm still curious what you're doing here."

"Are you asking me as a friend or as a cop? As far as friendship goes, I'm not sure those criteria apply anymore. And when it comes to law and order, there's this legal issue called probable cause. Unless I'm on your 'No Trespassing Wall'?"

The security team had a wall in the basement where they posted pictures of small-time crooks, vandals, and disturbers of the peace who had been warned they'd face arrest if they were found on the property again.

"Anyone in the mall is subject to a security interview if we deem it prudent," he said.

"A security interview?" I replied. "Since when? Are we taping an episode of *Mall Cops*? I don't see camera crews anywhere."

My reference to a reality TV show filmed on-site riled him. "Our security policy is on the mall website. You certainly should appreciate that where we're standing is the ultimate terrorist target."

He was correct about what's in a name. When the shopping complex first opened, the label was considered a stroke of marketing genius. But after the September 11 terrorist attacks, Minnesota braced for the worst. Pairing "America" with "Mall" had pros and cons. That's why the Mall of America employed a highly trained security team consisting of Israeli counterterror-ism experts, explosive-sniffing dogs, and more than a hundred officers. Bombings at the Nairobi mall and at the Boston Mar-athon had brought that fear home again, but I still didn't like Garnett's implication.

"Don't mess with me, Nick." I moved forward into his space, to see if he would step back. He didn't, and neither did I. We were both too close for comfort. "You didn't stop me because I'm suspicious. You stopped me because I'm me."

He didn't deny it.

I didn't remember our exact parting words, only that our breakup lacked good closure. While dating, we used to play a movie trivia game, weaving famous lines from film dialogue into our conversation, then goading the other into guessing their ori-gin. I'd long settled on what my final words to him should have been, and no coincidence, they came from a memorable breakup movie.

"You don't even know how much you'll miss me," I said.

Before he could answer, "Shirley MacLaine, *Terms of Endear-ment*, 1983," we heard screaming, and a red object came hurling toward us.

I don't know what he was thinking, but I had terrorism on my mind and envisioned blood. With only a split second to spare, Nick shoved me away as the thing hit him full in the chest and I fell flat on the floor.

CHAPTER 10

Applause and cheers filled the air around us as I turned in shock.

Nick was clutching a bridal bouquet.

Did he rescue me as a friend, someone he harbored feelings for, or as part of his cop duty? I decided his motivation didn't matter. The sight of him, holding roses and ribbons, was so comical, I stopped being mad and started to laugh.

"Well, Nick, I think that catch means you're the next to get married."

He was reaching a hand down to me, when a woman's voice interrupted any reconciliation. "Who do we have here?"

I recognized her as Velma Roberts, part of the mall's public relations team. She recognized me as a local television reporter. Whether she knew about my personal relationship with Garnett was unclear, but I'd interviewed her a couple of times as a mall spokesperson about consumer shopping trends.

"So, Riley Spartz," she said, "I heard talk you were around the place. But since you didn't stop by our office for media credentials, I'm quite certain you're not here on Channel 3 business, although I don't see a shopping bag."

From her trendy shoes to her blunt-cut bangs, Velma resembled a walking fashion plate in figure and dress. Her job was to promote all the mall had to offer. With auburn streaks through shoulder-skimming hair, she even looked good enough to anchor TV news, except that Velma had an irritating manner of speech in which she gave each word equal emphasis. I found her difficult to listen to, but apparently viewers could handle her in ten-second sound bites. I'd heard she was seeing a voice coach, but whenever she was nervous, Velma reverted back to her old habit.

Apparently, I made her nervous.

She didn't wait for me to answer, instead turning her attention toward Nick, who had seemed to forget I was still on the floor. She took the flowers from his hand and savored the scent of the fresh petals.

"Sweet."

Velma seemed momentarily wistful and I noticed her left ring finger was bare. I remembered hearing some gossip about her and a divorce. But her personal experience with marriage didn't seem to sour her on the idea of weddings in general. She waved the bouquet enthusiastically toward the mall's newest bride, who was skipping down the corridor in glee.

"Congratulations!" Velma called. "Come back on your anniversary!"

She glanced at an ornate wristwatch that seemed more decorative than functional, before tugging playfully at Garnett's sleeve in a way that conveyed familiarity.

"I'm almost off duty, Nick. Why don't we grab dinner and I'll fill you in on the mall's upcoming venture. It might pose some special security challenges."

That sounded like news so I scrambled to my feet and put myself back into the conversation. If I couldn't deliver a curfew story, maybe I could appease Bryce with some other Mall of America idea. Preferably one I could hand off to another reporter.

"So what's ahead for the mall, Velma?"

"You'll find out soon enough," she said. "But here's a hint: Hollywood loves weddings."

They both said good-bye to me, following in the bridal party's shadow, I waited, just in case Garnett glanced back at me
to wink, or even roll his eyes. But he kept walking, so I headed
in the opposite direction alone, resenting Bryce for making me
come there.

At the mall entrance, a security guard was still checking teens
for curfew. A woman with a large pile of packages and bags with
designer labels waited for a ride. She was leaving, proud of her
shopping spree, while I was leaving heavyhearted and empty-
handed.

I ducked back inside to buy some gourmet chocolate caramels
from a shop near the door—even though I suspected St. Apollonia would disapprove.

CHAPTER 11

The drive south to my high school reunion the next day took me past the headquarters of Hormel Foods. The best proof of the political clout wielded by the corporation was the seven freeway exits in a town with about 20,000 residents.

Having failed to RSVP, I essentially crashed the party, but nobody seemed to care. Some people had changed—gaining weight or losing hair—but I had no trouble recognizing who was a classmate and who was a mere spouse.

I could tell by their talk. And it all came down to one word: Hormel.

Anyone who grew up around Austin, Minnesota, pronounced the giant meatpacking company as HOR-mal, rhyming with "normal," just the way founder George A. Hormel did more than a century ago. Outsiders called it Hor-MEL. The change came about when an advertising agency taping a radio commercial thought Hor-MEL sounded better. Most people in the area continued to pronounce it the same way their ancestors did, despite the rest of the country making the switch.

"Riley Spartz!" A group of classmates flagged me over to the keg for a glass of foaming beer.

I waved back, mouthing, "No, thanks." I wandered over to the buffet table and saw a sad spread of sloppy joes and potato chips.

"Good to see you after so many years." A former cheerleader gave me a superficial hug, then glanced behind me. "Are you here alone?"

I realized high school had ended long ago, but I briefly regressed back to my teenage days grappling with the question of why no one had asked me to prom yet. At this stage of my life, I sure didn't want to admit I had no husband, no children, and not even a boyfriend. So I lied.

"He had to work tonight."

The funny thing was, if Garnett and I had remained a couple, he would have insisted we attend my reunion. He was a family history buff and would have considered it part of my—and thus our—life story. He would have paged through my yearbook ahead of time, asking who was popular, who was smart, who were the bullies, and which boys I had crushes on.

I shifted my thoughts back to the present when a former teacher mentioned seeing me on the news the other night. "How's life on TV?"

"Terrific." I continued to lie, rather than rob him of the belief that one of his students held a glamorous job. "News is one thing we never run out of."

That halted a nearby discussion on the price of corn and opened a rant on what's wrong with the media in America.

"Every time I watch your station, you seem to be reporting on crime," said Maureen Noterman, editor of the weekly newspaper. "Maybe you should try reporting good news. That's what *our* readers want."

Easy for her to say since her coverage area was far removed from most real lawlessness. And there was no sense in trying to explain that good news wasn't always *real* news, so I diplomatically agreed to pass that suggestion onto my boss and used the old ploy of needing to find a restroom to end our conversation.

The community bulletin board in the lobby caught my eye. A flyer with a photo of a dog stood out from the upcoming rummage sales and church dinners. It read MISSING across the top, while the bottom offered REWARD in the same bold letters.

It was a cute spaniel. Too bad.

"That's the second dog to disappear in two months." Maureen had followed me. "No sign of either of them. Maybe you could put it on the news."

While I'd had considerable experience covering missing people, missing dogs were a whole different issue. Dangerous things regularly happen to dogs out in the country. They can be hit by cars. Or bullets. Even poisoned. Savage animals can tear into their hides and leave them bleeding to death out of sight.

"Whose dogs?" I asked.

"The Kloeckners and Mertens," she said. "Not too far from your parents' place."

Like most news directors, Bryce liked animal stories because viewers like animal stories. That's why zoo babies get so much airtime. But I knew it would be an impossible pitch.

For starters, two missing dogs were *not* a trend. For all we knew, they ran away.

Most rural residents, including my parents, let their farm dogs run loose. It really isn't practical to chain them up, because part of their job is to keep wild creatures away from the buildings and bark an alert if strangers drive in the yard. To do that, they need freedom to roam.

Next, my hometown was far outside of Channel 3's broadcast area, which made it difficult to get stories approved because rural viewers watching the news on satellite television are less desirable to Twin Cities advertisers.

"Seems like a better fit for your paper," I said.

"We listed for readers to be on the watch for the pets, but we can't do much more. We cover school, sports, and community events. We don't have much of a staff. Mostly just me. We count on readers to send us news."

"The town's lucky to still have a local newspaper."

"Thanks. I'm sorry for how I sounded earlier."

"Don't worry about it, Maureen. I hear worse from viewers all day long."

"I have the same problem with constituents." A thin man in a plaid flannel shirt and jeans was holding a beer and listening to us talk.

Phillip McCarthy had also graduated in my class. He flashed me a smile, which was more attention than he had paid me all through high school. His claim to fame then was bringing home a state trophy for running the hundred-yard dash. A few years ago, Phil had been elected to serve as a state legislator when the current lawmaker from that district resigned midterm after a sex scandal.

"How are things going up at the Capitol?" I asked.

I seldom covered state government unless some kind of corruption was afoot, and only asked to be polite so he could sound important in front of our classmates. He went on and on about how the other political party wouldn't compromise. It was becoming tedious, and just when I was about to use that old ploy again about having to look for a restroom, he asked me out on what sounded like a date.

"How about you and I get together for dinner sometime, Riley?"

Just then the band started playing our prom song—"Everything I Do, I Do for You"—so I pretended I couldn't hear him. He pulled me out on the dance floor anyway, and during an instrumental part of the ballad, suggested again that we get together socially. "We could talk about old times."

By then I mustered a suitable answer that would save face for both of us. "Sorry, Phil, it could pose a conflict of interest, especially during the legislative session."

Other than sharing our single status and hometown, I doubted we had much in common and had no interest in getting in bed with a politician.

CHAPTER 12

Inmate 16780-59 hit the floor after being sucker-punched by a swaggering thug with a long braid of hair hanging down his back.

"If anyone asks," the brute whispered, "tell them you tripped."

"Tripped," a fellow ruffian echoed. "That's a good name for a clumsy punk like you. Trip. From now on, that's your handle. Understand?"

The first hood hauled him to his feet and pushed him against a wall. "So what's your name, punk?"

He wanted them to just leave so he could puke. "Trip. My name is Trip."

"Prove it."

He was confused and tried again to comply. "Call me Trip." He even smiled at them, hoping to pass their test.

"*Not* until you prove it," the man insisted.

"Fall on your face, idiot," the other man ordered. "*Trip.*"

So the inmate dropped to the floor and curled his arms over his head, trying to make himself invisible as he waited to be kicked.

The larger man leaned over him. "That's what I want to see happen anytime we meet. You hitting the ground."

The goons snickered as he limped back toward his cell to barf in the sink, and curl up with a thin prison pillow on a narrow vinyl mattress. His bunk mate was about half his age and called Kilo because he had landed in the slammer for dealing coke. Kilo had played nice by letting the old guy have the lower bed, but offered little sympathy regarding bullying behind bars.

"New guys, they get roughed up." Kilo shrugged at the inevitable. "Wait em out, Trip. When a new new guy arrives, they'll forget about you. Kind of like college hazing."

"Please don't call me Trip. My name is Jack."

"Not if they say it's Trip. Trip's what I'm calling you. I got to watch my own back."

That exchange wasn't reassuring for an incarcerated rookie who feared an escalation of violence. He inhaled deeply and told himself to stop acting like a patsy and start thinking like the Jack Clemens who used to rule Minneapolis finance circles. He had honed shrewd instincts about gauging who wielded real clout in business negotiations. He was used to making deals happen. And his future now depended on his ability to close one inside prison walls.

"Maybe we could look out for each other?" he suggested.

"Keep me out of it," Kilo replied. "Your problems are your problems."

"But say I wanted to discuss protection with someone, who?"

"Protection? In a place like this? Protection sometimes buys more trouble at a steep price. Better to stay out of their way."

"There must be someone running that type of operation."

Kilo paused and lowered his voice. "Okay, there's this guy— Scarface—but don't mention me."

"Scarface? You mean like in the Al Pacino movie?"

"I mean he has a scar across his face. I don't hand out the nicknames, Trip, I just use them."

The next morning, his head and gut still ached. And when Trip surveyed the damage to his face in a steel mirror mounted on the wall of the cell, he discovered a bruise over one eye. He touched the black-and-blue mark, wincing.

He kept on lookout for his tormentors and for deliverance from them. Later, in the lunch line, amid meat loaf, mashed potatoes, and brown gravy, he spotted a burly man with a twisted scar across one cheek in the company of an apparent entourage.

Trip carried his tray over toward the man, being careful not to get in his space. "Excuse me, sir, do you have a minute to chat?" He was reluctant to address him as Scarface without being introduced. After all, what if only his close personal friends were invited to use that name?

The man snorted impatiently at his dining being interrupted. "What does a skinny hood like you got to say that I want to hear?"

Trip struggled to answer even though he had practiced his pitch the night before in his bunk. But dressed in a prison-issued green shirt and pants rather than a dark custom-made wool suit and silk tie, he knew he resembled a pest instead of a seasoned dealmaker. He glanced around the room to make sure none of the man's associates were close enough to hear his hushed words.

"I got money. On the outside."

Scarface looked skeptical, but motioned for his gang to hang back and indicated that Trip should set his food on the table and take a seat. "Why you telling me this?"

"I'm hoping we can work out an arrangement. For protection."

"Protection?"

"Yes. You take care of me inside and I'll take care of you outside."

The man bit an apple from Trip's tray as he sized up the situation. "You certainly seem in need of protection." He put the fruit down and reached across the table for Trip's chin and pulled him close to get a look at his battered face. "We take care of our brothers. You're a stranger. Maybe even a snitch. You should show me this money. You might be all talk."

"It's hidden away. Outside. When I get out, I'll make it worth your while."

Scarface's expression darkened. "You asking me to *loan* you protection. I run a business. I expect to be paid for my services."

"I understand," Trip said. "Maybe we can negotiate a generous amount of interest."

"No." The man sounded firm and final. "I need to be paid up front." He grabbed a hard boiled egg from Trip's lunch and took a bite before setting it back on the tray. "So what did you say your name was?"

Inmate 16780-59 weighed how best to answer. "Jack. Jack Clemens out of Minnesota. And you?" he stammered. "Sir?"

"Call me Scarface." He pointed to the blemish with pride. "That should be easy to remember. So, Jack Clemens, if you have money, you have people. Have them take care of the financial details."

He disliked the man playing games with him. "You know I can't reach my people from in here." His voice squeaked in agitation, and he quickly shut his mouth to avoid appearing vulnerable.

The man smiled at his frustration. "Calm down, Jack. I'm trying to chow here."

He felt on the verge of vomiting again, but forced himself to sit silent. Bite by bite, the big man finished his new client's meal, then used the last bit of bread to wipe gravy from the plate and handed the morsel to his nervous companion, who swallowed it wordlessly.

When they left the cafeteria and reached the hallway, Scarface signaled some cronies, who gathered around them, blocking any view. He snapped his fingers and pointed at an inmate with a crew cut and glasses.

The guy reached inside his pants, around to his backside,

grunted and twitched, soon handing over to his boss what looked like a shrink-wrapped cell phone. The new prisoner among them caught a bad whiff and flinched, realizing the device was inside a condom—and where it had been hidden.

"Dial away, Jack." Scarface hit a series of buttons to unlock the cell before handing it to the latest addition to their gang. "No worries," the leader continued, "it's a burner. Good for maybe another couple weeks."

After his last prison rules debacle, Inmate 16780-59 took no reassurance knowing the phone was prepaid and untraceable. He glanced around nervously. "But what if . . . ?"

"This is part of the protection you requested, Jack. Now tell your people to expect a call from my people."

So he dialed a number he dared not call from the authorized prison telephone system.

CHAPTER 13

I stayed at the family farm that night. Because the southern part of the state had such a mild winter, it was an easy drive. With last year's drought, snow would have been most welcome, but little had fallen. The dogs were on their nocturnal patrol of the homestead when I arrived late, but they stopped barking and started slobbering when they recognized me, especially Husky, my favorite. He was a meek mutt who had lived with me briefly until it became clear my work schedule was not a good fit for a dog owner.

My parents had already gone to sleep, so I quietly crept up a narrow staircase to my cluttered childhood bedroom. When I turned the lights out, with a lumpy pillow and my old mattress, I fought to rid my mind of high school, but couldn't.

I turned on a lamp and skimmed through the reunion brochure I'd picked up. It had been stapled together by the organizers, with graduation pictures of the attendees, email addresses, and brief bios about what everybody was up to these days. I wasn't listed, because I hadn't RSVPed, but Phil McCarthy was. It said he lived about an hour north of the Twin Cities, even farther from our hometown than me. He served on the Minnesota House environmental and natural resources committee. When the legislature wasn't in session, he ran a car-wash business.

He seemed a decent enough guy and I felt bad for being so

dismissive at the reunion. But being in the news media makes you keep people at a distance because you're often not sure if they really want to be friends or just want to get their message on TV. I had no interest in finding out, but Phil making a move on me did make me feel a little better about myself.

My mind replayed my recent confrontation with Nick Garnett. Using my phone for Internet service was iffy because of the rural location, but standing next to a window I got enough cell juice to search the Mall of America website and found he was right about the security jargon. Along with a litany of warnings about visitors wearing shirts and shoes and not using skateboards, obscene gestures or posting graffiti, the mall rules included a line (in fine print) reading: "You may be subject to a security interview."

It didn't detail what types of behaviors triggered such attention, but seeing it in writing didn't make me feel any less annoyed about my experience with Garnett.

I grew more flustered lying there, watching out the window as red lights flashed on the wind turbines. I ventured back downstairs and coaxed Husky into the house to curl up on my bed. "Good dog." Soon he was snoring. The sound was like white noise. I felt safe, my loneliness banished, and slept better than I had in weeks.

That warm feeling lasted until morning, when I discovered him chewing one of my shoes. "Bad dog." I took a cell-phone picture of him licking my face anyway before turning him loose to run with the others.

Over a breakfast of ham and eggs, my mother was delighted when I showed her the group photo of my classmates on my phone. "It's amazing how much better the women look than the men. And you even combed your hair, Riley."

She seemed to intend her remark to be a compliment, but I let it pass. My style was a layered bob I was trying to grow out after a recent haircut disaster. I'd posted the reunion photo online late last night in case Bryce was checking up on me. Already viewers were "relating" to it with "likes" and "comments."

"Regretfully, Mom, my job depends not just on what I report, but how I look when I report it."

That was the sorry truth. TV was a young person's game. Now in my midthirties, I'd probably have more to show for my life if I'd spent less time chasing the reality of news and more time chasing the romance of dreams.

"Any bachelor farmers in the crowd?" Mom asked.

"None that interested me."

"Would it hurt you to go out with the next man who asked you?" she said.

"What if he ends up being a jerk?"

"Then you don't have to go on a second date."

My mom had given up trying to be subtle about her feelings concerning my single status. To hear her tell it, my broken engagement hurt her almost as much as it had me. Before she could ask whether I'd seen Nick Garnett recently, I steered the conversation from dates to dogs.

"Something weird did come up at the reunion," I said. "Missing dogs."

"That's been the talk of the neighborhood the last month." My dad shook his head sadly. "If they haven't been found by now, they probably won't be."

"How come neither of you mentioned this before?"

My mother was always suggesting story ideas to try to get me home to visit. "Didn't seem like much news value," she said. "You're always going on about needing news value."

"I didn't mean it as for a story. I was just curious."

"We can run over to the neighbors and see if they've heard anything if you want," Dad said.

Without any reason to rush back to the Cities, I grabbed a pair of old boots from the closet in case our journey turned cold. Husky enjoyed riding in motor vehicles, so when he saw

Dad with the keys, he scampered over to the pickup, and we all climbed in. Blackie, his Labrador pal, stood outside barking.

"I don't think we have room for one more," I said.

"He doesn't want inside," Dad said, "Blackie likes to ride in the bed of the truck," Dad said.

"That sounds risky."

"We'll take the back roads and go slow. Otherwise, he'll just chase after us. And that's even more dangerous."

At the neighbors', we found no new information from what Maureen had shared the night before. The lost dogs had disappeared on different days, and were still gone. "A real shame," Eugene Merten said. "My grandkids loved that animal. They won't stop searching for her."

Both families told the same story. Their pets had been fine, until they went missing. They couldn't believe it was a coincidence, but didn't want to believe it was a conspiracy.

"Sure our dog, Rocket, was getting old," John Kloeckner said. "But I don't for a minute think he went off alone to die."

"What do you think happened?" I asked.

"Something bad. There's always been talk of pets being stolen as bait for dog fighting rings or sold to research labs." He reached down to scratch behind Husky's ears. "Hold this guy close while you can."

Husky would certainly be vulnerable to being dog-napped, I had to admit. He had the soul of a lop-eared bunny and would probably hop in the back of a unfamiliar van if lured with a treat.

Luckily, Blackie was more suspicious of strangers. If threatened, he'd rather fight than flee.

My cell phone rang, with Mom on the other end. "One of my red-hat lady friends called. She said the Mullenbachs' dog is missing."

CHAPTER 14

Perhaps this hometown tip would turn out to have a real news angle. If so, Bryce would be even more pleased about my reunion. Dad and I drove over to the Mullenbach farm, watching carefully along the ditches in case their pet showed up as roadkill. The family was searching the barn and other outbuildings for their collie when we arrived.

"Lady!" A little girl was calling, upset. "Come home."

"Last time we saw her was late yesterday afternoon." Dan Mullenbach was upset. He farmed dairy cattle and helped with the church collection basket. "This morning she was gone."

Husky also seemed agitated by all the commotion, and was starting to whine. "Probably wondering where their dog is," Dad said. "Hounds know who lives where."

Blackie's nose was close to the frozen ground. Because of the mellow winter, there was no snow, and thus no tracks. But the cold weather had eliminated clutter odors, and the dog seemed to be following some kind of trail. Labs have an excellent sense of smell.

"Probably just a raccoon," my dad said. "Plenty of them around."

"We don't have any other leads," I said. "Anybody want to come with me?"

One of the Mullenbach boys stepped forward. My dad had

bad knees so I told him to take the truck and try and keep us in sight from the road. The others would continue searching the homestead.

"Come on, Blackie," I said. "Lead the way."

The dog took off barking, being careful not to get too far ahead. Husky stayed near me, behind his canine buddy. We promised to call the family if we found anything, but I was afraid of what we might find.

We left the windbreak of trees for a farm field that had held tall corn the season before, but was now mostly plowed under stubble. I could see in all directions, but nothing immediately caught my interest. Running on the uneven terrain grew difficult. Blackie raced down a ditch and crossed over a gravel road about a mile from where we started. I was losing speed. The Mullenbach boy moved ahead of me without any effort, then turned back.

"You okay?" he asked.

I motioned for him to keep going while I caught my breath, but he waited with me.

"How old are you?" I asked.

"Twelve."

My dad drove up, and I leaned against the hood of the pickup to rest. He unrolled the window. "Any sign?"

I shook my head and leaned over to briefly lock fingers with him against the steering wheel. I climbed in on the seat beside him and we followed the trio for another quarter mile before they stopped.

I scrambled out in time to hear Blackie growl as he approached a frozen stream, and lost sight of him in overgrown brush. Husky darted after him. Seconds later, wild yelping came from that direction. A howl. Then silence.

The Mullenbach boy took off. It took me a minute to locate him, near a culvert dripping water, sprawled in the dirt, cradling something close. A few more steps and I recognized the still body of a collie in his arms. The other two dogs huddled together quiet, keeping space between them and death.

Muffled sobs came from the kid. He was trying to talk, but I couldn't understand his words. I knelt down on the cold earth to rub his shoulder, wishing I had thought to ask his name when we first ventured out together. If I knew what to call him, comforting him would be easier. But I didn't, so I just told him how sorry I was.

"Let's find your family." I tried to pull him away from his dead pet.

He pushed me back, clinging to the furry corpse. "What is this thing?"

It wasn't until he lifted his face to look at me that I saw the piece of metal clamped tight against Lady's throat, and staked to the ground.

CHAPTER 15

The Mullenbachs had called the county sheriff to report what had happened, and were redirected to call the state Department of Natural Resources. All they told them was to fill out a form.

I grabbed the line and identified myself as a reporter from Channel 3. "I'm covering the story of how this dog died and would like to get some information."

I emailed a picture of the trap wrapped around Lady's head to the DNR and soon an officer called back to tell us she had died in a body grip trap—designed to capture raccoons, coyotes, and other wildlife. Trapping season was still underway, so it was legal—and lethal.

"Shame about the dog," the DNR officer said. "They sometimes get caught by mistake."

Again, he instructed us to make an "incident report" so Lady could become part of their statistical base.

"Does this happen a lot?" I asked.

"That's what we're trying to find out," he replied. "But the good thing is these traps are quick kill, so she probably didn't suffer much."

"That's not particularly reassuring." In a matter of seconds she went from being a pet to being paperwork. I told him I'd be in touch for a story, and hung up.

The property belonged to Abe Hayne, an elderly farmer up the road. His own dog, a German shepherd, was chained in the yard when we pulled in with a parade of vehicles. Lady's body was wrapped in a blanket in the back of the truck. The Hayne dog lunged and barked at our animals until a young man in a coonskin cap came outside.

"Abe around?" Dan Mullenbach asked.

"He's inside," the man said. "I'll get him."

The Davy Crocket look-alike was his son-in-law, Wayne. He and his wife had moved back to the farm last year to help Abe with the harvest, other heavy lifting, and ended up staying. The discussion about the dog trap didn't go so well. Both men were defensive.

"I've had problems with crop damage," Abe said. "Deer, raccoons, groundhogs. Nearly three grand from my pockets last year alone. We're not going to take it anymore."

Wayne pointed to his fur hat. "One less raccoon to eat our corn. You should be thanking me."

"Thanking you? You killed my dog!" Dan looked ready to throw a punch, but his kid was watching and glaring.

"Technically," Wayne said, "your dog was trespassing on private property."

That did it. If Dad hadn't grabbed Dan's arm and stepped between them just then, things would have gotten physical fast.

"Don't you think you should have told folks in the area you were setting these traps?" my dad asked.

Neither man seemed to have a good answer. "Sorry about the dog," Abe said. "We'll make it right." He headed to a small shed and threw open the door. Rows of animal pelts were hanging to dry. Others were stacked on a table. "Take your pick."

"No, thanks." Dan put his hand around his son's shoulder and walked away.

"What about the other two missing pets?" I asked. "Did they get trapped, too?"

Wayne tugged nervously at the striped tail sewn on his raccoon skin hat. "Don't know what you're talking about."

None of us believed him. The masked face above his own face made him look sneaky.

CHAPTER 16

B ryce was overseeing early construction of the new studio set the next morning when I gave him the bad word on curfew kids at the Mall of America. The sounds of heavy nail pounding and sawing interrupted our discussion, so my news director simply gestured his displeasure with a frown while turning his attention back on the building crew.

When the noise lulled, I told Bryce about the dead dog and showed him the gruesome picture of the trap clenched over the collie's face.

"It took two strong men to pull apart the springs and finally remove it," I said. "No animal would stand a chance against such a device."

"We can't show that photo on the air," Bryce said. "Too disturbing."

I've always found it strange that the same people who complain about stories featuring dead animals seem to have no problem with stories about dead people. But I knew what he meant. We couldn't do the story without airing the picture and we couldn't air the picture without offending most of our viewers. So, end of story. Or was it?

"I did some research, Bryce, and the use of these body grip traps is controversial. Maybe I should do a little more digging, especially since viewers tune in for animal stories."

"Not dead-animal stories, Riley. Happy ones. Tales of dogs traveling hundreds of miles to be reunited with their owner. Cats dressed in holiday costumes. Baby owls being rescued. Find me some animal news at the Mall of America that will spike our ratings and then we'll talk."

As much as I wanted to avoid crossing paths with Garnett, I also wanted to keep my job. So I tried playing chummy with my boss, even though I was certain he'd blow off my next idea.

"This has nothing to do with animals and hasn't been confirmed, but I got a sense the mall is planning another crazy wedding. Anything to land national media attention."

"What kind of wedding?" he asked.

"They do a stunt wedding every few years." Since he hadn't been in Minnesota long enough to see the mall's public relations machine in action, I tried to give him some perspective. "Couples married on the Ferris wheel. An arranged-marriage wedding. I-do's by the aquarium. They want to make the rest of the country envision the mall as a destination point for their big day. Sort of like Vegas without the casinos."

I started chuckling, figuring this was something my news director and I could yuk up together, sharing the absurdity. "Bride and grooms sometimes get a free ride on the roller coaster," I continued. "Couples with weak stomachs can opt for the merry-go-round instead."

Then I realized Bryce wasn't laughing. He was enthralled. "You can really get married at the Mall of America?"

"Absolutely." I raised my voice as the hammering on set again blended with the buzz of electric sawing. "Thousands of ceremonies have been performed there. You can shop for a wedding just like you shop for tennis shoes or a computer. They even have their own chapel."

Bryce yelled something, but the construction noise drowned out his words. I pointed to one ear and shook my head, so we left the production studio for the newsroom.

"So what kind of wedding are we talking about this time?" he said.

"I'm not sure there actually is one. I just overheard the Mall of America's PR and security people chatting, but believe me, if it's a go, they won't keep it secret. That place lusts for publicity."

"A wedding, huh?" Bryce's face was glowing like a new bride.

"None of this is for sure." I regretted deviating from my standard policy of never telling a news director about a specific story unless it was solid. Otherwise they felt robbed if you couldn't deliver.

Just then my cell phone rang, displaying the number for the city of Minneapolis switchboard, and giving me an escape from my boss.

CHAPTER 17

I was summoned to the Minneapolis police chief's office by his secretary. She sounded charming but ambiguous. I knew Chief Vince Capacasa generally kept his distance from the media unless there was something in it for him. My guess was the city's top cop wanted to leak negative happenings at city hall, so I stopped by at the suggested time and was ushered right in.

The chief was yelling into the phone. "If you don't like it, change the law." He hung up, abruptly.

"Anyone I know?" I asked.

"Mayor Skubic. He's mad about the police license plate–tracking data and wants it made private."

Thousands of vehicle plates and their public locations are scanned each day in Minneapolis by cameras mounted on squad cars and freeway bridges to help cops find wanted vehicles in real time—stolen cars or drivers with warrants out. Under the law, the data was deemed public and is stored for a year. A political fuss was underway because most of the licenses belonged to law-abiding citizens, not criminals.

"Not everyone wants the files private," I said. "Didn't some auto dealer recently buy the plate location records of a car the owner had stopped making payments on so he could repossess the vehicle?"

The mayor had appointed Capacasa to the job of police chief

years ago, but it was no secret the two were often at odds. Even though their offices were in the same building, they seldom met face-to-face. I waited to see if the chief had anything to add to the license flap, but that didn't seem the reason for my visit.

So I tried a little small talk. "How's the game going, Chief? Who's ahead?"

I motioned to a chessboard on a corner table where, it was well known, he continuously played a long-distance match with a murderer serving life in Minnesota's highest-security prison.

"He thinks he's beating me," the chief answered, "but I know I'm winning."

The two men snail-mailed moves to each other, so their competition advanced slowly. The chief, a chess master who had no shortage of law-abiding opponents, wouldn't disclose his motive for the game, but many of us in the media figured the two might have a side bet involving a confession about other unsolved homicides.

A knock at the door came just then, and Detective Delmonico entered, followed by a man in a dark suit. He seemed familiar, but avoided looking at me. Then I recognized him as an FBI agent I'd tangled with on a couple crime stories that fell under federal jurisdiction. I could never remember his name—FBI guys tend to look the same from the ground on up, from their black shoes to their short haircuts. If we had been outside, and he'd been wearing dark glasses, I probably wouldn't have pegged him at all.

"I believe we've met before." I introduced myself to both men anyway. "Riley Spartz, Channel 3 News."

Delmonico shook my hand without giving any indication he and I had seen each other lately.

The FBI guy paused, but couldn't refuse to divulge his name without confirming he was a true jerk. "Agent Jax, Federal Bureau of Investigation."

Now that I remembered him, I liked him even less. He always

gave his investigations Latin names to make them—and him—sound important.

He and Delmonico pulled up chairs around a conference table and joined me near the chief's desk. The meeting was a tad unconventional. When it comes to law enforcement, feds and locals aren't historically great collaborators, sharing some of the same tensions as television networks and affiliate stations.

Most police consider the FBI a one-way street when it comes to sharing information, while the feds fault police chiefs and sheriffs for being territorial. The players sometimes make a show of lining up together for news conferences, especially if the topic is terrorism, but much of the time they try to ignore each other.

Figuring this gathering had news potential, I leaned back to listen to what they had to say. Turns out, they wanted me to do the talking.

"Tell us what you know about this man." Delmonico held out a mug shot.

I reached for the picture. The man in the photo looked confident, despite his circumstances, though his eyes and smile seemed to hint at something furtive.

To me, he was a stranger. "I don't know anything about him."

"Hmmmm. We'll see." Chief Capacasa took control of the interview, maintaining eye contact with me as he asked the next question. "Was he a source of yours?"

"If he was, I'm not sure I'd tell you."

My answer didn't please my audience. "You don't need to worry about protecting his anonymity." Capacasa drummed his fingers impatiently against the desk. "He's dead."

With that news, I saw no point in playing coy. I realized I was on the verge of landing a scoop. After all, I was the only reporter in the room, and no one had mentioned anything about our discussion being off the record. Even if they had, I don't think I would have agreed to that kind of deal. I like to know more about what I'm trading silence for first.

"I've never seen him before." If the cops had the guy's mug, they also had his name. I knew the system enough to make them squirm. "Why don't you just tell me who he is? Maybe this will go faster."

"Leon Akume," Delmonico said. "His name is Leon Paul Akume."

That info didn't help. I tried to concentrate, closing my eyes as I repeated Leon Paul Akume to myself a few times. Ten seconds later, I opened my eyes and shrugged. "No. Never heard of him."

"Then why did you have his teeth?" the chief asked.

"So that's what this is about."

I hadn't expected the teeth to be identified so quickly. Forensics usually take more time because of the crime lab backlog. The teeth must be high priority. I stared at the mug shot again and tried to imagine Leon Akume without his cocky smile.

I glanced toward Delmonico, wishing he'd given me a head's up. "Certainly you read my statement. The teeth came in a package in the mail."

"But why you?" Delmonico asked. "What's your connection?"

"I have no idea, Detective," I said. "But for you to pull this identification together so fast, makes me think you already suspected whose mouth the teeth belonged in when I dropped them off. Why don't you tell me what else you know about Mr. Akume?"

Delmonico glanced over at Capacasa, who glared in the direction of the FBI guy. That move seemed odd to me. Even though we were sitting in the chief's office, who was actually in charge of this investigation?

"Agent Jax, what's your interest in this case?" I asked.

"That remains to be seen." His arms were crossed and he spoke in a grave voice as if discussing something important—a national security issue, maybe.

But I didn't believe him. I had the feeling the three men had deliberated their plan earlier and saw no option other than to share some information with me. If there was a chance I held a clue, they had to take it.

"So how long's our guy been dead?" I prompted them.

"About a week," the homicide cop said, explaining that the body had been found near a Dumpster in an alley in north Minneapolis.

The details sounded familiar. "Exactly where did this happen?" I asked.

"The Hawthorne neighborhood. A few blocks from Farview Park."

"I was there."

"We know." All three men answered simultaneously, making me feel outnumbered—three to one.

That part of the city was best known for vacant houses and drive-by shootings. I'd reported a routine live shot about the homicide a week or so ago and remembered standing just outside the yellow-and-black crime-scene tape with gawkers. Not much information had been available for viewers. No victim name, no suspects; the only witness was a homeless man who had discovered the corpse while foraging through garbage from alley to alley. I remembered him being disheveled, shaken, and too intoxicated for our on-camera interview. Who could blame him?

The only official comment from the police attributed the cause of death to foul play. Worthless. None of the other stations even showed up, figuring it just another gang killing.

"Your station was apparently the only one to send a live team," the chief said. "Any idea why?"

"Different news judgment or crew availability," I answered. "Happens frequently. News coverage is subjective."

That really wasn't the entire truth. The homicide had been delegated to me as a punishment, but I was too proud to let that gossip loose in cop circles.

The murder was the kind of no-brainer live shot given to new hires or that would have been busted down to a thirty-second voice-over because of its geography. I had been promised a day off the street to work on an in-depth report about nurses stealing drugs from patients, but Bryce and I had clashed during the news huddle, and when word of the homicide came over the police scanners, he ordered me out the door and sandwiched my live shot in the second block of the newscast. Definitely, a dis.

I hadn't given the homicide another thought since then. Neither had the assignment desk. And until now, the cops hadn't acted like they gave a damn either.

"No one on the scene mentioned the corpse lacking teeth," I said. "That might have turned it into a lead story."

"That word didn't come until the autopsy," Delmonico responded.

"Even later," I said, "that fact would have guaranteed another round of publicity."

My initial reaction was that the cops seemed to have been trying to keep this homicide quiet. Sacrificing media coverage for a closemouthed approach meant forgoing tips from the public. But why? Unless they already had a suspect in mind. "Any leads?"

"Just the postmark," Delmonico said.

He spread several large photographs across the chief's desk. They came from an exterior surveillance camera and each showed the same post office mailbox. Vehicles appeared beside the box in most of the pictures. While the plate numbers were visible, who was driving and what they dropped in the slot remained a mystery.

In three photos, people carried manila envelopes similar to the one the teeth came in. An older man walking a small dog. A teenage girl in a sweatshirt. A figure in a hooded winter parka who couldn't be recognized as either a man or a woman.

"Do any of these cars or people look familiar?" he asked.

"No. But I'm going to guess this was our sender." I pointed to the mysterious puffy coat. "He or she seems overdressed for the weather. The other two people aren't wearing heavy coats or hats."

"That may be," the detective said. "Do you recognize any of these names?"

He read off a list that I assumed were the owners of the vehicles. None meant anything to me, but they might not have even been driving.

Delmonico put the post office photos back in a file. Since our conversation wasn't yielding much about the perpetrator, I wanted to focus on our murder victim. I glanced at Leon Akume's mug shot while tapping my fingers against the table.

"Was he identified through fingerprints?" I asked.

No one volunteered anything.

"If he has a mug shot on file," I continued, "he should have fingerprints on file, too. Unless his fingers were cut off?"

Delmonico shook his head. "No, that didn't happen."

I started to think out loud. "So why did our killer yank the man's teeth, if not to thwart identification?" If the law men knew, they weren't saying, so I went for a gruesome question. "Were they removed before or after the victim died?"

That detail wouldn't be public record, but cops often leaked juicy aspects of a crime to the media for goodwill. I figured my brief ownership of the evidence gave me standing to inquire.

The chief cut in, not giving his detective even a chance to reply. "I think we'll hold tight to that piece of information just now."

I understood. The answer to my question fell under the category of Things Only the Killer Would Know. The fact that the victim's teeth had been pulled also fit that criteria, or at least had until I opened my mail.

Cops liked to keep those skeletons quiet to weed out false confessions. And this was a fresh murder, not a cold case. They weren't at the stage of the investigation where they'd take any evidence, real or not, just to close the file.

"Any chance you would discuss any of this on camera? I can have a photographer here in ten minutes."

They declined with a terse no.

"Well, thanks for all your help," I said. "And since mug shots are public, I'm sure you won't mind me keeping this."

I palmed the picture of Leon Paul Akume and slid it into my jacket pocket.

CHAPTER 18

I stopped by the coffee shop outside the Hennepin County medical examiner's office and bought a pricy coffee drink to take inside. Not for me—for Della Sax. Our paths had crossed numerous times in the name of news. I covered crime, she uncovered it.

But I knew her weakness.

"I've got a caramel cappuccino for Della," I told the man sitting at the front desk.

That was our code. If the chief medical examiner were available, I'd know soon enough. If not, the cappuccino would be mine. Within a minute, Della was reaching for her caffeine kickback and inviting me to follow her down the corridor.

She wore trademark pink scrubs and dangling crystal earrings on the job, her way of bringing elegance to a steel autopsy table. I could smell a whiff of formaldehyde in the air that neither perfume nor coffee could disguise.

Della closed the door when we reached her office, raised her cup in the air, then sipped her cappuccino with satisfaction. The office wall nearest her desk was covered with small pictures of faces with names and dates scrawled across the bottom of each. The earliest went back nearly five years. She called the montage her "murder wall"—victim photos of all the open homicides under her watch. Once a case was solved, the photo was moved into a desk file marked VICTORY.

"How many left?" I asked.

"Sixty-three." She savored another taste of caramel mixed with coffee and cream. "I'm no longer optimistic about justice. I used to count on good trumping evil and one day having an empty wall where I could hang pictures of my cats and kids instead of ghosts."

"That's not just on your back, Della. Chasing killers is a team sport. Cops want closure, too. But being smart isn't always enough. Sometimes you need dumb luck. Sometimes you even need the media."

"I know. I know."

We focused our attention on the wall of faces. Most of the photos depicted victims while they were alive, clueless to their unsettled destiny. Some came from the case files, given to the police by families for identification of their loved ones. Others were cut from newspaper articles or obituaries. A few of the photos—John and Jane Does—were taken after death and hard to view without recoiling from their pale skin and vacant eyes. Two had no faces, only sparse notes on Post-its to hold their place in her makeshift homicide row. The majority were mug shots.

Play tough; die rough.

"If a face doesn't come off my murder wall in the first couple weeks postmortem," she said, "I usually end up staring at it for a long time."

The same photo of Leon Akume in my pocket was the last in line. I leaned over to point him out. "I was just down at the cop shop about this guy."

"A messy murder indeed. I had feeling that's why you came looking for me, Riley. Your package is now in an evidence bag. Actually, two bags. One for the teeth, the other for the envelope."

"Like any concerned citizen, I turned what I had over to the authorities promptly and have been cooperating in their investigation."

She looked dubious.

"Of course," I continued, "now I feel invested in the outcome." I pulled out my copy of Leon's mug and held it next to hers. "Just like you do." I hoped he lost his life before losing his teeth. The alternative was too grisly to dwell on. "Has anyone claimed his body?" I figured that might give me a lead on friends or relatives, especially if a funeral was scheduled.

"Not yet," she said. "Maybe someone will see it on the news now. Did you have any relationship with the victim?"

That was the first question anyone wanted to know. I shook my head. "Didn't know his name. Never saw his face. Until today."

"If you have no connection to the victim, then we have to wonder whether you have a link with his killer," Della said. "This homicide is unusual on several levels."

"What was the cause of death?"

I knew better than to press for inside minutiae, but how the victim died was a fact of public record, so she didn't hesitate. "Homicidal aspiration."

That sounded ludicrous. "I don't understand. His ambition was to kill? Or be killed?"

"No," she said. "I mean 'aspiration' in the medical sense. Basically, he choked on his own blood."

A couple seconds passed before what she meant sunk in. I blanked out the rest of what she was saying because I was envisioning the horror of Leon Akume's dying moments. Retching sounds. Panicked eyes. Perhaps convulsions as his throat sought air and his world turned hellish.

"Riley?" She brought me back to the present.

"Did he suffer?" It was a useless question. Clearly he had.

"I'll discuss his death for context, but not talk specifics about the crime scene. You'll have to get that from the guys over in homicide."

I nodded, not sure how much more I wanted to know, still wishing the teeth had been lost in the mail.

"The body had no marks indicating he'd been restrained," Della said. "But he probably didn't struggle much. Drugs in the victim's blood suggest he was unconscious, yet alive, while his teeth were being yanked."

"You mean like novocaine?"

"More like meth, booze, pot. An addict's buffet."

"He didn't have meth mouth, did he?" That's when users' teeth rot and fall out. "From what I saw of his teeth, they looked okay."

"No. His teeth were fine," she said. "But each extraction—at least the first several—bled plenty—until he choked. At death the heart stops and blood flow ceases. So any remaining teeth wouldn't bleed."

"Any special training required to pull so many teeth?"

"Not really. The killer wouldn't have to be a licensed dentist, if that's what you're wondering. Just determined to get the job done. Judging by the damage to the gums, I'd guess it was an amateur."

I cringed again, reliving a unpleasant sensation when a couple of my teeth were removed for orthodontia work years earlier. My tongue remembered warm blood trickling from the gaps in my upper jaw. Suddenly, I wanted to gag.

I forced myself to concentrate on the murder at hand. "You'd have to have a tough stomach to slay someone like that when there are so many easier and faster ways."

"Yes, but just because the crime seems crazy to us, it doesn't mean the motive wouldn't make perfect sense from the killer's perspective," she said. "And there is always the possibility the suspect didn't intend for the victim to die."

"What do you mean?"

"Maybe the perpetrator was just playing dentist."

CHAPTER 19

Back at Channel 3, I photocopied several enlarged versions of the mug shot and ran my fingers along Leon Paul Akume's jawline. My own mouth ached out of sympathy. I ran my tongue across my top row of teeth, flinching again at the thought of St. Apollonia's demise.

That I was able to walk out of the cop shop with Akume's mug and name meant the police, despite playing hardball, were resigned to media coverage on the case. Were they rewarding me for turning in the teeth? Or were they somehow using me as a messenger? That didn't really matter, because I was also using them. We had different ambitions—finding a killer versus finding a story—but our goals sometimes intersected.

Right then, the cops knew more about our victim than I did. But that could change when the station broadcast his picture.

I wrote *"Leon Paul Akume"* across the bottom of one of the pictures and headed over to Lee Xiong, the newsroom's computer ace. Channel 3 had purchased numerous government computer databases over the years and Xiong had linked their information so he could retrieve the skinny on almost anyone in the state: whether they owned a car, or a home, or a business; whether they hunted, or fished, or voted. But especially whether they had ever been charged or convicted of a crime.

The latter held the most interest for me. If a dude had a mug shot he usually had a rap sheet, making it easy to read a biography of a life of crime.

"When you have a minute," I asked Xiong, "I'm interested in this guy. FYI—he's dead . . . as of last week."

"Do you have a date of birth?" For Xiong, knowing when someone was born was much more important than knowing when he died. DOBs confirmed identities and made his searches easier.

"No. But I'm hoping you can background him anyway. I'm most interested in Akume's criminal history." That seemed a likely avenue to find our murder motive.

I knew Xiong couldn't concentrate with me watching over his shoulder, so I headed to the assignment desk with the news that we had an ID on the city's latest homicide victim.

Ozzie had a hard time remembering the crime. "Is this a murder we even care about?"

He motioned for Bryce to join the discussion because we all knew that not all murders get equal treatment from the media or the cops. Certainly, there's a question of manpower and time. But there's also an intangible quality that simply makes some deaths more interesting than others, like those involving rich and famous victims or unusual murder weapons, such as a wood-chipper. My boss was indifferent to the mug shot because that suggested the Leon Akume was a lowlife, until I told him to imagine a toothless grin.

"You mean . . ."

"Yes, Bryce. We have a match."

He looked a little queasy now that he knew the teeth belonged to a dead man, but nevertheless, he quickly approved the story as the lead for that night's late news.

Besides the photo, I also had video close-ups Malik had reluctantly shot of the teeth. But when I checked for the unedited tape from the homicide coverage, I was too late. The raw crime scene video was gone, except for what had actually aired. I had hoped to find a visual lead. All that remained was thirty-seven seconds of cop cars, flashing lights, gawking bystanders, and a Dumpster next to a body shrouded with a sheet.

One of the changes Bryce made as news director was to order all video erased one week after the airdate. The strategy was meant to avoid having to comply with any subpoenas that might put the station in the middle of contentious litigants demanding copies of interviews. Without video, there'd be nothing to fight about in court. But for that tactic to work, the station had to be consistent. I felt the policy put us in legal jeopardy by destroying evidence of our solid work. But I was overruled.

I looked for the air check of the newscast and cued it up to my live shot. It was routine, overall.

((RILEY, LIVE))
BEHIND ME, A MAN'S BODY
WAS APPARENTLY
DISCOVERED NEAR THAT
DUMPSTER. POLICE ARE
CALLING THE DEATH A
HOMICIDE.

Had the killer been watching me at that moment on television as I gestured toward the alley? Or perhaps, even eyeing me from the sidelines among the crowd? Was that why the teeth ended up in my mail slot?

I assumed that the murder happened elsewhere. After all, pulling teeth is much more time-consuming than pulling a trigger. The alley was simply the body dump. I found it strange that the body hadn't been hidden in the Dumpster. That would have made it harder to discover. The display, along with mailing the teeth to the media, suggested secrecy was not a high priority for the murderer.

When I went back to the newsroom, through the glass walls of Bryce's office, I saw my boss spraying disinfectant on his desk where Leon Akume's teeth had once danced.

CHAPTER 20

Holding Leon's teeth in my hands, I hadn't thought I might also hold his fate. That idea crossed my mind as I started to write his story.

> ((ANCHOR, SOUND ON TAPE))
> A PACKAGE SENT TO
> OUR OWN RILEY SPARTZ
> HERE AT THE CHANNEL 3
> NEWSROOM NOW HAS THE
> ATTENTION OF POLICE.
> WHAT WAS INSIDE MAY
> JUST MAKE YOUR JAW DROP.
> SHE JOINS US NOW FROM
> NORTH MINNEAPOLIS WITH
> MORE ON THIS EXCLUSIVE
> STORY.

As I typed the narrow script, the computer timed my copy out to about a second a line to make reading the teleprompter easier. Because the newscast was broadcast live, a technician operated the machine from the control booth so reporters and anchors could stare straight ahead at the camera. Viewers don't trust television journalists with shifty eyes.

Out in the field, I had no teleprompter as crutch and had to rely on memory for the parts that weren't prerecorded and covered by video.

> ((RILEY, LIVE))
> INVESTIGATORS HAVE LINKED
> THE CONTENTS OF A PACKAGE
> I RECEIVED TO A
> RECENT HOMICIDE THAT I
> REPORTED FROM THIS VERY
> SPOT ONE WEEK AGO.

I stopped writing to open an email from Xiong that confirmed his progress in fleshing out the background of our homicide victim. The highlight: twenty-five-year-old Leon Paul Akume had been released from the Federal Prison Camp in Duluth two days prior to his murder after serving time for fraud. Leon had little time to enjoy his stint of freedom before his teeth were torn from his jaw. Xiong had included the name of a possible relative, but the number he was able to track down had been disconnected.

> ((RILEY, SOT))
> THE VICTIM . . . LEON PAUL
> AKUME . . . WAS FOUND NEAR
> THIS DUMPSTER . . . DURING
> HIS AUTOPSY, AUTHORITIES
> DISCOVERED HE WAS MISSING
> SOMETHING—HIS TEETH.
> AND THAT'S WHAT SHOWED UP
> IN MY MAIL.
>
> I TURNED THIS EVIDENCE
> OVER TO THE POLICE AFTER

FIRST SHOWING THE TEETH
TO A LOCAL DENTIST.

((DENTIST, SOT))
NO DOUBT IN MY MIND THE
TEETH ARE HUMAN.

((RILEY CLOSE-UP))
THE POLICE HAVE RELEASED
NO MOTIVE FOR THE MURDER,
THOUGH CHANNEL 3 HAS
LEARNED THE VICTIM WAS
RELEASED FROM PRISON
RECENTLY. WHY SEND SUCH A
GRISLY CLUE TO US?
WE HAVE NO IDEA.

As I skimmed back through my script and stored it, I realized there was someone else who might have additional insight about the victim. Toby Elness, an animal rights activist, was serving a manslaughter sentence in the same prison for his role in a misguided plan to bomb wind turbines to protect migrating bats. Toby had started out as a news source regarding a pet cremation scam, and we'd later become pals. I'd introduced him to his former wife, my previous news director, Noreen Banks. Even after their divorce, she'd continued to visit him in prison and care for all the animals he'd adopted. After her death, I'd found homes for their menagerie.

Reaching out to him meant facing up to self-reproach. He and I hadn't spoken for months. He had sent me a letter, desperate for a visit, but I'd written back that regretfully, I was swamped with work. Even I could admit it was a lame excuse, but we'd both changed. Toby's extremist cronies also shunned him, but for an entirely different reason. They wanted to avoid their names appearing on any government watch lists.

Seeing him meant a two-hour drive north to Duluth. I called the prison and learned that I remained on Toby Elness's visitor list and that the next visiting day was tomorrow. I hated myself for reaching out to him now just because I needed something. But I did it anyway.

The Duluth prison camp housed under a thousand inmates, but Toby was a social butterfly. I had a hunch he might have run into Leon before the young man's death and was interested in his impressions. Toby was an odd one, but he was also astute, one of the qualities that first drew me to him—that and his quest for justice.

He reminded me of an eco–Don Quixote. I'd taken him once to see a stage performance of *Man of La Mancha* and we'd left the theater, arm in arm, singing of righting unrightable wrongs.

((RILEY, GRAPHIC))
IF YOU KNOW SOMETHING
ABOUT THIS HOMICIDE,
PLEASE CONTACT THE
MINNEAPOLIS POLICE.

I added the final line to my piece and forwarded the script to the newscast producer before leaving for mirror, makeup, and my live shot . . . the melody of "The Impossible Dream" stuck in my head. Even though I'd tagged out the Akume murder story with the police phone number, I hoped viewers might call the station directly with tips.

After all, somebody out there must care about Leon Paul Akume—and I wanted to be the first one on the case.

CHAPTER 21

I drove north, toward Lake Superior the next morning, tracking a hundred-fifty miles on my odometer before reaching the prison gate. No cameras were allowed, so I made the trip alone, in the name of research. I didn't mind. The weather was clear, the roads dry, the radio reception good. I was glad to have a break from Channel 3.

A uniformed woman in the guard shack flipped through some papers before circling my name and allowing me to enter the grounds of the Duluth Federal Prison Camp.

After I stuck my purse and cell phone in a wall locker, another guard searched to make sure I wasn't bringing in contraband. They didn't just mean drugs or weapons. Smuggling in a newspaper, cash, or even chewing gum, could get a visitor booted permanently and could also land the inmate in trouble.

But prisoners who followed the rules enjoyed an easy sentence. *Forbes* magazine had recently ranked it among the top-dozen cushiest prisons to do time. The place was a minimum-security detention facility without guard towers or even a fence. Visitors and inmates weren't separated by glass partitions, gathering together on couches or around tables in a large community room instead.

Toby and I relaxed on some upholstered chairs and checked each other out. "How are Blackie and Husky doing?" I wasn't surprised that he asked about the welfare of the dogs that had once been his before asking about me. Animals always topped his priority list.

"They're happy to be farm dogs." Usually, when someone says a dog went "to live on a farm," they're being euphemistic. But Toby trusted me, and had met my parents. "I was actually down visiting them over the weekend, but something nasty happened."

I told him about finding the dead collie with the trap snapped across her throat. "Even my boss said it was too gruesome to air."

Toby had long opposed trapping and disagreed about shielding viewers from grim reality. "Sometimes you have to expose ugliness to bring change. Viewers should see the cruelty of these devices, like you did. Very few animals survive body grip traps. Most die within a minute, their windpipe crushed. No chance to even whimper for help. At least with leghold traps, if the wrong animal is caught, release is an option."

I told him about the other missing dogs.

"Odds are, they're dead," he replied. "Shoot, shovel, shut up."

"Excuse me?" I said.

He repeated the line. "Shoot. Shovel. Shut up. Some trappers kill unwanted animals and bury the evidence. Happens to protected species that are pests, or pets that get in the way. One of those hush-hush things."

He explained that when it came to trapping, some hunters were siding with animal rights activists. "Enough hunting dogs have been killed while tracking through the woods with their owners that lawmakers are being pushed to pass restrictions."

"Like what?" I asked.

"Requiring the traps to be five feet off the ground on a tree or pole. That way, climbing animals like raccoons could still be caught but dogs wouldn't become victims." Toby encouraged me to check state records. "The DNR is supposed to be keeping statistics. Even one dog's death is too many, but you might be surprised how many you find."

Tony's passion reminded me why I was glad we were still in touch. I loosened up as he chatted about a prison program in which he helped train dogs for disabled people. Then we discussed the earliest he might get out for good behavior. Finally I brought up the real reason for my visit: Leon Akume.

"Sure, I know who he is." Toby leaned forward and lowered his voice so the other visitors couldn't hear our conversation. "Everybody does. He's a snitch."

"A snitch?" I whispered back.

"Someone who rats out other people."

"I know what a snitch is." In news, we call them "sources" to make them sound noble. Suddenly Leon's murder and lack of teeth had an obvious and punitive motive. "So who'd he squeal on?"

"He was serving time for some kind of credit card fraud," Toby said. "Word out was that he flipped for a shorter sentence and nicer digs. That's how he ended up here instead of somewhere fierce."

"Did you know him at all?" I asked.

"We used the same dentist. But then, everyone here does. That's how I first met him. We had back-to-back appointments."

That explained how the cops were able to identify the teeth in the envelope as Leon's so quickly. The prison likely had sent current dental X-rays of his mouth to Minneapolis Police when informed about the unusual circumstance of his murder.

So I told Toby the latest on his former fellow inmate. "He's dead."

Judging Toby's emotions was difficult because his face resembled a perpetually sad bassett hound even when he was perfectly content. Though he and Leon weren't buddies, I could tell he was upset by the savagery of his murder when a throaty gasp escaped his droopy jowls.

"Hush," I said, noting that other visitors were glancing in our direction, including a family with young children. "We don't want to attract unwelcome attention here. If anyone asks what's wrong, tell them you got bad news about one of your dogs."

He gripped the arms of the chair before calming down. "I feel awful, Riley. I'd run into Leon Akume now and then, and he'd try to chat, but I'd steer clear because of his reputation."

"Reputation?"

"For informing. Whether it was true or not, nobody wanted to risk being his friend."

"He must have looked forward to his release."

"That's the funny thing. I can't wait to be out of here. I count the days—four hundred eighty-seven still to go. But he once mentioned not caring about going back to the real world."

"What do you think he meant?"

"I don't know. Some of the guys here sort of dig it. Especially those who don't have real family. We got comfy quarters. Easy jobs. Decent food. Free health care. Every once in a while someone jokes that it's better than working for a living. But now I'm wondering if he felt safer inside than outside."

I pondered that morose concept much of the drive home, and speculated how Leon had spent his last hours of life. In hiding? If so, he hadn't been good enough. Trying to gain an upper hand over those he feared? Again, failure. His final minutes were, perhaps, filled with excruciating dread. The kind that would make any man grit his teeth.

On my return trip, I stopped in Hinckley, the halfway point between Duluth and the Twin Cities. A bakery off the freeway was famous for caramel rolls, and even though I sensed St. Apollonia's displeasure, I bought one to go.

Her revenge came when a news story over the radio reported that a recent poll showed America's trust in TV news was at an all-time low.

CHAPTER 22

When the courthouse opened the next morning, I was waiting outside to retrieve Leon Akume's conviction file from the records counter. Normally, I merely skim through the legal paperwork and photocopy the juicy parts to save the station money. But in this case, I wasn't sure which documents might be key, so I paid for the entire folder.

I tucked the pages in my black shoulder bag and made a second stop at the cop shop to check their criminal records, which typically contain extra details, but this counter clerk told me that Leon Akume's file was "not available."

"Why not?" I asked, even though I already suspected the answer.

"It's part of an active criminal investigation."

The homicide cops had closed the police file while they searched for Akume's killer, but luckily they hadn't thought to pull the court records.

I waved the file at Ozzie, who was on the phone at the assignment desk, this time explaining to a viewer that daylight saving time wouldn't kick in for another month.

"I'm working on a follow-up to the teeth murder," I told him.

He nodded that he heard me and I headed back to my office and hung my coat on a hook on the back of the door. Reading through the documents was discouraging, because I didn't know exactly what I was looking for. But I quickly perked up when I saw a grand jury indictment alleging that Leon had been part of a multimillion-dollar identity-theft ring.

Even though he pleaded guilty to a lesser crime, I was surprised he hadn't received a longer prison term. But the file reflected a delay between his charges and his sentencing. That hinted that perhaps Toby's buzz might be correct—perhaps Leon was attempting to work a deal by leaking information on other criminal colleagues. Too late for him to go scot-free, but sufficient for a reduced penalty.

I taped Leon's mug shot to a white board hanging on my office wall where I like to track complicated stories, then started to make a chart with dates, names, and arrows.

I called the federal prosecutor who had handled the case. "What can you tell me about Leon Paul Akume?"

"Now you're interested," he fumed. "Last year I tried to get some media coverage about identity fraud, but nobody cared."

"Well, I care now."

"You're only interested because there's a dead body. You want details, call homicide." Then he slammed down the phone.

His criticism was spot-on. There's no way Channel 3 would give me time to chase financial crime unless the case involved armed bank robbers holding hostages. We aren't CNBC; our audience isn't into business and math.

When TV journalists say, "If it bleeds, it leads," they're talking about real blood, not companies bleeding money or making a killing in the stock market. That's not entirely the media's fault. Unless it's their own checking account, viewers are more attracted to loss of life than financial losses.

But Leon Akume's murder combined both.

My legwork on the case continued with a call to Detective Delmonico, which ended poorly.

"I told you I'd stay in touch. Remember?" I said. "Just checking to see if you got any leads regarding our murder victim after last night's story? I'm pushing for a follow-up on tonight's news, but I need something fresh."

"Sorry, Riley, can't help you. Not my case."

"Since when? You're the lead homicide detective."

"Not anymore. The feds are claiming jurisdiction. Everything has to go through them."

"How did they manage to make a federal case out of this murder?"

"You'll have to ask them," he said.

"Can you give me some direction here?"

"I don't dare."

Typically, murder is not a federal crime. Unless . . . and that word covers a lot of ground.

Unless the killing happens on US government property. Unless it involves a federal official. Unless it's rooted in the violation of another federal law—such as hate crimes and civil rights, organized crime syndicates, or crimes that cross state lines, such as kidnapping and drug or sex trafficking.

While those might be obvious cause for a federal investigation, the FBI has also demonstrated a creative ability to become involved if the victim is from a prominent, politically connected family.

I wasn't sure how Leon Paul Akume's death merited all this interest, but his fraud case had been prosecuted by the feds, so that seemed the place to start. I left a message for FBI agent Jax, asking him to call me back regarding the homicide.

Leon's defense lawyer hadn't heard that his former client had been murdered and seemed genuinely shocked on the phone. "We hadn't stayed in touch and frankly, I don't watch the news anymore unless I'm on it. Too depressing."

Benny Walsh was a criminal attorney who had developed an enviable legal reputation years earlier after convincing a jury that an obviously guilty client was the victim of a vast government conspiracy. Prosecutors found him tiresome, but the media appreciated him because he was always willing to appear on camera as a legal analyst whether he knew anything about a particular case or not.

"Well, Benny, my experience as a journalist tells me attorneys are a curious bunch, so I imagine you might have some questions about Leon Akume's death."

He agreed to meet with me on one condition: he wanted to first confirm his client was actually dead. "Not that I don't trust you, but I don't."

A couple hours later we met for a late lunch in uptown Minneapolis at The Bulldog, known for bar food and beer—and it was far enough from our downtown offices that we were unlikely to be noticed by anyone who knew us. At a table in an empty corner, I filled him in on Leon's homicide. The specifics about the missing teeth in the mail rattled him more than I expected because he had often demonstrated an unsettling ability to remain emotionally detached from his cases.

"It's possible his murder had nothing to do with his criminal life," I said. "But I feel a personal obligation to see where this leads."

"Honestly, Riley, I'm not sure how much information I'll be able to share. Attorney-client privilege can be tricky and doesn't necessarily end after death."

"How could talking to me hurt him?"

"It's not that simple."

"But much of what you know is part of the public record." I pulled out the meager court file and spread it between onion rings and burgers. "The cops were unusually quiet about this homicide until I showed up with the victim's teeth. And now the feds are taking over the murder investigation. I'm trying to figure out why. I'm hoping you can give me the highlights."

"I'm going to pass," he said.

"You're turning down a chance to appear on TV? I thought sound bites helped advertise your law firm."

"Dead clients are bad for business."

Leon Paul Akume's mug shot was in the paperwork, and I pushed it toward him. "What would your client want you to do?"

Benny was not sentimental and ignored my maneuver, choosing instead to concentrate on a plate of tater tots. I noticed he'd gained weight, but didn't mention that.

"I can certainly keep your name out of the news and use our chat on background only," I assured him. "Otherwise I'll have to report that 'the victim's attorney Benny Walsh declined to comment,' and you'll be connected with the murder anyway."

"You'd do that to me after all I've done for you?"

I'd once retained Benny myself to resolve an unpleasant legal matter. "I paid for your services, plus you got loads of publicity."

"You're wasting your talent in news," he said. "You really ought to go to law school. But you'd probably end up a prosecutor, and I'd hate to face you in court."

"I just need to understand a few things, Benny, and I'd like to start with your client's role in this identity fraud case. An obituary, of sorts. And I promise, nothing you tell me will be attributed to you."

"His criminal history is too complicated for TV," he said.

"Let my boss be the one to shut down the story. And between us, he probably will. But I'd still like to try."

So we paged through the indictment, the witness list for the sentencing hearing, and other documents as he explained that his client had been part of an identity-theft team that combined high-tech and low-tech means to run a lucrative swindling empire.

"How lucrative?" I was taking notes.

"He was able to afford me," Benny laughed. "Seriously, he was on the hook for a long prison term because of the sheer amount of money stolen. Twenty million, at least. Of course, it's split between a lot of players. And these people incur certain expenses that most of us don't, like money laundering."

Usually prosecutors dread chasing complex crimes. Juries get bored so verdicts can be unpredictable. Careers can be ruined. "How come you didn't take this to trial and try to get him off?" I asked.

"Overwhelming evidence. Social security numbers, bank accounts, stolen credit cards. They found a dozen drivers' licenses, all with his photo but different names. Victims who had been defrauded were anxious to testify. See, Leon started out small. Buying data from hoods who broke into cars and stole letters out of mailboxes, using it to get fake credit cards and hire runners to charge up a storm in gift cards and merchandise that could be resold online. If he had stuck with that operation, the law wouldn't have paid any attention. There's too much of the same con out there."

I started to speak, but he held his hand up to stop me.

"Let me finish," he said. "Akume got greedy and wanted to expand. He began setting up loans under false identities, aided by a banking insider. That's where the real money came from. I would have liked to have argued that the evidence against him was planted, but his computer showed he was quite involved in closed Internet chat rooms with international crime rings."

"How'd the feds get onto him?"

"The old-fashioned way. He'd insulated himself with cyberscreen names and other cute computer forensic tricks, but someone down the chain ratted him out. Even then he might not have been a big deal because the feds had always been too busy chasing guns and drugs to go after intricate financial crimes, but with the new US attorney coming to office, their priorities shifted. Akume was doing the wrong crime at the wrong time."

I was still scribbling when Benny glanced at his watch. "Last question," he said.

Benny had alluded to an informant playing a role in his client's downfall. Already one source—Toby—had mentioned Leon himself being a snitch, but Toby really had no firsthand knowledge, just jailhouse gossip. I needed better confirmation, so I cut to the chase.

"Was Leon Paul Akume a government informant?"

My inquiry surprised him. His eyes narrowed as he responded with a question of his own. "What are you planning to do with my answer?"

"Depends on what it is, Benny. But I wouldn't be asking unless I already had information suggesting he was."

"And if I verify your theory?"

I leaned across the table, lowering my voice. "I'll keep your name out of it and report something like 'Channel 3 has learned . . .'"

"Ask me another question instead."

"Who did he squeal on?"

Benny shook his head. "We're finished here." He picked up his briefcase and headed for the door.

I threw enough cash on the table to cover our check and followed him—fast.

CHAPTER 23

Benny had clicked a key remote to unlock his Lexus, but I reached the vehicle just in time to duck in the backseat and slam the door behind me.

"Get out." He gunned the engine, to show he was serious.

I buckled my seat belt to show I wasn't leaving, even if it meant a road trip. "You met me here because you know something's off. You want an explanation just as much as I do. Help me out, and I'll keep you in the loop, but off the air."

We both stayed quiet, evaluating each other through the rearview mirror.

"You can't blame me for asking, Benny. That plea bargain was a sweetheart deal, even for you."

"Yes, Leon Paul Akume turned informant."

"Who?"

"You might be better off not knowing."

"Come on," I pressed. "I just want to know what the cops know. Otherwise I'm at a disadvantage."

"Here's my terms," he said. "You can know it, but you can't report it."

A tough off-the-record deal. But he had the name, so he had the leverage.

I always like repeating source arrangements to avoid misunderstandings. "Just so we're straight, I can report Akume was an informant as long as I don't attribute it to you. You'll give me the name of who he rolled on, but I can't use it unless I verify it another way." That wasn't as difficult as it sounded. As a journalist, once you know what you're looking for, you know where to look.

"He gave up Jack Clemens."

I knew the name. When a rich guy falls, it makes news.

CHAPTER 24

One secret phone call transformed Inmate 16780-59's prison standing from chump to champ. Nobody dared call him Trip. He had regular access to a cell phone and the kind of respect only someone like Jack Clemens could buy.

The voice on the other end of the line had been surprised to hear from him in prison, but greeted him warmly and promised to work out a weekly payment plan with Scarface's outside people.

Kilo tried to weasel in on his good fortune, but this time his cell mate relished shutting him down. "Your problems are your problems, remember?"

"You know I didn't mean that, Jack. I was just joshing. Hey, you look like you're losing weight. That's hard to do on a high-carb prison diet."

He was momentarily startled by Kilo's compliment, and muttered something about getting "plenty of exercise folding towels." He didn't care that he had to work a menial job at the prison laundry for twenty cents an hour anymore. Knowing Scarface had his back gave him confidence walking the corridors. And that combination of protection and nerve kept other thugs at bay.

His first hint that something was wrong came during an off-the-books phone call to check in with his benefactor, who mentioned being irked by the price increase.

"What do you mean?" he asked.

"Don't get me wrong, Jack," the voice said. "I'm willing to pay to keep you safe, but I was just informed the cost is doubling. And apparently there's no guarantee it won't keep going up."

The inmate felt double-crossed by his prison partners, but didn't react because he was surrounded by them. "I had no idea. I'll see what I can find out on this end. I want you to know, I appreciate all you've done for me."

"Don't worry about it," the voice said. "No amount of money is enough for what you've done for me."

He didn't worry, because he knew what the voice said was true. They both needed each other.

Approaching Scarface about the finances was problematic. He decided not to take the scam personally, but simply treat it as a business misunderstanding.

"About our deal?" He brought the subject up when they left the cafeteria together later that day. "My people need to budget, and I thought our price had already been fixed."

Scarface stopped walking, placed his hand on his colleague's shoulder and squeezed hard. "Well, Jack, if you're unhappy with my services, we don't need to continue this arrangement."

"No, that's not what I'm saying." He backed out from the big man's grip. "I'm just wondering how you arrive at your rate?"

"My people handle the numbers."

"Well, my bill keeps going up, and I'm wondering why?"

"My people never charge more than they think a client can pay. Apparently they think you can afford the best we have to offer."

"That sounds more like blackmail than services rendered." He tried to make it sound like a joke.

"It is what it is. You made some negotiating mistakes, Jack. If I took advantage of your inexperience with prison life, that just makes me a better businessman."

"What do you mean, mistakes?"

Scarface headed over to a metal bleacher bolted to the floor and motioned for him to sit down. "Feel my scar, Jack Clemens."

He shook his head. "No, thanks."

"I didn't ask if you wanted to touch my scar. I ordered you to touch it."

So he reached out his hand tentatively and traced the twisted blemish from the big man's eye, where it started, to his lips, where it ended. The texture was smoother than the surrounding skin, like a snake sleeping on warm concrete.

"That mark is to me what a purple heart is to a soldier," Scarface said. "It proves that unlike you, I've mastered the rules of surviving time in the pen. I see you're confused, so I'll explain. Rule number one—*never* tell your real name." Scarface counted down on his fingers as if tutoring a child. "Rule number two—*never* tell you have money. Rule number three—*never* tell how to reach your outside friends. You violated every rule, Jack."

That's when Inmate 16780-59 realized that while there was safety in numbers, there was also safety in anonymity. He was no longer a client, but a hostage. And in his quest to protect his body and his pride, he had put himself in greater jeopardy.

CHAPTER 25

None of the TV stations had covered the mechanics of Jack Clemens's downfall, just the highlights. Fraud. Divorce. Guilt. Prison.

The business section of the newspaper had followed the financial drama in considerable detail, so back at Channel 3, I pulled up the archived articles on my computer. No time—or need—to read them all just then. I was looking for one thing: a date. Jack Clemens had motive to kill Leon, but did he have opportunity?

Thirty seconds later, I determined my theory was flawed. Jack had the ultimate alibi. He was behind bars at the time of the murder. His incarceration began a week before Leon's release from the same northern Minnesota prison camp. I wondered if their paths had crossed in the slammer.

I was counting on Bryce's business background to gain support for my investigation, but he cut me off cold.

"Identity fraud?" he said. "Dull."

"But it's the crime wave of the future," I insisted.

"Then we'll cover it in the future," he countered.

"That will be too late."

I laid out the twists I'd discovered about Leon's homicide. As far as scoops went, it wasn't bad. The FBI still hadn't returned

my phone call, but my deadline loomed and Channel 3 ran with
what I had confirmed.

((ANCHOR CU))
TONIGHT WE LEAD WITH AN
EXCLUSIVE REPORT INTO A
POSSIBLE MOTIVE FOR THE
MURDER OF THE MAN WHOSE
TEETH WERE MAILED TO
CHANNEL 3.

((ANCHOR TWOSHOT))
RILEY SPARTZ JOINS US NOW
WITH THE LATEST.

((RILEY, BOX))
TWO WEEKS BEFORE LEON
PAUL AKUME WAS
KILLED . . . HE WAS RELEASED
FROM THE FEDERAL PRISON IN
DULUTH AFTER SERVING A
ONE-YEAR SENTENCE FOR
CREDIT CARD AND BANK
FRAUD . . .

CHANNEL 3 HAS LEARNED
THAT AKUME WAS A
GOVERNMENT INFORMANT IN
A SOPHISTICATED IDENTITY
THEFT RING.
MINNEAPOLIS POLICE TELL US
THEY ARE NO LONGER
HANDLING HIS HOMICIDE . . .
AND THAT THE FBI HAS

TAKEN OVER THE
INVESTIGATION.

The newscast producer had opted for me to read the script on
the news set because the story lacked visuals and so Scott, our
new anchor, could debrief me and look like a real journalist. I'd
given him a few ideas for questions while we were putting on
makeup in the green room. At first, it went as planned.

((ANCHOR TWOSHOT))
DOES THE FBI HAVE ANY
LEADS?

((RILEY TWOSHOT))
IF THEY DO, THEY AREN'T
SAYING. I PHONED THEM
HOURS AGO AND THEY HAVE
YET TO CALL BACK.

((ANCHOR CU))
ANY WORD ON WHO THIS
GUY RATTED OUT?

((RILEY, CU))
THAT'S THE FIRST QUESTION
WE'D LIKE TO ASK THE FBI.

((ANCHOR TWOSHOT))
SINCE WE NOW KNOW THE
MURDER VICTIM WAS A
SNITCH . . .
WOULD IT HAVE MADE MORE
SENSE FOR THE KILLER TO

CUT OUT HIS TONGUE THAN PULL
HIS TEETH?

I was mortified and couldn't believe Scott had asked me such an over-the-top question on live television, especially following an investigative report in which each word is vetted by our attorney. I stumbled through an answer reiterating that we didn't know if there was any connection between the homicide and the victim's status as an informer, but would keep investigating.

Scott thanked me and then introduced a pretaped story about the controversies involving Minnesota's wolf-hunting season.

As soon as the floor director indicated we were clear of air and our audio wasn't hot anymore, I screamed at Scott. "Are you insane? That was gross!"

"It was a good question," he said. "You're just jealous you didn't think of it."

The producer rushed over. "Calm down. We'll deal with this later. Standby. Camera back on Scott in ten seconds."

I unclipped my microphone and walked off the set. Scott teased our upcoming weather forecast; then the newscast went to a commercial break featuring a denture commercial, a subtle reminder that Channel 3 has the oldest viewer demographics in the market.

Scott had beaten out several candidates with hometown connections for the anchor slot. Our longtime medical reporter had been the internal favorite in the newsroom because he worked hard and didn't have an attitude. Bryce's top pick was reportedly a blond weekend anchor from Chicago, who had grown up in northern Minnesota. But the network recruited Scott from a Baltimore station that competed against, and regularly beat, one of its other owned-and-operated TV stations. With one hire, the execs hoped to boost Channel 3 and hurt a rival a time zone away.

Scott realized he was in demand and had insisted on being called *managing editor* as well as anchor. It was a made-up title that meant nothing, but Bryce had agreed because it didn't cost money.

I was heading to my office to lay my head on my desk when my cell phone rang. The screen said UNKNOWN CALLER, but I answered anyway and heard Agent Jax yelling on the other end.

He sounded madder at me than I had been at Scott, but for an entirely different reason. "Do you have any idea the damage you have caused? Not just for us, but for all law enforcement?"

"What are you talking about?"

"One of the hardest challenges in my job is convincing people to become informants," he said. "You basically told everybody listening to the news that cooperating with the government will get you killed."

"Isn't it possible that's what happened here?" I said. "A revenge killing for snitching? A warning to others to zip their lips? Is that why you all were trying to keep Akume's death quiet?"

The line went dead before I could ask him about Jack Clemens.

CHAPTER 26

I grabbed a black coffee in anticipation of a long night ahead and went back to the newspaper archives on my computer.

Jack's troubles started when the economy tanked. As new investors for one of his companies dried up, Jack had propped up his financial enterprise by selling elite client identities to an identity fraud ring for fake home equity lines of credit and other fraudulent loans. He knew which investors were easy marks—aging clients, those on extended vacations, ones who didn't monitor their credit reports.

After the news hit, most of Jack's wealthy friends ran the other way, not wanting to be associated with him.

Benny had filled me in on something more—something not in the public court file or any of the previous articles—Leon Akume was his identity-theft contact. The scheme might have bought Jack enough time and money to stay ahead, except that Leon turned informant.

Checking Jack's online incarceration record, I noticed he had been recently moved from a Minnesota prison to one in New Jersey. With more than a thousand miles separating us, the chances of traveling to see him were dim. Even so, white-collar criminals tend to enjoy whining to an audience, and mail with a Channel 3 logo on the envelope would undoubtably make Jack homesick for Minnesota. I drafted a letter requesting an interview, but stayed vague about specifics.

CHAPTER 27

Bryce raised a cup of coffee to me in the employee break room as he beamed about the overnight ratings spike. I thought he was being sarcastic until he told me Channel 3 had held the lead-in audience of a popular forensics crime drama by aggressively promoting my informant murder motive story during each commercial break, along with a plug for the soon-to-come new studio set.

"The feds are unhappy." I hated to break his good mood, but needed to play straight with him in case he got an angry phone call. But that had already happened.

"They ranted at me, too," he replied. "I offered to let them come here and say that on camera, and they declined."

"So you want me to ease up?"

"No, Riley, all this is costing us is airtime, not cash. I want you to push harder."

I'd told Channel 3's attorney about the connection between Leon and Jack Clemens, but hadn't shared that detail with my news director. I didn't trust him to keep his mouth shut long enough for me to land a second source, but I was considering confiding the secret to him after the morning huddle.

Just then we were distracted from the day's news by Ozzie singing a rendition of "Here Comes the Bride" at the assignment desk. When he had our attention, he asked, "Anyone interested in a Mall of America wedding?"

"Do you know something about it?" Bryce asked.

"Just what it says in the news release," Ozzie said. "I'll hit print."

Bryce moved toward the newsroom printer ahead of anyone else, pulled a sheet of paper from the tray, and began reading out loud.

HOLLYWOOD TO FILM MASS WEDDING AT THE MALL OF AMERICA

Sublime Studios will shoot a scene from their upcoming movie, "We Do," at the Mall of America on Valentine's Day, February 14.

The film features a young couple whose wedding plans go awry because of family and financial troubles. They decide to forgo their traditional dream wedding and instead exchange vows in a giant ceremony with one hundred other engaged couples.

The starring roles will be played by Rachel Neuzil and Ricky Sand. Rachel is best known as the child actor from the popular television comedy *Cat Heaven and Hell*. Ricky, a native Minnesotan and Grammy winner, first came to fame through the Internet as the lead vocal in the boy band Rebel Fever.

The film will require hundreds of local extras as brides, grooms, and wedding guests. Couples with valid Minnesota marriage licenses will be allowed to be legally wed during the ceremony for free and participate in a reception following the event. Pictures of all of the newlyweds will appear at the end of the film during the closing credits.

Bryce stopped reading and a huge smile spread across his face like when the Grinch's small heart grew three sizes in the children's Christmas classic. Seeing such joy from him was unusual, and thus unsettling. That's when I learned my boss was a wedding zealot, just as his predecessor had been an animal fanatic.

"Viewers *love* weddings," he said. "If we play this right, we could net decent ratings cheap. This could be Minnesota's version of a royal wedding."

"I'm not sure this counts as news," I said. "It feels more like reality TV gone bad."

Now his expression changed and he looked like the evil Grinch with termites in his smile and garlic in his soul. "If I say it's news, it's news."

I let him have the final word as he assembled the rest of the news staff to talk about news coverage. Both daily papers were on the table, various articles circled for possible inclusion in a newscast or interview.

"Hollywood, plus wedding bells," Bryce said. "Who wants to own this story?"

The news release was lying in front of him and listed Velma as the media contact person, so I kept quiet. After all, what did I care if Bryce wanted to ring in newscast nuptials each night? Plenty of Channel 3 reporters would fight for such a soft, safe news assignment.

Me, I'd rather cover murder than marriage.

Sure enough, Nicole volunteered with no hesitation. "I think it sounds exciting. We can profile some of the couples who are choosing to get married for real and run features leading up to the big day."

If journalism ever died, Nicole would be an excellent wedding planner. She would fit in well with the mall culture, and as a rookie reporter she hadn't experienced enough of life to be disillusioned about weddings. We were friends, so I withheld my opinion about the story's paltry news value.

"What if no real brides or grooms take them up on it?" Ozzie asked.

That was my initial reaction to the mass wedding. Like throwing a party that no one attends, but still being stuck with the bill.

The late-news producer weighed in. "I think they'll have to turn people away. Some might do it to save money or avoid feuding relatives. But a lot of people will be attracted by the thrill of being in a movie."

"Yeah," Nicole said. "They can brag that Rachel Neuzil and Ricky Sand came to their wedding."

"Good discussion," Bryce said. "Nicole, get the mall on board and arrange so we have exclusive coverage of the actual wedding scene."

That idea seemed doomed to me. The mall would want publicity from all media outlets, not just one. There was no way Channel 3 could land this exclusively.

Nicole chewed her lower lip, suggesting that she might also have doubts. But if she did, she was wise enough not to share them.

CHAPTER 28

I n news, the best way to make viewers care about a crime is for them to care about the victim. As a homicide mark, Leon was a hard sell for compassion because he was a criminal himself. And while banks and credit card companies take big financial hits when it comes to identity fraud, ordinary people are the ones who are ruined.

So that's who I went looking for and how I ended up knocking on Lisa Melby's door. Her name was in Akume's court file as a witness making a victim impact statement at his sentencing. A woman who was taller than me, younger than me, and in better shape than me, answered the door.

"Hello, Lisa? I'm from Channel 3 News and would like to talk to you about a man named Leon Akume." I showed her his mug shot. "Do you remember him?"

"How could I forget? He basically wrecked my life." She recognized me from TV and invited me into her apartment. We sat on a shabby couch under a religious picture of an old man praying over bread. The same print had hung in my grandmother's house.

"Well, crime doesn't pay," I said. "He's dead now."

"I know. I saw it on the news. Very confusing. But I am glad that the harm he caused is finally getting some attention."

"So what did you tell the court when you testified?" I asked.

"That when you steal someone's identity, it's forever. They can't get it back. Insurance may cover the replacement value of stolen cars or jewelry, but it doesn't cover reputations."

She had been clueless until it was too late.

It was only after her student loan was denied that she learned her credit score resembled that of a deadbeat. Unpaid loans and overdue credit and debit cards were listed under her name at addresses across the country. She dropped out of school, struggling to find work because most employers insisted on credit background checks. And Lisa was so weary of phoning customer service representatives and filling out affidavits swearing she was not responsible for any of the charges incurred.

"It's been a three-year nightmare," she continued. "I'm still trying to get my credit history cleared, but the bad information keeps popping up and collection agencies keep calling."

"How is this affecting your day-to-day life?" I was fishing for tangible examples viewers might understand.

"My car is an old beater that doesn't even have air bags, but even though I have a job, I can't get a loan for a newer one," she said. "I'd like to move to a nicer neighborhood, but no one else will take me as a tenant because I look so bad on paper. So I'm basically stuck in a status quo of misery."

"Did testifying give you any sense of catharsis?" I was always fascinated about the dynamics when convicts and witnesses faced each other in court—one in handcuffs, the other with hand on a Bible.

"No. I felt rushed. Like I was just a formality. But here now, with you, it feels like someone is finally listening to my pain."

"That assures me that I'm doing my job right." We'd spent the last hour together. She talking, me taking notes. She was an articulate interview. "How crowded was the courtroom? Any friends of Leon around?"

"Basically empty. No spectators. Just me and him, the attorneys, the judge and other court employees."

"Did you look at each other that day?"

"Yeah, I looked at him. I was hoping he might look ashamed or at least sorry. But his arms were crossed, and he smiled the whole time I spoke."

"Really? What kind of smile?"

"Bold. He had more at stake than me, yet I was more nervous. We had a stare down, but I looked away first." She looked away from me then, seemingly reliving that moment. "Afterward, when he got such a lenient sentence, I blamed myself for not doing better on the stand."

"You did fine. Akume and the feds already had a deal. Nothing you said was going to make any difference." I changed the subject because my questions were making her dejected. A sob might be near, and there was no point in letting her get all emotional unless a camera was rolling. "You mentioned school. What were you studying?"

"I wanted to be a doctor."

"That's an admirable profession. It's a path that takes a lot of dedication, both before and after getting your degree."

"I had the grades and the passion. I got robbed by Leon Akume."

"Well, you certainly did. What would you think about doing a camera interview about identity theft? It would warn people about the problem."

That suggestion made her uncomfortable. "I don't want people to know I'm a loser."

"You're not a loser," I said.

"They'll think I am," she insisted. "I work in a funeral home, and that's only because my aunt knows one of the owners. I'm surrounded by dead people. Most of my time is spent mopping floors and loading and unloading caskets and flowers from vans. I dreamed of saving people, not burying them."

That sounded like a dismal way to make a living. But while she put a negative spin on her job, I tried staying positive. "Funerals give solace to those in despair and are an important part of our culture. Don't downplay your contributions. You are helping people, just in a different way."

"I don't mean to sound ungrateful, but it just wasn't my dream."

"Lisa, there may not have been an audience listening to your story in that courtroom, but I can guarantee, plenty of folks will be watching and rooting for you when they hear your story on Channel 3."

I left with a "maybe" regarding an interview, but internally confident the next time we met would be in front of a camera and lights. On the street, I noticed an old clunker parked in front of her building and reminded myself that my life, most days, was pretty good.

Benny called me on my way back to the station to thank me for keeping his name and Jack Clemens's out of my informant story.

"No need to thank me," I said. "That was our deal. But I am working on confirming the information another way."

"Good luck with that. But I did hear something about Jack that you might be interested in. The government is auctioning off some of his possessions in a couple days. It's open to the public. It'll probably attract a fun crowd. Might be worth some news."

"Really? Are you going?"

"Me, buy used? Especially linked to a jerk like him? I may be a lawyer, but I have an image to protect."

"Hmmm. Maybe some of his friends will show up."

"Are you kidding? He's a man without friends. Besides, this is lower-end stuff. His cars, Rolexes, and top art were already sent to speciality auction houses. This is more like what a rich person would donate to Goodwill. *You* might even be able to afford something."

Back in the newsroom, Bryce's office door was closed and through the glass wall I saw him scrolling down his computer screen. I tapped and he waved me inside. Soon I was pitching the auction story, again not mentioning my growing interest in Jack Clemens. He was intrigued with the idea of watching the spoils of fraud sold to the highest bidder "unless something better breaks."

I also told him about Lisa and her firsthand experience with identity fraud, and his reaction was much the same. But I pushed him on the concept that viewers care about crime victims, especially if there was a chance they could end up like them.

"She humanizes the identity-theft problem," I said. "We can use Leon Akume's murder as a news peg."

"Will she cry?" he asked, bluntly.

That was a hard question to answer. Even though I did suspect Lisa was in need of a good cry, that did not assure the interview would deliver that on-air magic TV photographers refer to as "sound up tears." But I told Bryce what all news directors wanted to hear when discussing crime victims in these circumstances. "Absolutely."

CHAPTER 29

An email from the Department of Natural Resources was waiting in my inbox when I returned to the station, part of my goal to put a wider scope on the trapping story. I'd requested copies of state paperwork documenting the number of dogs killed in body grip traps since the season opened last fall. Attached were twenty-seven Trap Incident Reports from across Minnesota.

Thirteen dogs were killed; eight were injured seriously enough to require veterinary care. Most of the accidents happened on public land, but not all involved hunting dogs off in deep woods or far fields. Several were simply folks walking their pets in public parks or near trails. One even took place in the metro area. The DNR had determined that all the traps had been legally set—under the current regulations.

The names of the animal owners had been blacked out, for privacy, I was told. That didn't deter me. The data was sound. I was confident that with specific dates and locations, I'd find enough people to interview for Bryce to approve the story.

I'd also figured out a way to get around the problem of pictures. I'd simply tell viewers the photographs were too disturbing to show. Imagination can be even more effective than reality.

• • •

Nicole closed the door to my office and told me that her efforts to get the Mall of America to give Channel 3 a wedding exclusive had failed badly.

"Their media spokesperson, Velma, laughed at me," Nicole said. "She told me all credentialed media will receive the same access. I'm so embarrassed. What am I going to tell Bryce?"

"Tell him it's a no-go," I said, "but that you'll do your best to make your stories stand out from the rest of the competition."

"That won't be good enough for him."

I could see she was beginning to panic, so tried a little gallows humor. "Then offer to get married with the rest of the pack. It can be an arranged marriage between you and one lucky viewer. Bryce is big on reporter-participation stories."

"Stop joking, Riley. He's going to be upset. I wish I'd steered clear of the whole wedding business."

I told her to stop acting like a nervous bride. "He'd probably have made you cover it anyway. At least this way you get credit for being a team player."

"Well, I'm going to wait until the huddle to tell him the bad news. That way he'll have to act civil in front of witnesses."

"Don't bet on it, Nicole. The odds were always against landing that scoop. But for him to recognize that would be admitting he was off base. That doesn't sound like the boss we know."

But Bryce surprised us. Instead of spouting off, he merely acted disappointed in Nicole and mentioned her "inexperience." Then he scrutinized the rest of the news staff. "Does anybody else think they have what it takes to negotiate an exclusive deal here?"

Nobody responded.

"Then I guess I'll have to show you journalists how it's done." He excused himself from the huddle, turning the day's coverage decisions over to Ozzie and the newscast producers.

We all looked at each other and toward the glass-walled office where Bryce was already on the phone. I remember thinking, no good can come of that. Hours later, I learned I was right.

I missed the afternoon huddle while chasing a story about a milk truck rolling over in a freeway tunnel and blocking traffic, but I heard plenty, starting with a text from Nicole: CAN U TALK? BRYCE GOT MOA EXCLUSIVE.

I phoned her immediately. She skipped hello and went straight to the problem. "Riley, I feel like such a washout."

"I don't believe Bryce. The mall would never agree."

"He says he took a business approach. Apparently, the corporation that owns Channel 3 also owns the studio making the wedding movie. Somehow he convinced them to only allow our news cameras. Synergy, he called it. And cross-promotion."

Bryce's business brain was trumping our journalism skills. "Well, Nicole, at least you have an exclusive."

"Not anymore. Scott wants to cover the story and Bryce thinks it's the perfect way to showcase Channel 3's new anchor. He dumped me."

I'm always aware of audio, and noticed her voice had turned from miffed to truly mournful in five seconds.

I took her out for a drink that night and tried to tell her that working for a television station was a lot like being wed to someone you could never please. "Think of it as a job, not a relationship. Lot less hurt feelings down the road."

"Is that what you do?" she asked.

"No. In my mind I'm married to my job; that's why I'm so messed up when it comes to finding true love. But it's not too late for you."

"Do you really believe that, Riley?"

"About me or you?

"Both."

I wasn't sure how to answer, so we sat there for a few minutes, not talking, before heading to our cars and home. In bed, while I channel-surfed between newscasts, I had to admit true love might have slipped away from me.

CHAPTER 30

Inmate 16780-59 hadn't received a letter since his prison relocation, so the Channel 3 stationery made him anxious. The envelope already had been opened by prison screeners to make sure it contained no drugs, money, or sexually explicit material.

Dear Mr. Clemens,
  I am a television reporter in Minneapolis and have been following your court case since it unfolded. I am interested in conducting an interview with you regarding your situation. I'd be happy to accept a collect phone call to answer any questions you may have and work out any visiting details with prison authorities. I look forward to hearing from you and hope that you have been able to follow the news back home.
  Sincerely,
  Riley Spartz
  Channel 3

The note contained both desk and cell-phone numbers, and the writer's email and snail mail addresses. He recognized the reporter's name, could visualize her face, and had no doubt she was who she claimed.

He was glad to not be forgotten, but realized an interview was impossible.

As he considered the implications of the letter, he started coughing and had difficulty stopping until he laid down on his bunk. His chest felt tight. He knew he needed to make a call, but not to the TV station. He didn't want his cellmate finding the letter and asking questions, so he folded it several times and stuck it under his mattress.

Scarface passed him the burner phone and Inmate 16780-59 dialed the number, slowly, as if he wasn't sure this was a good idea.

"Jack," said the voice on the other end of the line, "something going on?"

He summarized the letter from the reporter. "Do you think she knows?"

The voice was silent. This was not something either of them had anticipated. "You must not communicate with her. No interviews. That would ruin all our plans."

"I know. I know."

"You need to stay calm."

"I'm feeling jumpy, is all. What if she knows?"

"I will take care of this, Jack," the voice said. "I promise."

And then the line went dead.

CHAPTER 31

"O pen wide," Dr. Mendes said.

I'd scheduled my dental appointment like I'd promised him, and told Ozzie I'd be a little late for work. Turned out, I would be a lot late.

"I'm sorry, Riley, but you have a cavity," my dentist said.

"A cavity? I haven't had a cavity for years." Teeth were important in TV news.

"That's why we urge patients to have regular checkups." His voice had an I-told-you-so tone. "Seriously, didn't this tooth bother you at all?" He poked it with a pointy tool and I winced.

"I thought it was psychosomatic pain, related to that earlier story we discussed." I tried to stay obscure about the teeth in the mail because I didn't want to gross out the young woman having work done on her mouth across the hall.

"No, it's the real thing. And you need a filling."

Another patient had canceled at the last minute, so we decided to finish the job then. I closed my eyes as he stuck a needle in my jaw. My mouth grew numb and during the drilling sound I tried imagining myself in the production studio where work was being completed on the new set instead of my teeth.

"You're good to go." Dr. Mendes gave me his usual parting lecture about not forgetting to brush and floss. "Any questions?"

"Well actually, I do have one about that other matter."

He knew what I was talking about. The other day, the teeth had just been teeth. Now they were evidence in a homicide. Banter was unseemly. "Let's continue this discussion in my office."

I'd never been in his back office before. I didn't even know he had one. A couple of white plaster of paris teeth molds sat on a desk along with a photo of his son's championship soccer team. He was the coach, so I was about to congratulate him on the win when a gilded picture stuck in the corner of his dental diploma caught my attention.

It was St. Apollonia.

A different depiction of the martyr than the one I'd seen, this image showed a pale woman in heavy Renaissance garb with one hand against her mouth and the other holding a set of pliers. Dr. Mendes gave me the same history as Father Mountain, minus the religious debate.

"My dental school presents a copy to students when they enter the program as a symbol of the hard work ahead," he said. "Study hard and pray to St. Apollonia. That's the road to graduation."

That was the perfect transition to share intimate details of Leon Akume's murder, such as him choking on his own blood.

Dr. Mendes shuddered. "For such a bloody extraction, the gums must have been badly torn."

Now I shuddered. "All the more blood to choke on?"

"Definitely."

"So how hard is it to pull healthy teeth?"

"Without the patient's cooperation? Difficult."

"What if he were drugged?"

"That would make it easier. And determination might count for more than brute strength."

The same thing might be said about the TV news business: in some cases tenacity can get a reporter farther than raw talent. That had always been my philosophy, anyway.

CHAPTER 32

Luther Auction House in North St. Paul resembled an indoor flea market. There was already a line for auction numbers. I didn't intend to leave with any souvenirs, but filled out the paperwork anyway, just in case. I handed over a credit card with my driver's license to the cashier and was told to sign across the bottom of a legal-looking form.

"It verifies you have no personal connection to the Clemens case," she said.

That seemed a bit Big Brotherish to me. "Why would that be any of your business?"

"These are assets seized by the federal government," she explained. "The money raised goes into a fund for the crime victims. This screening is to prevent the crooks or their friends and relatives from using insider knowledge to buy possessions back cheap."

A flick of my pen, and bid number 139 was mine.

The auction stage was surrounded by rows of folding chairs, most of which were already occupied. I preferred to move around to check out the surrounding artwork, furniture, jewelry, and collectibles. A flyer described the items and the order in which they would be sold.

A couple of items did draw my attention. One was a framed picture, where it looked like real fish—sunnies, bullheads, and minnows from their sizes—had been brushed with paint, then pressed against the oceans of a printed world map. A blending of actual and abstract. The scales and gills had interesting texture, but the art was too large to be practical for most homes. It hung high above an intricately carved buffet I admired before moving on.

US marshals stood near the front and back doors, and I figured they must be an extra precaution, called to duty whenever the auction house sold federal-seized property, just in case a hothead showed up.

The Channel 3 crew arrived. Malik had a live truck and ran cable inside so we could broadcast with the auction proceeding in the background. We interviewed attendees about whether an item previously owned by a white-collar criminal carried curses or cachet.

> ((LADY, SOT))
> I'M HERE OUT OF CURIOSITY.
> I WANTED TO SEE HOW THE
> ONE PERCENT LIVE.

> ((MAN SOT))
> I'M HOPING TO GET A DEAL
> ON SOMETHING UNUSUAL.

The auctioneer knew his job. He spoke fast, pointed with authority, and moved the merchandise along with plenty of personality. "The next lot contains a jeweled money clip that was once likely in the pants pocket of Jack Clemens."

Some things went for more than I would ever have imagined, like a cement sculpture of a bull covered in one-hundred-dollar-bills—titled "Bull Market" and signed by the artist.

"Ostentatious or merely tacky? You decide," the auctioneer said before accepting a final bid of four grand. It made me wonder if there was gold inside instead of solid concrete.

Some of the bids came in by phone. A woman sat at a table on the stage calling out-of-towners who had expressed interest in acquiring specific items.

One of them came out on top, buying a Bob Dylan vinyl album for three grand. A monogrammed briefcase with the letters JRC netted thirty bucks. A safe went for fifty. Signed sports jerseys drew multiple bids, as did a personalized memoir from a former governor thanking Jack for his "friendship during these difficult economic and political times."

A mounted moose head and a bearskin rug from Jack's northern Minnesota cabin also attracted considerable admiration from the crowd.

"Our featured white-collar criminal was also a great white hunter," the auctioneer explained. "And since the hunter became the hunted, we are selling these distinctive wildlife trophies, both shot dead by Jack Clemens."

He started with the bearskin rug, which brought an easy grand. Then he moved on to the moose head, and because the moose population in Minnesota is dwindling, bidding was fast and furious until reaching a cool five thousand dollars.

The competition between rivals was entertaining, and Malik shot video of customers nodding or waving their numbers until that magic word: "Gone!"

Some items drew little interest. A treadmill brought no bids despite the auctioneer insisting it still had Jack's sweat on its surface.

Then the fish painting came up on the stage. The crowd was told, "This was from Jack's home office." On an impulse, I decided to go for the experience of bidding so Scott could ask me a question about it after my live shot. News directors like reporter participation in stories.

The auctioneer called out, "Sixty. Anybody give me sixty?"

I held up my number. He pointed toward me. "I have sixty dollars. Anybody give me seventy?"

"Seventy here," the auctioneer called out. I scanned the room to size up my competition, and noticed the woman with the phone was holding up a bidding card.

"Do I have eighty?" the auctioneer looked over. Malik nudged me in the shoulder, so I raised my card again to make good TV.

"Eighty dollars," the auctioneer repeated. "How about ninety?" He looked toward the phone clerk. She shook her head and shrugged like the mystery bidder had hung up.

"Eighty once." He eyeballed the crowd. "A very unique piece of artwork. Eighty twice." He paused three seconds before proclaiming, "Gone. Sold to the bidder by the camera."

I glanced around in case he was talking about someone else, but Malik shook his head. "Not me. You. You just bought one crazy huge fish painting. Good thing we have a van."

A couple of people laughed as I claimed my prize and leaned it against the wall behind us as I finished writing my story for the news. The fish painting would be a good prop to hold up on the air. Then maybe I could write it off on my taxes.

>((RILEY, LIVE))
>A BIG CROWD TURNED
>OUT FOR THE SALE OF
>ITEMS BELONGING TO
>WHITE-COLLAR CRIMINAL
>JACK CLEMENS.
>
>((RILEY, NATURAL SOUND))
>THE GOODS WERE SEIZED BY
>THE GOVERNMENT . . . AND
>ALL MONEY RAISED GOES
>INTO A VICTIM'S FUND.

Sound bites from people at the auction aired next, and I finished my report with pictures of items and the amount they netted.

>   ((RILEY, LIVE))
>   IT'S REALLY PENNIES ON
>   THE DOLLAR COMPARED TO
>   THE MILLIONS IN FRAUD.

>   ((SCOTT, DOUBLE BOX))
>   WERE YOU TEMPTED TO BUY
>   ANYTHING, RILEY?

I'd fed him that question ahead of time.

>   ((RILEY, LIVE))
>   AS A MATTER OF FACT,
>   SCOTT . . . I'M THE PROUD
>   OWNER OF THIS ARTWORK.

I'd recruited two spectators to hold the fish painting in front of the camera and signaled some others to applaud in the background.

>   ((SCOTT, DOUBLE BOX))
>   WELL, IT'S CERTAINLY
>   DIFFERENT. HOW MUCH DID
>   YOU PAY?

>   ((RILEY, LIVE))
>   EIGHTY BUCKS . . . WHAT CAN I
>   SAY . . . I CAUGHT A CASE OF
>   AUCTION FEVER.

Already I regretted the purchase. Loading and unloading the painting was a two-person job, so I was grateful for Malik's help transporting the picture to the station.

"Maybe you should buy it from me," I said. "You were the one who urged me to keep bidding."

"No way," he said. "Missy would kill me if I brought home something that big and ugly."

I took down a cluttered bulletin board from a wall in my office and we gingerly centered the painting's wire on the nail.

We both stepped back to survey the result. "Maybe it will remind me to always be fishing for stories," I said.

"Luckily, in news," Malik said, "there's no limit to that."

CHAPTER 33

Winter may have been late coming to Minnesota, but Mother Nature was making up for lost time with an overnight storm aggregating six inches of white stuff with strong winds. By morning the city had declared a snow emergency, unleashing plows and complicated rules regarding which side of the street cars could park on.

I paid a neighbor with a plow blade on the front of his pickup to clear my driveway but had to shovel the back sidewalk to reach my garage before sitting in rush hour traffic. A leased monthly parking space was waiting for me in a downtown ramp; however, that didn't stop my face from becoming red and chapped from having to run through subzero wind to reach the station.

Bryce's commute was easier. As boss, he'd reserved a space for himself in the basement of Channel 3. So while most of us were cold and crabby at the news huddle, he was in a cheerful mood.

"People are calling to complain about being towed," Ozzie said. "That always happens after the first storm."

"Send a crew to the impound lot," Bryce said.

I dodged that field assignment, knowing that people who get towed yell at everybody around them. Once our camera was even pelted with a snowball during a live shot by a man upset by the long line to reclaim his vehicle. Instead, I offered to check around, calculating the storm basics—number of cars towed, number of accidents, and severity of injuries. Actually, I used the phone time as a cover while trying to reach Lisa and lock in her identity-fraud interview.

My desk phone rang as I was walking into my office. Most people I want to talk to have my cell number, so I often let desk calls roll to my voicemail to screen out the junk and crazies. But I remembered there was a chance inmate Jack Clemens could be calling collect from prison. Reaching for the phone, I was disappointed to see the caller ID indicated the call was being transferred from the Channel 3 switchboard.

It was some guy who'd seen me on the news the night before. "Are you the woman who bought the fish painting?"

"Yes, I am."

"I collect art and would love to purchase it from you."

There's nothing like having someone express interest in something you don't want to make you treasure it. "Thanks, but I'm not interested in selling."

"Perhaps I can change your mind. Since we share the same taste in art, perhaps we could share lunch and discuss an offer."

I wasn't into meeting strangers, even if it was in a public place, unless an intriguing story was on the line. Too many stalkers presume an intimacy with TV reporters simply because they've watched us on the air or are friends on Facebook.

"I work in TV news. I rarely get time for lunch. And I'm especially busy with storm coverage."

"How about joining me for dinner, then?" The man was persistent and I was about to hang up when he softened his sell. "I understand your hesitation. You don't know me, but if you advertised the painting on Craigslist, you'd be showing it to strangers at your house."

"That would never happen. I'm smarter than that." I'd covered several Craigslist crimes, ranging from robbery to murder, and knew the risk of answering or posting such ads.

"Exactly. So how about we meet tonight at Stella's? They're known for their fresh fish, and that symbolism might bode well for me. Say eight o'clock?"

Stella's was a popular seafood restaurant in south Minneapolis. I'd only been there once, with Garnett, celebrating our first anniversary of dating. That evening still ranked as one of my favorite meals. I'd ordered the scallops, he'd gone for wild caught salmon. But it was our mood rather than the food that made the night special. We'd started with a champagne toast to our future and ended by boxing up our dinners to rush back to my place.

I decided the best way to erase an old memory was to create a new one. If Garnett was moving on, maybe I should as well. And I had promised my mom I'd say yes to the next man who asked me out. Even though this was a business meeting, I decided to think of this guy as dating practice.

"All right, I'll swing by, but I can't promise I'll be able to stay for dinner."

"Excellent. The reservation will be under the name Johnson."

"In the interests of full disclosure, Mr. Johnson, I'm not inclined to part with my fish art." That wasn't exactly true. Everything had a price. I may have bought it for a bargain, but that didn't mean I would sell it cheap. "I've developed a sentimental attachment to the painting."

"You've only owned the artwork about twelve hours. I wouldn't have pegged you to fall in love so fast."

I was beginning to rue agreeing to the meeting, but figured even if my dining companion turned out to be insufferable, the food was sure to be splendid. And, as before, I could always eat and run.

CHAPTER 34

Hollywood proved me wrong. I had underestimated the interest real people had in pledging to love and cherish each other until death as part of a wedding stunt.

The word from the Minnesota Film and TV Board later that day was that hundreds of couples had applied to be extras by submitting photos of themselves dressed in their would-be wedding garb. The only apparent rule—men in black, women in white. Getting the moviemakers to use Minnesota as a location was a victory for the state, which had recently approved ten million dollars in tax rebates to create jobs by luring film projects here.

Scott had already parlayed his reporting assignment into a cameo in the film as a news reporter covering the event. He was bragging to the rest of the Channel 3 staff that he even had a line of dialogue in the screenplay. Because there would be no teleprompter on-site, he kept practicing at his desk, in the halls and even, sources told me, in the men's room.

He had left the script on his desk while anchoring the newscast, so I took a peek to see what his role looked like on paper.

INTERIOR—MALL OF AMERICA

Camera pans a giant crowd of brides and grooms before pausing at a TV reporter with microphone in hand.

SCOTT
Love reigns strong here behind me where I'm reporting live
amidst a large-scale community wedding.

Hearing him experiment all day with the inflection was annoy-
ing. First he stressed the word "love." Then he switched the emphasis to the word "strong." He kept asking anyone who would
listen which way they preferred. I stewed quietly because I was
avoiding speaking to him after our confrontation about tongues
versus teeth.

Scott took every opportunity to remind viewers about the latest development regarding the upcoming movie, even teasing
the meteorologist while tossing to Channel 3's weather report
during the five o'clock news.

> ((SCOTT TWOSHOT))
> THE STUDIO IS LOOKING
> FOR A DIVERSE MIX OF AGE
> AND RACE FOR THE COUPLES . . .
> EVEN THOUGH THE
> MARRIAGE SCENE IS BEING
> FILMED IN MINNESOTA,
> THEY DON'T JUST WANT
> BLOND SCANDINAVIANS.

Our meteorologist, Ingrid, who happened to be a blonde with
the last name of Anderson, looked momentarily miffed, then cut
him off. "Thanks, Scott, but I'm already happily married."

He pressed her for what the extended forecast looked like for
the wedding day. "Rain or shine?"

"It's indoors, so it really doesn't matter," Ingrid replied.

The ceremony would take place in the Mall of America rotunda, the site of celebrity appearances ranging from A-list movie
stars and controversial politicians to *American Idol* winners.

Casting priority for *We Do* was being given to couples who wanted to actually tie the knot. In addition to an audition photo, they had to provide a copy of a valid Minnesota marriage license, and furnish the names of two witnesses who would attend on their behalf.

Brides and grooms would gather on the ground floor while witnesses could observe the festivities by looking down over the circular rails of the upper three levels. After the vows, the witnesses would drop rose petals while the newlyweds kissed. The mall would be open for business, but shoppers and sightseers would remain behind security lines.

I was so glad to not be covering the event.

My cell phone rang, with Mom on the other end. She'd been watching news coverage of the Mall of America wedding. "That sure sounds exciting. Maybe Dad and I will come up for it. We could stay with you."

I tried discouraging her. "It's going to be crowded and unpredictable. Sort of like the State Fair, but without livestock."

"We love the State Fair," she said. "And we don't get invited to many weddings anymore. We weren't even invited to yours."

That was a continuing sore point in our relationship. "Mom, Hugh and I eloped. It was a spontaneous moment. The kind that only happens once in a lifetime." It was true. We were engaged less than ten minutes before we were husband and wife.

"Well, you better never get married without me again," she said.

I didn't see much likelihood of that happening, so I promised.

"How come you never mentioned Phil McCarthy asking you to dance at the reunion?"

"Nothing came of it and nothing will. Who told you about that?"

"You have your sources. So do I."

If she was going to act like that, I didn't see any reason to tell her about my dinner plans.

CHAPTER 35

Stella's Fish Cafe was in the heart of Minneapolis's funky Uptown neighborhood with an art deco neon sign of a large trout over the door. I'd parked in a ramp a block away because I didn't want to risk being towed like the gray sedan around the corner being hoisted by its bumper. I took a photo with my phone for a "relatable" on Facebook and Twitter. I posted: Sorry to see this vehicle on its way to join the 316 already in the Minneapolis impound lot.

Inside the restaurant, I approached the hostess. "I'm with the Johnson party." She took me to a table near a window.

Mr. Johnson stood and welcomed me. His head was bald, his beard trimmed and graying. He wore a leather jacket, dark turtleneck sweater and jeans.

"I'm David Johnson. Thanks for joining me. Please sit down."

He'd already ordered a white wine and offered me one as well, but I declined. "I need to stay sharp through dessert, or I might be out a fish painting."

He laughed. "Dinner before business."

"Actually, I never drink if I'm driving," I explained. "The cops would love to hit me with a DUI and land my name in the newspaper. Plus, it would give my boss an excuse to fire me." Channel 3's talent contracts contained an unsuitability clause allowing termination for criminal or immoral behavior.

The restaurant setting was casual, the menu interesting. We started with skillet corn bread and salads, and David settled on walleye while I went for mahimahi. The food and company were both pleasant. I told him about the desperate life of a journalist and he told me about the "dull in comparison"—his words, not mine—world of academia.

"Does that mean I should call you Professor Johnson? Or even Doctor Johnson?"

"Please, call me David."

He was a visiting college professor on sabbatical and enjoyed buying art from every place he lived or worked. One ear had a gold earring that lent a hip appearance despite his age.

"When you showed the painting off on the news last night, it was like destiny."

"Why don't you commission your own?" I offered to give him the name of the artist.

He dismissed that idea. "That would be contrived. It destroys the thrill of discovery."

I got what he was saying, but still liked the backstory behind how I acquired the piece enough to want to keep the fish painting. Until he started talking money.

"You demonstrated a good eye for art at that auction," he said. "You should profit from it. I'm prepared to offer you two thousand dollars."

I switched back and forth between wavering and fantasizing. Two grand was more than twenty times what I paid. An excellent investment return. But perhaps my picture was one of those extraordinary finds, bought at a garage sale but worth a small fortune, as seen on *Antiques Roadshow* or that pawn shop cable TV series.

I decided to play coy. "I'll think about your offer."

"What's to think about? Surely there's something you need? A fur coat? A vacation? Car repairs?"

I held firm. "I'll think about your offer."

"I'll call you," he replied.

I smiled. "That's a line men give women when they don't want to see them again. But I think you will call, if only for the painting."

As far as blind dates went, he wasn't as bad as I expected. And his next line hinted at a shared reaction.

"Is this the part where you invite me to come upstairs to see your etchings?" he asked.

Now I laughed. "There's an old-fashioned euphemism," I said. "Maybe I would invite you over if I thought you really wanted to see my etchings, but you just want my fish painting." I showed him a picture of it on my cell phone. "Like I said, I've grown fond of it."

The waiter brought our bill and even though I reached for my purse, David insisted on picking up the tab. He paid cash, with a generous tip, and offered to give me a ride home.

"Thanks, but I drove myself."

We said good-bye at the door and left for home in different directions.

That night, while reading in bed, alone, I thought about David Johnson and whether some chemistry might develop between us. Mostly I thought about what two thousand dollars could buy. I had plenty of vacation time saved up, and a trip to a warm ocean resort held appeal during a Minnesota winter.

By habit I turned on the late news to channel-surf between our station and our competitors. Ashamed to see Channel 3 promoting an exclusive breaking development about the wedding movie, I burrowed under the blankets to avoid what was sure to be a journalistic train wreck. Yet curiosity kicked in, and I persuaded myself I needed to watch, if only to criticize.

((SCOTT BOX))
THE WINNING COUPLES HAVE
JUST BEEN NAMED TO PLAY

EXTRAS FOR THE MOVIE . . .
WE DO . . . TO BE FILMED AT
THE MALL OF AMERICA.
WE'VE POSTED THE LINK ON
OUR WEBSITE SO YOU CAN
SEE THE PHOTOS OF ALL
ONE HUNDRED. HERE'S A
SAMPLE.

Quick cuts of smiling couples covered about ten seconds of wedding march music until Channel 3 broke for commercial. All I could think, pillow over my face, was that at least the station didn't lead with it.

CHAPTER 36

The next morning, Bryce announced that the wedding extras link had generated a record number of visits to Channel 3's website. And the clicks were still coming, even temporarily crashing the system a couple hours earlier.

"That proves there's genuine interest in this story," he said. "Each of the featured couples have families and friends who want the latest news about the ceremony. This is our chance to gain new viewers virtually overnight. Ideas?"

"We can begin profiling some of the couples," Ozzie said.

"Excellent." Bryce nodded his approval. "I'd like to see a mention of it on every newscast. Anything else we should address?"

Xiong brought up the issue of the license plate tracking data kept by Minneapolis police. He didn't normally say much during the news huddles, so we listened.

"The information is currently deemed public and is retained for one year. Political pressure is underway to reclassify the data as private and only save it for a brief period of time. I think Channel 3 should purchase the entire computer database before that happens."

"What's it good for?" Bryce asked.

Xiong was starting to fidget under the pressure of everyone watching him. His computer skills were better than his people skills. "The police use it to identify criminals. When the plate

number is scanned, they pull over the driver. We have the benefit of the history they have assembled. With a particular license
plate number we can learn where a vehicle has been seen."

"So what does that get us?" Bryce said. "If this data is all from
the past, won't it be outdated?"

Xiong was no match for Bryce's condescension, so I jumped
in. "I can envision how it might be useful if we were going to
conduct surveillance to determine a target's travel patterns."

Bryce mulled over my point. "How much does it cost?" The
bottom line was our news director's primary focus for decision
making.

"A few hundred dollars."

"What? For a bunch of computer files?"

Xiong said. "But if we wait, the law might be changed and it
will be too late."

"And you're sure this will actually work?" Bryce asked. "It will
help us locate cars and people?"

"Not in actual time," Xiong said. "But it will show where a
person's vehicle has been documented in the past, and help us
predict what area it is mostly likely to be found again."

"Here in Minnesota," I said, "we are likely to have more complete data than in other states because our law requires plates
on both the front and the back of vehicles."

That was because 3M, another Fortune 500 company based
in Minnesota, made the reflective tape used on the license plates
and lobbied hard for the statute, campaigning that it would help
law enforcement. But everyone knew it was so they could make
more money.

"Vehicles here have a greater chance of winding up in the
computer list," I said. "I think a story might come along where it
could pay off."

"Well, you caught me in a good mood," Bryce said. "Fine.
Go for it. So does anyone want to know why I'm in such a good
mood?"

"The heavy hits to our website?" Ozzie asked.

"Yes, but this is something more."

"Is it your birthday?" Nicole asked.

I hoped not, or we would have to run out and buy him a present.

"No, it's not about me. Today's a big day for the entire newsroom. You'll see."

A semitrailer from California slowed outside Channel 3, backing up against the rear of the building. Word spread through the station that, after a cross-country journey, the new studio set had arrived and some assembly would be required.

Most of us had thought it was being built from scratch, like our previous ones. But apparently all that sawing and pounding was just prep work for the coronation to come.

Bryce scoffed at our lack of sophistication about the digital age of television engineering. "The technology requires special skills. Our set was designed by the same experts who created that game show stage with the spinning wheel.

"And besides, the corporation that owns us, owns them."

CHAPTER 37

Two grand?" Malik said.

I'd just told him about the offer I had for the fish painting while we were headed to an interview. He was the kind of driver who usually kept his eyes straight on the road, like looking through a camera viewfinder, but this time he glanced over at me to see if I was kidding.

I assured him I wasn't. "Two grand."

"I deserve a cut," he insisted. "I'm the one who encouraged you to buy it."

"I haven't decided whether to sell or not."

"What's to decide? Take the money."

Malik made sense.

What I didn't tell him was that part of the reason I hadn't closed the deal was a possible personal interest in the man behind the money. An articulate guy with nothing to do with law enforcement or the media might help me find a new path away from my all-too-frequent thoughts of Nick Garnett. So I was delaying the sale in case that was the last I saw of him.

A few minutes earlier, out of curiosity, I'd searched "David Johnson" and "professor" and found about four hundred thousand hits—far too many to scroll through. That's when I realized I should have spent more time at dinner learning about him rather than discussing art.

• • •

Lisa Melby had been skittish when I had first broached the idea of telling her story on TV. Her life had been stolen by thieves. She worried that her privacy was next. But she had contemplated the idea and decided that if I actually followed through, so would she.

"I wasn't sure you would really contact me again," she said.

"I told you, as a victim, you're an essential part of this story. I can't tell it without you."

Malik and I were a few miles from Lisa's place when Ozzie diverted us. He was shouting on the phone, something about a wild protest at the Mall of America.

"Inside?" I asked.

"Affirmative," he said. "Apparently, the wedding extras in the mall movie include five gay couples. A group opposed to same-sex marriage is staging a demonstration. You're my closest crew. Can you head over?"

"It means busting my identity-theft victim interview." While I normally thrived on breaking news, I was still trying to steer clear of the mall.

"But that doesn't even have an airdate yet and this is happening now," Ozzie remind me.

I didn't see any way out. "There might not be much to shoot by the time we arrive. The mall doesn't allow groups to wave signs and demonstrate. They'll be evicted immediately, and it's so cold they'll scatter once they get outside."

"I know," Ozzie said, "but maybe you can catch up with them when they're kicked out. Or find somebody who shot cell video of the commotion. Give me an ETA"

Malik exited the interstate and headed east on the Crosstown highway. "Tell him, fifteen minutes tops."

I phoned Lisa and told her about the change in plans, assuring her the station was still committed to her story. "This is just one of those out-of-nowhere news events we have to chase. I promise we'll reschedule."

The issue of same-sex marriage had undergone a contentious battle in Minnesota. The fight wasn't just political. Fervor came from the Catholic pulpit as well, pitting parishioner against parishioner in the debate. At the polls, voters had rejected an amendment to the state constitution to define marriage as "one man–one woman." Months later, in a surprise move, lawmakers inserted the word "civil" before all references to the word "marriage" and passed a law making gay weddings legal in the state.

That didn't mean everyone was happy. While thousands of same-sex couples had already exchanged vows, opponents vowed to repeal the law once the political climate changed. And protests kept the issue in the news.

When we arrived on the scene, about a hundred people were gathered in front of the mall, and two police cars with flashing lights blocked the entrances. A middle-aged man and a heavyset woman carried a long banner reading: TODAY GAY MARRIAGE, TOMORROW POLYGAMY, while other folks marched behind chanting "Don't mock marriage. *We Don't*"—a play on the film's title.

Malik pulled over, grabbing his camera from the back of the van to shoot cover video of the crowd. As I changed seats in the van, two protesters waved their signs in front of us to get their messages on TV. One read: ALL BORN OF A FATHER AND MOTHER. The other said: TESTICLES DON'T HAVE EGGS.

"Good luck, Malik." I left him to look for parking. Word of the rally was apparently attracting supporters of gay marriage to turn out for a counter protest. I passed two women in the ramp waving a flag that read: EQUAL LOVE.

Minutes later, when I caught up with my cameraman, more protesters were being ushered outside. This rally presented more of an embarrassment to the mall than an actual security threat. I nudged Malik and made sure he shot a man with a handmade sign that read, GAYS SHOP AT MOA. WHAT'S THE FUSS ABOUT MARRYING?

We rushed around for sound bites and learned the riot had been mobilized through Facebook and Twitter by opponents to same-sex marriage who used the film as an excuse to face off. We were surrounded by proof of the power of social media. People were taking pictures of the demonstration with their cell phones and posting them online. One woman texted me some interior video she shot before being kicked out, in which the protest leaders spoke of not wanting straight and gay couples wed in a joint ceremony during the movie.

"Hollywood is Satan!" one of the speakers shouted. I forwarded that scene to the Channel 3 assignment desk.

We spotted Velma waving her arms to keep the crowd back while balancing a cell phone between her shoulder and chin. I would have liked to dodge her, but Malik was already moving in with his camera to get official Mall of America reaction. At the same time that we reached her, so did Nick Garnett.

He and Malik greeted each other like old buddies. He and Velma acted like colleagues in a hurry. Neither of them had coats, and her dress, while stylish, offered little protection from the winter wind. Garnett and I squirmed like the testy exes we were, waiting to see who would speak to the other first, but we both stuck to our jobs.

While security guards tried to disperse the crowd, I clipped a wireless microphone on Velma for an interview. She was familiar with the drill. "What can you tell us about the protest?"

"While the mall recognizes the right to free speech, we are a place of business and can't allow this action to interfere with our customers' shopping experience."

Once again, Velma's weird speech pattern was noticeable, but there was nothing we could do to fix it. A photographer from a competing station shoved his camera into our Q&A with Velma. There wasn't much we could do to oust him.

"What will happen once they begin filming the movie, *We Do?* Is there a chance we'll see more of this?" I gestured to the pushing and shouting around us.

"The movie is a comedy," Velma said. "It is not making a political statement."

"What about the gay couples in the wedding scene? That's apparently what set off this commotion."

"Straight or gay, anyone can marry at the mall," she said. "One hundred couples were cast as extras in a film. All this brouhaha over their sexual orientation is misplaced."

Her voice was lost after that because a cop with a blow horn began urging everyone to leave the grounds or risk being cited for trespassing. That didn't apply to us because courts give broad latitude to media covering news events in public places.

Velma halted the interview, saying she was freezing and had to head back inside. I heard her swear and mutter something about her PR predecessor having it much easier with *Jingle All the Way* and *The Mighty Ducks*. But by then she'd turned off the mic and started marching away in high-heeled ankle boots made out of some reptile.

"This one surprised us." Garnett was explaining to a Bloomington Police captain that, while mall security analysts monitor social media for references to MOA, this protest was imminent by the time they caught track of it.

I signaled to Malik that we should hang back and try and get some of that info on video, when Velma returned to tap Garnett on the arm and tell him, "No media interviews. I gave them all they need."

After our years as a couple, I could still read Garnett and at that moment I knew he was peeved that a communications flack was telling the mall's head of security what to do. Especially in front of me.

A female security guard hanging in the background removed her coat and wrapped it around Velma's shoulders and they

walked back into the mall, heads together like they were whis-
pering. I wondered if they were talking about me, then told myself to stop being so insecure.

Garnett was a better on-camera interview than Velma, and he
knew it. His voice inflection sounded more natural. As much as
I wanted to test his resolve following Velma's orders, I decided
to walk away and prepare for my live shot. This time I didn't
bother turning to see if he was watching me leave. Because if he
wasn't, I didn't want to know.

I had no proof that their relationship was more than professional, but they had the advantage of proximity. And were both
on the rebound. Him from me. Velma from a nasty divorce. As a
TV reporter, my job required me to look good, but nobody looks
better than a recently divorced woman.

Back at Channel 3, I listened to a voicemail message from David
Johnson, apologizing for not calling me sooner. "Good thing you
didn't need a ride home that night. My car got towed after that
blasted snow." He wanted to know if I'd had a chance to think
about his offer.

I leaned back in my desk chair to admire the fish painting and
imagine myself snorkeling in some tropical reef with my profit.

CHAPTER 38

Scarface flashed the taboo cell phone like it was an extra ace. "Jack, your turn to call out if you want."

As the rest of the gang hovered, he dialed, taking assurance from the fact that the voice answered his call. If the day came when the phone kept ringing and no one picked up, he would know his penitentiary predicament was about to get much worse. Right now, just hearing an outside "hello" soothed any anxiety.

Inmate 16780-59 turned his back as if that would give him some semblance of privacy in a place where none existed, and lowered his speech to a whisper. "Fine, I guess. Anything I should know?"

The brief conversation instantly came to a halt when he dropped the phone as he reached to protect his neck from a hairy arm that had wrapped around his throat.

He tried calling for help as his knees collapsed. The floor was hard, but the grip against his windpipe was harder. No scream left his lips, just a muffled gasp of confusion. He heard the voice from the phone speaker calling out his name and he stretched his fingers toward the device as he struggled against the acute pain.

A hand retrieved the cell and held it close to his foaming mouth. "Say good-bye to your people." The prisoner recognized

Scarface's voice and tried twisting to look at the big man, but the arm kept squeezing tight.

"What's happening?" the phone voice kept asking. "Are you okay? Jack, talk to me."

Scarface loomed over him and snapped his fingers, instructing whoever had the hold on his neck to ease up. "Last words."

"Why?" he sputtered.

Scarface shrugged. "You got outbid."

"Help me," He pleaded to the voice on the phone. His heart was beating too fast and he could no longer speak.

"Finish it," Scarface told the man with the choke hold.

After ten seconds of spastic jerking, he lost consciousness and slumped. The last sound he heard was his name echoing from the phone. "Jack, are you there?"

The assailant kept up the pressure until the whites of the dead man's eyes oozed red. By then his face was swollen and his body was still and quiet on the prison floor.

The voice on the phone spoke urgently. "Somebody, talk to me. Is everything okay?"

"Yep," Scarface answered. "We're done here."

"Good," the voice replied.

CHAPTER 39

By the time I woke up the next morning, the Associated Press had moved a news story out of New Jersey reporting that Jack Clemens, a multimillionaire fraudster, had died in prison. They'd picked it up from a local television station whose crime reporter had probably called the medical examiner in a routine check for "unusuals."

Facts were sketchy. *Minnesota Businessman Dies Behind Bars.*

I always knew that landing a camera interview with him was a long shot, but I fully expected Jack to at least phone me. I'd even programmed my voicemail to instruct the prison operator that I accepted collect calls, even from correctional facilities, so he could leave a message in case we missed each other.

If Jack was dead, so was my plan for confirming that Leon had ratted him out. I volunteered to cover the news of his demise, and since nobody else seemed to want the story, the assignment was mine.

I started out by contacting the prison to learn a cause of death. That would determine our news coverage. Plenty of incarcerated people die of natural causes, but if prison violence was involved, we might be looking at a national story. And I might even be able to sell Bryce on a trip out east.

"I'm sorry," their public information officer said. "But we are awaiting an autopsy report before commenting."

"Can you give me a sense of what happened?" I asked. "Did he drop dead or have some help? Off the record, are we looking at foul play?"

The guy wouldn't engage. "We will be releasing information as it becomes public."

Another two hours passed before that happened. And when it did, the wire story called it murder. *White-collar criminal Jack Clemens was found dead in prison, apparently strangled by another inmate. Clemens had pleaded guilty to conspiracy and fraud charges and was serving a ten-year sentence.*

I was just leaving a message for his attorney, seeking his reaction and asking why his client had been moved to an out-of-state prison, when Bryce entered my office and closed the door. Considering what I knew about his history of harassing women, that move made me uncomfortable. In the past, Nicole and I had texted each other if one of us was alone with Bryce so the other could casually interrupt the meeting. We hadn't needed that plan recently and my cell phone was out of reach.

"Is there something you'd like to discuss?" I stood up before he could sit down. "I was just making some calls, but I can join you in your office." That way the rest of the newsroom could keep an eye on us through the glass walls, and Bryce would keep his hands on his side of the desk.

"Let's chat here for a bit, Riley. Why does the FBI want to talk to you about Jack Clemens?"

"What?"

"An Agent Jax is waiting in the lobby right now."

"Really." I sat back down. I hadn't expected that. My desk was a mess of paper. I sorted through a stack and handed him a copy of the letter I'd mailed to Clemens in prison. "It's possible they know about this."

He looked impressed as he read. "Why did you want to interview Jack Clemens?"

A knock came on my door and Miles Lewis stuck his head in.

"The FBI apparently wants to ask you some questions. There's an agent here who is losing patience."

Miles was Channel 3's media attorney. He vetted investigative news stories, advised reporters on open government meetings and public data, and handled subpoenas and other legal affairs.

"What a coincidence," I said. "I'd like to ask him some questions as well."

"It might not work that way," Miles responded.

"Agent Jax has a lot of nerve showing up here. I've left numerous messages for him and he's not returned my calls."

"Is he the same jerk who screamed about us running the snitch story?" Bryce asked.

"That's him," I said.

"So how is he connected to both those cases?" my boss asked.

That was the pivotal question. I looked at Miles—who already knew the answer—and he nodded. Bryce wasn't going to be happy when he learned we'd cut him out of the loop. But maybe he wouldn't recognize the slight.

"What I'm about to tell you is very off the record," I cautioned. "We can't report this unless we confirm it with a second source. We can't even talk about it within earshot of anyone else, it's so very off the record. Understand?"

"Of course I understand. I'm the boss. What's the big secret?"

So I explained that I believed that the person Leon Akume had informed on was Jack Clemens.

"And now they're both dead," Bryce said.

"It would appear so," I answered.

He handed the letter to Miles. "Check the date."

Miles's eyes widened. "So in a matter of days after receiving a request from you for a media interview, Jack is killed."

"Yep," I agreed, "but that doesn't mean the story's dead."

CHAPTER 40

We were heading up the stairs toward the station's conference room to speak with Agent Jax. The FBI guy had wanted us to come to headquarters, but Miles had vetoed that idea.

My attorney spent the whole walk to our meeting talking like the lawyer he was. "Remember, I'll be there the whole time. Don't speak except to answer a question. Don't answer any questions unless I authorize you."

"What about me?" Bryce asked.

"I think it's best to keep you out of this," Miles said. "Otherwise, there's a chance he'll want to question you, too."

Bryce seemed disappointed, like the unpopular middle school kid left off the party guest list. "But I'm the boss."

"That's right," Miles said. "You're the news director. If somebody ends up in jail for not divulging sources or information, we can't have it be you. After all, look what happened to Jack."

That remark certainly changed Bryce's attitude. "Well, good luck. Keep me posted on the latest." He then left us to take the elevator back to the newsroom, giving me a thumbs-up as the doors closed.

"Jail?" I said to Miles. "Nobody's going to jail. What about the shield law?" Minnesota has the strongest law in the country allowing journalists to protect confidential sources and unpublished information.

"That's a state law, not a federal one," he said. "And the FBI has been known to work outside the rules. Our goal here is to make him go away."

Agent Jax kept his sunglasses on even though we were indoors in the Channel 3 conference room, probably thinking he held more power if we couldn't see his eyes. He opened his briefcase and pulled out a copy of my "Dear Jack" letter. "What did Mr. Clemens say in regards to your request?"

I glanced at Miles, and he nodded that it was okay for me to answer.

"If you have the letter, then you know I didn't get any response," I said. "Prisons track inmate communications. If Jack had telephoned me, my number would have showed up on his call list. If he'd written to me, prison screeners would have read his reply before it was mailed. So why am I here, telling you what you already know?"

Miles kicked me under the table, signaling me to calm down.

"It just seems peculiar your name would come up in another homicide," Agent Jax said. "Why did you want to interview him?"

"I'm a journalist. That's what I get paid to do: interview people."

"Have you ever met Mr. Clemens in person?"

"Nope. Just followed the news accounts."

"So what were you hoping to learn?"

We were both dancing around the facts, Agent Jax waltzing slowly back and forth to find out how much I knew.

Me, I was doing the twist.

I could have kept my answers vague, noting how eager viewers always are to hear a white-collar convict whining about life behind bars. But I sensed an opportunity and decided it was time to tango with Agent Jax.

"I wanted to get a sense of how angry he was about Leon Akume ratting him out." I said.

Miles kicked me again, under the table, this time harder.

"How did you know about that?" Agent Jax asked.

"I'm a journalist. That's what I get paid to do. Find things out." Sometimes reporters confirm information by bluffing what they already suspect to be true. That's what was happening with me and Agent Jax. He was quickly becoming my second source.

"Who told you about Akume and Clemens?" he insisted.

"We're not going to discuss sources," Miles said. "Otherwise I'll shut down this interview."

Agent Jax ignored him, raising his voice. "Who told you about this? That's classified. I want the name!"

"You did."

His eyes widened as he realized what he'd done.

I thanked him for his cooperation. "And tonight Channel 3 will broadcast that Jack Clemens was killed in prison and that the informant who helped build the case against him was Leon Akume, who died violently soon after being released from prison. Would the FBI care to comment?"

CHAPTER 41

Agent Jax left mad.

His investigation into identity theft had spanned six states and thus far resulted in charges against nine individuals involving thirty million dollars in fraud. He'd dubbed it Operation *Dissimulo*—Latin for "Disguise." Though neither of us realized it then, he would rue using that particular nickname.

He'd given me this background for context and in an attempt to get me to hold off reporting on the Jack Clemens/Leon Akume link.

"You'd have to trade me something better than that," I said. But if he had anything, he didn't offer it up.

Miles escorted him out of the station, while I went to check what kind of file video we had on Jack Clemens besides what I'd used for the auction story. Not much: fifteen seconds of him walking across the street into the courthouse, his arrest mug shot from a year ago, and exteriors of a mansion on White Bear Lake that the government had seized.

Xiong emailed me another mug shot of Jack, this one from the federal prison inmate website. I forwarded it to Malik, who was going to be editing the piece. "He looks thinner," he observed.

"I suppose knowing you're headed to the slammer for ten years might make you lose your appetite," I said.

"Not me," Malik said. "I'd be chowing down all my favorite foods while I could. Like a bear going into hibernation."

"Except spring is ten years away."

"My point exactly. Hey how about your fish art?" Malik asked. "Did you sell it yet?"

"No. The guy's left a couple messages, but I've been too busy to call him back."

"Does the value increase with Jack Clemens's death?"

That hadn't occurred to me. Did his ownership and demise add to the painting's provenance? The only way to find out might be to call David Johnson. I wondered if he'd heard about the murder. But he didn't answer his phone, so I hung up before being connected to his voicemail and went back to my desk to finish writing the story linking two murders, more than a thousand miles apart.

CHAPTER 42

By the time it was completed, Channel 3's new set was the size of a penthouse apartment. The news desk was dwarfed by a panoramic screen that covered an entire wall and was flanked by a weather center and sports area. The anchor close-up shot had an unflattering orange background. Across the room was an L-shaped couch for guest interviews, surrounded by brushed metal and faux stone.

Bryce considered it a masterpiece. To me, it was a monstrosity. It was rumored to have cost more than half a million dollars. The price buzz gained credibility when Bryce laid off the teleprompter technicians, presumably to save money.

A massive promotion campaign was underway, and Bryce called a newsroom meeting to announce that after some test runs the new set would be unveiled on air within the week.

"How are we going to read the news without a teleprompter?" Nicole asked.

"Don't worry," Bryce said. "As part of the studio makeover we've installed a new teleprompter that on-air talent can run with foot pedals."

"Like one of those old-fashioned sewing machines?" My grandmother had mended clothes on a 1900s Singer treadle, now crammed in the attic at the farm with other junk. I remembered her getting angry and throwing spools of thread against the wall every time it jammed.

"No," he said. "This is like driving a Porsche."

I waited for Scott to lead the argument for common sense. After all, as anchor, he had more at stake in having a functional teleprompter than the rest of us. But he disappointed me by buying into the luxury car comparison. He'd also used a similar product while working in a smaller television market in Indiana. "It wasn't so bad. You get used to it."

Bryce gave him a high five and punch in the shoulder, like they were comrades in news. "That's the spirit I like to see here at Channel 3."

Our news director sent us all back to work, and Scott and I ended up in the green room fighting over mirror space to put on airbrush makeup before the newscast.

"I can tell you're mad at me," he said.

I pretended to be concentrating on perfecting my eyeliner.

"You're just jealous because I'm going to be featured in the wedding movie and you're not," he continued.

That was so far wrong I couldn't ignore him anymore. "I don't care about being in the damn movie."

"Keep telling yourself that, but everyone on the small screen wants to be on the big screen."

"You think you have movie potential? Prove it, Scott. Let's hear your line."

"My line?" he asked.

"Your line from the film. Your big break. Say it."

"Love," he stammered. "Love rules. No, love reigns. Yes, that's it. Love reigns—"

"For cripe's sake," I said. " 'Love reigns strong here behind me where I'm reporting live amidst a large scale community wedding.' It's not even my line and I know it better than you do. Big screen talent? Hah! Without a teleprompter, you're noth-ing."

((SCOTT, BOX))
GOOD EVENING. TONIGHT WE
LEAD WITH A CHANNEL 3
EXCLUSIVE IN THE MURDER
OF IMPRISONED MULTIMILLION-
DOLLAR CROOK JACK
CLEMENS.

((SCOTT TWOSHOT))
RILEY SPARTZ JOINS US WITH
HER INVESTIGATION.

Scott and I ignored each other during the newscast, each looking straight at the camera. The shots of us side by side appeared stilted. He didn't thank me for my report about one murder victim informing on another. And I had told the producer that because of the investigative nature of my story, Miles had advised against any live follow-up questions. I simply tagged out the story that prison officials in New Jersey were planning to release more details tomorrow.

Father Mountain called that night, suggesting I stop by for morning Mass as it was the feast day for St. Apollonia. "I have a special homily planned to honor her."

I hadn't thought about Apollonia since my dental checkup, probably because my teeth no longer hurt. While I was intrigued to hear his remarks, I actually decided to go to church because I was feeling guilty about snapping at Scott.

Yeah, he was a jerk. But he was Channel 3's jerk. And that made him my jerk.

CHAPTER 43

The church wasn't crowded, as it would have been for an Ash Wednesday service. I didn't grab a spot in front because that seemed to falsely imply God and I were tight, but I also didn't head for the back, because that could be interpreted as hiding something. I knelt down in a middle pew, all the better to blend in with other parishioners.

Because it wasn't yet Lent, Father Mountain wore a green vestment instead of violet. I caught myself daydreaming during the service, comparing the ornate altar to Channel 3's new set. But unlike Scott, Father Mountain didn't need a teleprompter to rock his sermon.

First, he read from a liturgical text. "What energy was thine, Apollonia!"

He reiterated the story of how she voluntarily threw herself into the flames rather than renounce her Lord. "A momentary pain leading thy soul to eternal bliss, nothing when we compare it with the everlasting fire of hell to which grave sinners condemn themselves."

And then, addressing my previous criticism, he discussed how the difference between martyrdom and suicide comes down to intent. "For Apollonia, her goal was not to bring about her death, but to bring glory to God."

I still found his explanation fuzzy, but did appreciate when he spoke of how the Church's teaching on suicide had changed over the years from condemnation to pity in recognizing the role of psychological distress.

"Reach out to those experiencing inner pain," he urged. "For they may not bring themselves to ask for help."

I didn't appreciate that he seemed to look in my direction during those words. I stuck around after the church was empty to inform him that I was doing fine, but the first thing Father Mountain brought up was the murder investigation involving the teeth. I felt sacrilegious discussing homicide in church, but then glanced up at the Stations of the Cross and remembered the Bible was filled with tales of violent death by man, nature, and even God.

"Any leads?" he asked.

"No, I took your advice and prayed to St. Apollonia, but she yielded no clues."

"You might be praying for the wrong thing, Riley. The job of prayer is not to give us answers, but to help us find them."

That tip felt too broad to be useful, and I told him so.

"Ah, you would prefer a faster solution," he said. "That's not how faith works. Faith requires a long-term commitment."

"You mean, like marriage?"

"Well, yes."

Rather than risk him bringing up my romantic future, I took the conversation in a different direction. "That reminds me of another story in the news." I told him about covering the protest at the Mall of America and asked about his views on the Catholic Church and same-sex marriage.

Father Mountain paused, looking over at a painted wall. It was no Sistine Chapel, but it was still a lovely depiction of Mary, Joseph, and baby Jesus. "I believe the Church needs to work to be more welcoming to all God's children."

That wasn't a definitive answer, but at least he didn't quote scripture about immorality. I decided this discussion would be too complex to explore before I needed to leave for work.

CHAPTER 44

The prison warden stepped up to a podium crowded with microphones and plastic TV logos. Bryce had nixed traveling east for the news conference, determining we could follow the proceedings from a live transmission shot by our sister station in New York City without sacrificing much beyond the cosmetics of a reporter standup in front of the prison.

Although unhappy not to chase this story out of town, I saw his point. Anyway, we assumed officials were simply going to announce further details about the investigation into Jack's murder or, in a best case scenario, release the name of his assailant.

The motives behind prison violence can be trivial by most standards; sometimes inmates are simply killed by another prisoner having a real bad day, and nothing to lose. I suspected there was more to Jack's death, and watched the video feed intently on a monitor screen in the newsroom while it was being recorded in a station editing room.

The warden introduced himself. "I'm here to talk about the murder of Inmate 16780-59, who was strangled two days ago within these walls. I want to start out by clarifying that the victim was not Jack Clemens, as had earlier been stated."

It took me a few seconds to process that remark, and even then I was sure I'd misheard or he'd misspoke, but he repeated the key line. "Again, the homicide victim was not Jack Clemens."

I dropped my pen as I gasped at the significance. The media on that end were also silent before firing questions simultaneously. "So who died?" "Is Jack alive?" "How did he escape?"

The warden tapped the mic to make a shrill feedback noise and shut them down.

"Quiet, please," he said. "I'm going to read a statement. An unknown man assumed the identity of Jack Clemens and was serving his sentence. We are working to determine who he is. The discrepancy was discovered during the autopsy process."

"How did someone change places with him?" one of the reporters asked. "Was it an inside job?"

That was my thought as well—a classic case of the old switcheroo—especially since we then knew that Jack had been moved in and out of several corrections institutions en route to New Jersey.

The warden disputed that theory. "This was not a prison break. We believe Jack Clemens was never in federal custody and that a substitute turned himself in at the prison camp in Duluth, Minnesota."

Sounded like a security breach on this end. And that seemed to be the message that the warden was trying to communicate—yes, he had a dead body on his watch, but the bigger screw-up happened more than a thousand miles away outside his jurisdiction.

"How come nobody caught on at the time?" another reporter asked.

"Mistakes happen," the warden said. "Here's what we know. This man was processed in the federal prison system as Jack Clemens about a month ago. He presented a valid driver's license under that name."

A prison mug shot—the same one Channel 3 broadcast on the news—appeared on a large screen behind the warden who was using a laptop computer for the presentation, and clicked to a second picture.

"This is a mug shot of Jack Clemens taken after he was first arrested for fraud and booked in a county jail in Minnesota where he was briefly held last year before posting bail."

Then he pulled up a split screen of the two photographs side by side. Both men had blue eyes and a receding dark hairline. Their foreheads were similar, but their jawlines didn't quite match. The man on the right's chin was square, while his counterpart had thinner features. Close enough that neither Malik nor I had doubted we were looking at the same person the day before.

I remember admiring the warden's production technique and thinking he might make a fine television news producer if he ended up being fired over this fiasco.

"Both men share a physical resemblance and are approximately the same height," he said. "The real Jack Clemens is on the left. The fake is on the right. If anyone sees the man on the left, or recognizes the impostor, call the police."

"So who killed this other man and why?" another journalist asked.

"That is still under investigation. What we know is that at the time of his death, he was wearing an arm bracelet that identified him as Inmate 16780-59—known in our system as Jack Clemens."

I'd discussed the case with the reporter at the New Jersey TV station earlier when it had seemed a more routine murder. I now texted her a question. Soon I heard it being asked. "Will officials at the Minnesota prison be available for questions?"

The warden shook his head. "Because the homicide investigation is being handled here, we're taking all media inquiries."

Darn. I imagined whoever handled Jack's intake in Duluth probably had some explaining to do. Was the error merely due to sloppiness or had the switch been facilitated through bribery? Neither explanation made them look good. I texted another question: HOW DID U DETERMINE MAN NOT JACK?

But then the warden stopped questions, ending the news conference. He likely figured he'd said enough to guarantee coast-to-coast media coverage. At that moment, I thought there was a good chance he'd have the genuine Jack in custody and phony Jack's name in twenty-four hours.

The camera pulled wide, shooting video cutaways of the other journalists and the warden from different angles for editing purposes. As the lens panned the room I saw two men in dark suits standing against the wall, conferring. One of them was Agent Jax.

CHAPTER 45

It was one thing to assume someone's identity to gain money through fraud. And people do fake their own deaths all the time. But to take a felon's place in prison seemed implausibly complicated. Mark Twain's *The Prince and the Pauper* came to mind, as did Shakespeare's *Comedy of Errors,* and I realized that for mistaken identity to be such a popular plot twist for authors, they had to get their ideas from somewhere.

After all, art was more likely to imitate life than life was to imitate art.

Bryce stuck his head in my office. "Do you need anything?"

"Yeah. Answers."

"Well, get busy. Showtime's ahead. And you're the lead."

I didn't bother reminding him that we air a newscast, not a show—a vocabulary pet peeve of mine.

Even though we'd left on poor terms, I dialed Agent Jax on the East Coast. Instead of letting me ring into voicemail oblivion, he picked up my call. Maybe he figured not talking to me hadn't worked out so well. Or maybe he was just fishing to see if I knew anything useful.

"We should call a truce," I said. "And acknowledge we have similar goals."

"What are you offering?"

"I'm offering publicity to help you catch a killer."

"That's nothing. You'll publicize this anyway. And his killer is already behind bars. Ultimately we'll zero in on the perpetrator. I'm more interested in the identity of the victim."

"You mean the fake Jack? I can help with that, too," I said. "But the killer I was referring to is Leon Akume's murderer. Even though Jack Clemens had motive, I'd crossed him off as a suspect because he lacked opportunity. But since he wasn't in prison at the time of Leon's homicide, I think he should lead the list of possible perpetrators."

Agent Jax didn't respond. I couldn't tell if he was taking me seriously, or if something in New Jersey was more interesting than our conversation.

"So, how do you think the wrong guy got inside?" I nudged.

"I'm not going to speculate," he said. "Mistakes happen."

That was the same line the warden gave. I figured they must have practiced their talking points. "How about if you promise to call me first if there's an arrest?"

"I'm not going to agree to that bargain unless you trade me something," he said.

That was the deal I had offered him when we were arguing about me broadcasting the news that Leon had ratted on Jack. The FBI guy was using my own maneuver against me. I had nothing to trade, and he knew it. But what neither of us knew just then was that balance would soon shift.

In the meantime, I decided acting petty might be the best approach. "What if I promise to forget that you dubbed this case Operation *Dissimulo*. How unfortunate that you feds fell for a disguise behind bars. You'll probably be the opening skit on *Saturday Night Live*."

Either he was breathing heavy or his cell phone was malfunctioning. I had no body language cues. "Let me get this straight. You're threatening to make me look stupid unless I cooperate with you?"

"You give me too much credit, Agent Jax. I can't make you look stupid. I just report facts."

He hung up.

I found myself wishing I could reach out to Nick Garnett and pick his law-enforcement brain about how prison intake worked. Before we were lovers we had been friends. But before that, our relationship was reporter-source.

It was worth a try. But calling and being ignored might feel even worse than him not turning to look at me while he walked away. I'd symbolically moved his phone number off my cell favorites, so had to search through my digital contact list. I never realized, until then, that I hadn't memorized his number. That alone might have hinted at a rocky future. Maybe love *is* in the details.

His phone rang and rang before a recording of his voice was asking me to leave a message. The familiarity was so soothing, that had it actually been him live on the line, I might have pleaded with him to meet me later that night. Before I could hang up, a jarring beep signaled that his phone was recording my breathing. I resumed news mode and pretended nothing was unusual. I hoped he would do the same.

"Hello, Nick. This is Riley Spartz from Channel 3, calling to see if you might have some insight into this latest Jack Clemens development. Please call me if you have a moment. Thanks."

I even left my telephone number, just to keep it strictly business.

And just in case he'd forgotten it.

CHAPTER 46

Nicole was taping afternoon promos for the local newscasts at the anchor desk when I walked by on my way back from Keys Café down the block with a late take-out lunch.

"Is Scott sick?" I'd been thinking about apologizing to him and rebuilding our working relationship.

"No, he took an overnight flight to Los Angeles to interview those two movie stars for *We Do*. I'm anchoring for him today."

"What? Scott flew to California?"

She offered to fill me in after she finished, but I headed for Bryce's office and barged in without even a courtesy knock. "How come the station couldn't afford to fly me to the East Coast for an actual news story, but Scott gets to go to Hollywood for a puff piece?"

"Relax." Bryce instructed me to sit down. "The big difference is that Channel 3's not paying for his plane ticket. The studio's covering the costs. And our sister station in Los Angeles is furnishing the cameras. We each air the interview exclusively in our markets. Plus, the story is made available to affiliates across the country on our news feed. It's great exposure for Scott. And us. Our station logo will be displayed in the corner of the screen."

Because the network was invested in Scott, Bryce's job was to make Scott look good. So I tried another approach rather than dissing both of them.

"But the movie production company is essentially paying for the interview," I argued. "That makes it a conflict of interest for us."

"No, that just makes it smart business. The same corporation that owns them owns us. Recognizing our shared goals enables both of our bottom lines to prosper in a tough economy."

"But, Bryce, news is supposed to be objective when it comes to covering stories. Aren't you worried you're risking your job by doing this?"

He looked at me with what seemed to be sympathy, which made me uneasy. The last thing I wanted was for Bryce to pity me.

"Riley, you just don't get it. The news industry is changing, and with it, the business model for journalism. My approach is much more likely to get me promoted than fired."

"And while you have already hit the peak of your career in broadcasting," he continued, "it's only a matter of time before *I'm* your boss's boss's boss."

CHAPTER 47

((NICOLE CU))
FEDERAL AUTHORITIES ARE
INVESTIGATING THE UNUSUAL
MURDER OF A MAN BEHIND
BARS IN A NEW JERSEY
FEDERAL PRISON . . . AND ARE
NOW OFFERING A 25-
THOUSAND-DOLLAR
REWARD IN THE CASE.

((NICOLE TWO SHOT))
CHANNEL 3'S RILEY SPARTZ
IS HERE TO TELL US ABOUT
THE MINNESOTA CONNECTION
TO THIS HOMICIDE.

((RILEY BOX))
THE DEAD MAN—STILL
UNIDENTIFIED—
APPARENTLY WAS POSING AS
WHITE-COLLAR CRIMINAL
JACK CLEMENS AND SERVING
HIS SENTENCE.

I summarized what we knew and what we didn't know about how Jack Clemens came to be on the list of America's Most Wanted Fugitives.

((RILEY CU))
IRONICALLY, CLEMENS WAS
CONVICTED AS PART OF A
FEDERAL INVESTIGATION
INTO IDENTITY THEFT THAT
WAS CALLED OPERATION
DISSIMULO—THAT'S LATIN
FOR DISGUISE.

((NICOLE, TWOSHOT))
WHAT DO YOU KNOW ABOUT
HOW THIS MAN DIED,
RILEY? WITH ALL THE
SECURITY IN PRISON . . .
SHOULDN'T THAT BE THE
LEAST LIKELY PLACE FOR A
HOMICIDE?

Jack Clemens turned off the television.

He didn't want to listen to any more details of his stand-in's death, because the man had been his last friend. Asphyxia due to neck compression was the official cause, according to an online report he'd read, and that jibed with the gasping sounds Jack had heard over the phone during the final minutes of the fatal struggle.

Deep down, Jack knew that simply hoping the feds wouldn't figure out he wasn't the dead man had probably been unrealistic. After all, homicides lead to questions. Had that ploy worked, Jack's new life would have been considerably less complicated. And it had seemed worth the chance because he couldn't risk his impostor confiding their secret to wild prison cohorts or a nosy TV reporter.

Jack had already been squealed on once, so he convinced himself that what happened wasn't murder, just business. The gangsters-for-hire didn't know his true identity. Not those inside the pen furnishing protection, nor those outside handling the payments. The only link they had to him was wired cash and a cell-phone number, which he'd ditched after his impersonator was killed.

He wished he could leave town. Only one thing still stood in his way.

CHAPTER 48

Downtown. Meet for coffee in five."

The text on my phone came midmorning from Garnett. He must have spent the night debating whether or not to reply to my message.

I didn't bother checking my appearance in the mirror because I did not want to pretend this was anything but a professional courtesy on his part, nor did I want him to think this was a scheme to win him back. I might no longer have a boyfriend, but I still had my pride. At least that's how I consoled myself as I walked toward the coffee shop.

Garnett was sipping a hot brew outside and handed one to me.

"Thanks," I said. "I appreciate you stopping by."

"No problem. I was in the area. Let's walk and talk. I've been sitting the last couple hours."

I figured he wanted to stay on the move to avoid looking me in the eye. We headed north on Nicollet Mall, window shopping and watching buses speed by. "You heard about the Jack Clemens business?"

He nodded. "Your basic public relations disaster."

I wondered at his choice of words: public relations. Had he already had a similar conversation with Velma? Being envious made me feel anxious. *Stick to business,* I reminded myself.

"So how could the feds not know he wasn't in custody?" I asked.

"Sloppy processing," he said. "Every year, there's a couple cases where the wrong inmate gets released by mistake."

"But this is the opposite problem. The wrong person got *in*."

"That doesn't actually surprise me," he said. "On the intake end, there's even less reason for scrutiny. Nobody's expecting a body double to show up for voluntary jail time, so as long as the guy resembles the mug, has some ID, and shows up when he's supposed to . . . he becomes whoever he says he is."

"But what about DNA?" I asked. "Don't they check that?"

"That's way too sophisticated and expensive for prison intake. And as a white-collar criminal, Clemens probably wouldn't have had his cheek swabbed for DNA until he arrived at prison, so there might not be any samples to compare it to. Truth is, often law-enforcement agencies get confused over who's doing what, and tens of thousands of ex-felons who should have DNA on file don't because of human error."

"That sounds like another good story." I made a mental note to check into it later.

"With Jack Clemens," Garnett continued, "their best bet to having figured out they had the wrong man would have been comparing his fingerprints at intake to his original arrest fingerprints. But that clearly didn't happen."

I saw where he was heading. "So the dead man must not have a criminal record himself, or the authorities would already know his identity from his fingerprints."

"Right. Their John Doe is clean, so they had to stage a show for the media and ask the public's help in identifying the guy." He shook his head. "Embarrassing."

"Why would anyone agree to trade places with Jack Clemens?"

"Money, most likely. The practice is well documented in China," he said. "The wealthy pay the poor to serve their sentences. There's even a name for it. *Ding zui*. Substitute criminal."

"That's fascinating," I said. "*Ding zui*. What is the price of freedom? Even in a tough economy, that seems a hard way to earn a paycheck."

"He probably didn't expect to die on the job. And Duluth would have been an easy gig to serve if he hadn't been moved. White-collar criminals pull strings to land there."

"What's so great about it?"

"Things are relatively lax. There's no fence for one. There's talk about inmates who walk off the grounds to go to a liquor store or even a motel for a conjugal visit. As long as they return, no harm."

I wished Toby had told me about some of those perks. That would have made for interesting surveillance footage and block-buster TV ratings. But I imagined that wasn't the kind of thing the prisoners wanted publicized.

"Why don't inmates just take off?" I asked.

"When they're caught," Garnett said, "they'll be labeled an escape risk and sent somewhere much worse."

"Without a fence, is it possible the switch happened when the real Jack walked off and the fake Jack walked back in?"

"Could be. They'd have to transfer the wristband ID, but that's not impossible."

"So where's Jack Clemens?" I asked.

"Long gone, if he's smart. And I suspect he's quite smart."

We were approaching the iconic Mary Tyler Moore statue, my favorite spot in downtown Minneapolis. As I ran my hand along her bronze briefcase, the theme song from the television series ran through my mind. "*Love is all around, no need to waste it.*"

"She and I both spent careers in a TV newsroom," I said. "Why can't I be cheerful, like her?"

"Hers was fiction," Garnett said. "Real life isn't happily ever after."

We both knew we weren't discussing life in general, but rather our particular situation. I dumped my coffee cup in a garbage can and sat down on the base of the sculpture, chin in my hands, while Garnett remained standing.

I said what needed to be said. "Our paths will continue to cross, yours and mine. On the job and off. There's no avoiding that. I just don't want those times to be awkward."

"I'll be honest with you," he said. "It's hard for me to be around you."

"Okay, I'll be honest, too. It's harder for me *not* to be around you than it is for you to be around me."

"Is that a line from a movie?" he asked.

"No."

"Well, it should be. It's good dialogue."

That made me smile. "Dialogue might have been the best part of our relationship. Maybe we should have just stuck with talking."

He pulled me to my feet, and for a few seconds our bodies were close enough for me to sense he wasn't as detached as he pretended to be. "No. Our best moments together were when we stopped talking. Talking was what always got us in trouble."

So he wanted me to be quiet? I gave him the silent treatment.

"You know that's not what I meant, Riley."

As long as I said nothing, I suspected there was a chance we might kiss. But he knew how to make me talk.

"A relationship, I think, is like a shark," he said. "You know? It has to constantly move forward or it dies. And I think what we got on our hands is a dead shark."

The instant passed, unrequited. So I replied, "Woody Allen, *Annie Hall*, 1977."

"Those two didn't end up happily ever after either," Garnett said. "I need to get back to work now. I'm parked in a ramp around the corner."

"Sure, Nick." I started to walk away, but suddenly turned with an impulse. "Just one more question. What's my phone number?"

"Why are you asking me that?"

"I just want to know if you know." My heart beat faster.

He recited both my desk and cell numbers. And that convinced me the shark wasn't dead, after all.

On my way back to the station, I hummed the Mary Tyler Moore chorus: *"You're going to make it after all."*

CHAPTER 49

Scott returned from Hollywood with the certainty that he was on the verge of being discovered for something bigger than Channel 3. "I don't want to waste my whole career in Minneapolis, like you," he told me during rehearsal on the new set.

After that, I no longer felt I owed Scott any apology.

He'd tweeted a picture of himself with his arms draped around Rachel and Ricky's shoulders to promote his interview with the two movie stars, which was airing during the set unveiling. Viewers were promised a new look and a big story for tuning in.

Bryce was keeping details of the interview quiet, even from the rest of the newsroom during the huddle. "I don't want those celebrity gossip rags stealing our scoop."

"Are we giving viewers their first glimpse of her wedding costume?" I didn't use the word gown because I considered the whole event a farce.

"No," my news director said, "this is much bigger. This is significant enough to lead with."

"I thought we were leading with my story about domestic dogs being killed by traps."

I'd landed prime examples and even had actual traps to use on set as props.

"No, we're holding that," Bryce said. "This has the potential to go viral across all social media. This exclusive will help our new set get maximum exposure. Rachel and Ricky appeal to younger demos—their local fans will watch Channel 3, and their national fans will click on our website."

That night, I tuned in, along with the majority of viewers in our TV market, as would be proven by the overnight rating numbers the following morning.

> ((SCOTT CU))
> GOOD EVENING, EVERYONE . . .
> WELCOME TO OUR NEW
> STUDIO . . .
> HERE'S A BRIEF LOOK AT HOW
> CHANNEL 3 UNDERWENT THIS
> MAGNIFICENT
> TRANSFORMATION TO BETTER
> BRING YOU THE NEWS.

A time-lapsed video rolled of the assembly of the new set, from empty room to Taj Mahal. Bryce was clearly very proud of his accomplishment.

> ((SCOTT, CU))
> NOW FOR OUR LEAD STORY . . .
> THE COUNTDOWN CONTINUES
> FOR FILMING THE "WE DO"
> WEDDING SCENE AT THE MALL
> OF AMERICA . . . AND CHANNEL 3
> HAS SOME EXCITING NEWS
> TO SHARE.
> I JUST RETURNED FROM
> HOLLYWOOD WITH THIS
> EXCLUSIVE INTERVIEW WITH
> THE STARS OF THE MOVIE.

Rachel and Ricky flashed carefree smiles to the camera. Rachel had grown from a child star into a young beauty. She'd been cast at age six in her first acting role for a television comedy about a family with four cats—one for each child.

Ricky had come onto the national scene more recently as a wavy-haired pop singer. He'd grown up in Le Sueur, Minnesota—also the home of the Jolly Green Giant. This would be his first appearance on the big screen.

> ((SCOTT, SOT))
> FOR ONE OF YOU, THIS IS
> A TRIP BACK TO YOUR HOME
> STATE OF MINNESOTA. HOW
> DOES THAT FEEL?

The interview was done as a three-camera shoot, meaning one camera was on Scott, the other shifting between the two actors, seated on a couch. The third, locked in a side view for cutaways. The questions and answers were edited back and forth.

> ((RICKY, SOT))
> I AM SO LOOKING FORWARD
> TO HAVING MY FRIENDS AND
> FAMILY MEET RACHEL . . .

> ((RACHEL CU))
> AND I AM LOOKING FORWARD
> TO THAT BECAUSE WE HAVE A
> SPECIAL ANNOUNCEMENT.

> ((RACHEL, RICKY TWOSHOT))
> WE'RE GETTING MARRIED . . .
> FOR REAL!

The happy couple laughed and kissed and laughed some more. A reaction shot was edited in of Scott looking shocked, then pleased. He congratulated them on camera. They explained they'd met and fallen in love during the filming of *We Do*.

((RACHEL SOT))
SEE MY RING? ISN'T IT
BEAUTIFUL!

((RICKY, SOT))
WE KEPT OUR RELATIONSHIP
A SECRET SO WE WOULDN'T BE
CHASED BY THE PAPARAZZI.

((SCOTT, CU))
SO WHEN EXACTLY IS YOUR
BIG DAY?

((RICKY TWOSHOT))
DURING THE MOVIE! WE'RE
GETTING MARRIED IN THE
GIANT WEDDING SCENE AT
THE MALL OF AMERICA
ALONG WITH EVERYONE
ELSE!

They smooched, once more, this time as if they'd rehearsed for the camera. His arms were wrapped around her waist from behind, her neck tilted back to reach his lips, matching the choreography of the famous film kiss on the bow of the *Titanic*.

News control dissolved the video back to Scott on set, who seemed lost in the moment until a floor director cued him. Even then, he took so long to react that I thought the producer might order the newscast to go black while they regrouped. To go black—off the air—is the worst thing that can happen to an anchor on a live program. But Scott suddenly reverted to professional mode.

> ((SCOTT, CU))
> THAT'S NOT ALL FOLKS . . .
> RACHEL AND RICKY WILL
> SELECT TWO FANS TO BE
> THEIR OFFICIAL WEDDING
> WITNESSES.
> GO TO OUR WEBSITE AT
> CHANNEL 3 AND YOU CAN
> APPLY FOR THE HONOR.

The line between news and gossip is always narrowing, but there was no doubt in my mind that the station had crossed over. I turned on my computer to click on Channel 3's website to leave a mean comment under a sock puppet name, but found the system had once again crashed because of heavy user traffic.

CHAPTER 50

I considered calling in sick the next morning so I wouldn't have to listen to Bryce gush about the wedding exclusive, but then I remembered we'd rescheduled Lisa's interview, and I didn't want to cancel on her twice.

Those good intentions fell apart when Keith Brunn, Channel 3's medical reporter, showed up at the news meeting with a copy of an email he'd received. He'd blocked out the name of the sender.

"My source wants to stay confidential," Keith said, "but I thought you might want to see this. I checked and another cancer clinic got the same message."

The email contained a photograph of the mug shot of the fake Jack Clemens. "Here's the best part," Keith said, reading it out loud.

> We are asking the medical community, particularly those treating oncology patients, for help in identifying this man. He was a homicide victim, but our autopsy also found that he had stage four colon cancer, which had metastasized to his brain.
>
> His blood type was A positive.
> His height was 5 feet 10 inches.
> He is believed to be between the ages of 40 and 50.

If you recognize this man, please contact the Federal Bureau of Investigation.

You can remain anonymous and may be eligible for a reward.

Keith handed me the email. I looked at the sender line. It was from Agent Jax.

"I'll let you determine if it's authentic," he said.

"It looks genuine, but I'll definitely confirm that first. In the meantime, do you know what the rules are regarding doctor-patient confidentiality after death?"

"I'd venture they'd be fuzzy in this case," he said, "Who's going to file a complaint about a breach of privacy if the patient is dead?"

"And how about the prognosis for stage-four colon cancer?" I asked.

"Terminal. Just how long can depend on several factors, but no doubt, even if this guy wasn't murdered, he would have died in prison anyway. Most likely within a year."

Bryce applauded, and made us both give him high fives. "Keep me posted. I'm expecting a team report from the two of you. We'll want to be promoting this so viewers tune in for another look at our new set."

I tuned out my boss, and the rest of the day's discussion of news, weather, and sports, instead pondering the mystery man and his connection to Jack. Theirs was not the kind of deal struck by strangers. Does the price of freedom increase or decrease as the end of life nears? I imagined the two men negotiating a furtive contract more binding than wedding vows. *Till death us do part.*

Back in my office I reached for the phone. The first call was to Lisa. I felt terrible bailing on her identity-theft interview yet again. Last time, she sounded disappointed. This time, she was mildly perturbed. I worried that my window to tell her story was closing.

"So do you want to try again tomorrow?" she offered.

"I really hope so," I answered. "But I have to chase down this other lead concerning the prison murder of that guy impersonating Jack Clemens."

I explained how the genealogy was also linked to her—that Leon, the man who ripped her off, had snitched on Jack. "It's the circle of crime."

"So you'll call me?" she asked.

"Absolutely."

The list of people I was supposed to phone was growing. David Johnson had left another message about the fish painting. But Agent Jax was a higher priority, so he was my next call. He didn't answer.

"Riley Spartz here at Channel 3. Just checking to see if you've had any leads from area cancer clinics about the identity of our John Doe prisoner."

> ((RILEY, BOX))
> CHANNEL 3 HAS LEARNED
> THAT THE MYSTERY MAN
> POSING AS JACK CLEMENS
> IN PRISON HAD TERMINAL
> CANCER.

My first time with the new teleprompter was rough. My foot-eye coordination sucked. The script stalled when my heel got caught in the pedal, so I had to ad-lib my way before my voice package rolled—risky because TV investigations are vetted line by line, and messing up or skipping a word can change the meaning of a story. After all, there were only three letters' difference between guilty and not guilty.

> ((RILEY, SOT))
> FEDERAL AGENTS HAVE

CIRCULATED HIS PICTURE
TO CANCER CLINICS . . .
APPARENTLY HOPING
SOMEONE MIGHT RECOGNIZE
HIM AS A PATIENT.

I finished out the story asking viewers to contact authorities if they knew the man's identity, but skipped giving them the number because I had lost my place with the teleprompter.

Afterward I asked Nicole for any tips, and she told me to remember to kick off my shoes under the set. "Seriously, ask Scott to do it. He runs the teleprompter for me."

"Really? Did you ask or did he offer?"

"He offered, and didn't seem to mind," she said. "The speed was fine. He has to read so much, he's a real pedal pro."

He hadn't suggested helping me, so I figured he was waiting for me to beg. But that would never happen. I'd rather learn braille and follow my script with my fingertips.

CHAPTER 51

By the end of her interview the next day, Lisa had cried in all the right places.

Bryce was very proud of me when I showed him the video. "Nobody gets tears the way you do, Riley. I wish I knew your secret."

If I told him, he wouldn't understand. Some journalists think they can bully a victim into crying, but it doesn't work that way. People only cry on camera when they trust a reporter enough to forget about the camera. Bryce would never be able to muster enough empathy to make that happen.

While tears can make good TV, a paper trail isn't very visual. Malik shot video of stacks of bills and credit card statements crooks had racked up in Lisa's name, casual shots of her at home, and exteriors of the University of Minnesota, where she had attended school.

The owner of Rest in Peace Funeral Home, where she worked in Columbia Heights, an inner-ring suburb just north of Minneapolis, agreed to let us follow Lisa on the job, but only videotape-approved areas. "Our clients trust us to protect their privacy." That meant no taking pictures of corpses, which was fine with me. I'd seen enough dead people in my news career.

He ended up giving us a tour of the mortuary. "We offer once-in-a-lifetime service," he said.

I complimented him on his "deadpan" delivery and we were off to a good start. He took me on a tour through their showroom—a display of half a dozen caskets in various price ranges. The exteriors were smooth and shiny. The lids were open to display embroidered satin interiors. It had the feel of an auto dealership, except with no test drives allowed.

Malik rolled video while Lisa vacuumed carpets in the public places, then mopped floors in the back areas. We passed a giant steel refrigerator where bodies were kept awaiting burial, but that stayed closed. So did another door marked STORAGE. A hearse pulled into the garage and Malik shot Lisa helping load a casket amid vases of flowers.

"Ahead of us is the embalming room," our guide explained. The name conjured up dread and a sign on that door read: DANGER—FLAMMABLE LIQUIDS—NO SMOKING. The warning puzzled me.

"Embalming fluid is very flammable," I was told.

The room was empty, so we were allowed to videotape Lisa wiping a low white table on wheels. A tray beside it gave the illusion we were in an operating room. And in a way, we were. Prior to a viewing, a body would be prepared by draining blood and injecting embalming fluid to slow decomposition so the deceased would appear natural when friends and relatives said their extended good-byes.

As a Muslim, Malik was fascinated by all the fuss. "We bury our dead within twenty-four hours, to hasten their meeting Allah, and thus have no need for embalming. We lay the bodies in the ground without caskets on their right side to face Mecca."

The owner spoke of a growing interest in what he called "green" funerals by non-Muslims, but said that while the practice was not required by law in Minnesota, embalming was the norm for most funerals.

"Don't forget to take care of the embalming fluid," he told Lisa, who carried three plastic bottles of pink and orange liquids from the counter to a cabinet, then turned a key to lock the door.

"Why does it need special security?" I asked.

"In case we have a break-in," the owner answered. "We can't take chances."

"But why would anyone steal embalming fluid?"

"To get a longer high." He explained about a drug trend called "wet"—marijuana or cigarettes dipped in embalming fluid, dried, then smoked. "It's an unpredictable drug and can even cause users to lose consciousness or turn violent."

That sounded like an interesting story by itself, if I could verify the problem with the cops. I already had some video and sound ready to go. I promised Lisa I'd let her know when her story would air. I still needed to fit some research in around my other news assignments to give the story breadth, but having a real victim was the centerpiece.

The owner turned on overhead bluish ultraviolet lights, telling us the heat helped sanitize the embalming room. But it gave the place a creepy, paranormal feel, and I was anxious to leave. Other than the front sitting rooms for mourners, the place had no windows for natural light.

Lisa and I walked out together, and I could tell that she felt better about herself. She seemed confident, even proud. My experience as a journalist has taught me that crime victims who speak out often suffer less than those who stay silent.

I hoped that would be the case with Lisa.

CHAPTER 52

I alerted my parents that my trapping story was running on the late news that night. Even though it was not the kind of upbeat animal story that television stations traditionally push, Bryce could see the potential for impact, so he ran a dual promotion: *"Tune in for an exclusive investigation from Channel 3's new set. The life you save may be your dog's."*

> ((STAN CU))
> LIKE HUNTING, TRAPPING IS
> AN OUTDOOR TRADITION IN
> MINNESOTA. BUT AS RILEY
> SPARTZ TELLS US . . . NOT JUST
> WILD ANIMALS ARE AT RISK . . .
> YOUR PET DOG COULD FALL
> VICTIM TO A CRUEL DEATH
> THAT YOU MAY BE
> POWERLESS TO PREVENT.

I opened the story by holding up an actual trap as a prop.

> ((RILEY HOLD PROP ON SET))
> THIS IS CALLED A BODY GRIP

TRAP . . . IT MAY NOT LOOK LIKE
MUCH . . . BUT IT CAN BREAK AN
ANIMAL'S NECK, KILLING
IT INSTANTLY.

I'd prerecorded my voice on the package so I didn't have to read so much teleprompter.

((RILEY TRACK))
IT'S A POPULAR TRAP FOR
CATCHING RACCOONS,
BOBCATS AND OTHER
WILDLIFE SOUGHT FOR
THEIR PELTS.

((RILEY GRAPHIC))
BUT A CHANNEL 3
INVESTIGATION HAS FOUND
THAT AT LEAST 13 DOGS
HAVE BEEN KILLED
SINCE TRAPPING
SEASON BEGAN LAST
FALL . . . AND MANY
OTHERS INJURED.

((OWNER 1/SOT))
ALL I HEARD WAS A SNAP.
THEN MY PUPPY WAS DEAD.

((OWNER 2/SOT))
MY DOG WAS MY BEST
FRIEND. WE WERE OUT HUNTING
TOGETHER. I TRIED TO
GET THE TRAP OFF HIS NECK,

BUT HE WAS DEAD IN LESS
THAN 30 SECONDS.

((OWNER 3/SOT))
MY DOG WAS KILLED, AND
THEY TOLD ME THE TRAP
WAS PERFECTLY LEGAL. AND I
SHOULD HAVE KEPT MY PET
ON A LEASH.

((RILEY, CU))
PICTURES OF METAL TRAPS
CLAMPED TIGHT ON THE
THROATS OF DOGS ARE TOO
DISTURBING TO SHOW YOU.

I was counting on viewers shuddering at those words.

((RILEY SOT))
ANIMAL RIGHTS ACTIVISTS
AND HUNTERS ARE PUSHING
FOR A LAW REQUIRING BODY
GRIP TRAPS TO BE ELEVATED
FIVE FEET ABOVE THE
GROUND OR SUBMERGED
UNDERWATER TO AVOID
KILLING DOGS. BUT
TRAPPING ORGANIZATIONS
ARE RELUCTANT TO
COMPROMISE.

((TRAPPER SOT))
YOU CAN'T OUTLAW
EVERYTHING.

> CONSIDERING THE AMOUNT
> OF TRAPS SET, THE NUMBER
> OF DOGS KILLED IS SMALL.

The studio camera cut to a wide shot of Scott and me at the anchor desk. I handed him one of the traps.

> ((RILEY TWOSHOT))
> THIS IS THE TYPE OF TRAP
> WE'VE BEEN TALKING ABOUT.
> SEE HOW FAR YOU CAN PRY
> IT.

Scott was in top shape. He wrestled with the trap's spring but could barely open it.

> ((SCOTT, TWOSHOT))
> WOW, IMAGINE THAT
> SLAMMING AGAINST THE
> WINDPIPE OF A FAMILY PET.
> NOT EVEN I COULD GET IT OFF
> IN TIME.

Next, I handed him a leghold trap and explained how, if a nontarget animal was caught, at least it could be freed.

This was the kind of story that was unlikely to change adamant minds, so I was pleased when I got back to my desk to find a voice message from Phil McCarthy, my old classmate, and a member of the Minnesota House environmental and natural resources committee. "I'll sponsor that bill for the elevated traps. Let's see what kind of support we can get."

CHAPTER 53

Viewer feedback on the new set was consistent: they hated it. "This is Minnesota, not Miami." "Folks here aren't into glitz unless it's the Holidazzle Parade."

Bryce didn't seem concerned. "Older viewers may not appreciate it, but they don't deliver advertising revenue. Our new look will pay off by attracting a younger demographic and those viewers will be the foundation for Channel 3's success."

The station continued running promo after promo about the new set, but it was all flash and no substance—like an action movie trailer without the car chases.

I was still contemplating the idea of building a friendship with David. Neither of us knew much about the other, so it was refreshing to be around someone who couldn't throw my past in my face. That's part of the reason I was in no rush to part with the fish painting.

This time, we ordered lunch at The Oak Grill on the twelfth floor of Macy's—formerly Dayton's—department store. The restaurant, best known for its popovers, was a downtown tradition with dark paneling and white linen.

I steered our conversation away from me even though David was modest and didn't like to go on about himself. "Enough with

TV news. Tell me something about you. How about your child-hood."

"Well, I hadn't been back to Minnesota for nearly twenty years, but I still consider it my home, and your artwork re-minded me of fishing with my dad. But it also reflected a bigger world beyond Minnesota. I felt like it was a visual balance of the two most important parts of my life."

His voice sounded so sentimental I was about ready to give him the painting for free. Small talk became more of a struggle with the "deal" still out there, unresolved.

"So where were you born, David?"

"Southern part of the state," he answered. "I grew up in Aus-tin."

"Really? I was raised south of Austin, on a corn and cattle farm along the Iowa border. What did your family do?"

He seemed startled by our shared history. "Well, like most of the town, my father worked at the Hormel plant."

Those words should have bonded us like high school sweet-hearts meeting decades after graduation. I should have imag-ined taking him home to introduce him to my parents. But the minute he uttered the name Hormel, I knew something was off.

His pronunciation or rather, *mispronunciation*, of Austin's corporate giant might have seemed minor, but it made me ner-vous enough to reach for my cell phone and pretend to read a text message.

"Excuse me, David. I need to call the newsroom. I'll be back in a moment."

I left him at our table near the antique fireplace and headed out to front of the restaurant. I reached Xiong on speed dial back at Channel 3 to ask him to check a name for me from his computer databases.

"Something odd just happened," I told him. "I don't have time to explain, but I need to confirm a Minnesota birth certificate for someone from Mower County. Probably during the early 1960s.

Name of David Johnson. I don't know a middle name. Yeah, I know, there's tons of Johnsons there."

Xiong verified the spelling. "I will call you back."

"Thanks. I don't want to be a jerk here, but I need this fast. The guy I'm inquiring about is waiting for me to return for lunch."

I grew tense as I waited for Xiong's report. Maybe David had lived away from Minnesota so long, he'd left his roots behind. Yet if his father had actually worked at Hormel during that time period, I was convinced there was no way he could forget how the locals spoke. Five minutes later, my cell phone buzzed with Xiong on the other end. "I have information for you. David Nathan Johnson was born July 25, 1963, at 1:36 PM at Austin Medical Center. Parents were—"

I cut him off. "I don't need to know the rest. Sorry, Xiong. I must just be edgy. I was starting to doubt someone was who he said he was. But now I can settle down."

"You might be correct to have doubts," he said. "I found more. Not just a birth record, but an obituary."

For a few seconds, I couldn't stop coughing. "What do you mean?"

"The same David Nathan Johnson who was born on July 25, 1963, in Austin, Minnesota, appears to have died on December 2 of last year. About two months ago."

"What?"

"His obit says he was killed near Rapid City, South Dakota, in a motor vehicle accident," he said. "He had been a college professor at Wartburg College in Waverly, Iowa.

I believed him. Identity thieves often trolled obituaries for names, addresses, birth dates, and sometimes even mother's maiden names. With that information, it's easy to illicitly purchase the deceased's Social Security number.

"I cannot tell you who your friend is, but he is not the David Nathan Johnson born in Mower County," Xiong said.

"I'm sure the family doesn't have a clue this is going on," I said.

Xiong agreed. "It generally takes six months for credit-reporting agencies and the Social Security Administration to update their death certificates."

By now the professor probably had credit cards, a driver's license, maybe even a passport issued under the dead David's name.

I wanted to walk out of the restaurant and put some distance between this man and myself, but I also didn't want to make him suspicious. I forced myself to head back to our table. My chicken potpie was already there, as was his chicken avocado salad. He hadn't started eating yet; he was politely waiting for me.

"I'm so sorry, David. You must be starving. There's a problem back at the station and I have to run. This is the liability of lunching with a TV reporter. Our day belongs to the news. We'll wrap up our business later."

He offered to drive me to Channel 3, but I laughed. "Thanks, but by the time you get your car out of the ramp, I'll already be there through the skyway."

He also suggested having the waiter box up my meal, but prying that potpie out of its crock would destroy it. I told him to help himself. "Well, Riley, at least let me have one more look at the painting before you go."

I pulled up the picture on my phone and handed it to him. I tried to make a joke, like nothing was unusual about his fixation—or my wish to leave his presence.

"He wants the precious," I rasped. "Always he is looking for it."

If Garnett had been there, he would have responded, Gollum, *Lord of the Rings: The Two Towers*, 2002. But David looked momentarily confused, then flicked his thumb and finger across the screen to enlarge the fish painting before returning it to me with a wistful smile.

CHAPTER 54

David—or whoever he was—had first reached out to me via the fish painting. His offer to buy it had always had the ring of something too good to be true. But I'd pushed that notion away rather than trust my instincts because I was feeling insecure about myself and had forgotten that I was a skilled investigative journalist.

The auction had taken place less than a week ago, so the raw video still existed. I replayed it in my office, storing it on my computer so I'd retain a copy after it was erased.

I watched closely as the fish painting was carried onto the stage. Malik had missed my first bid, but his camera panned to capture the bid against me as it came over the phone. "Seventy here." I froze the video and zoomed in on the bid card. Number eleven. "Do I have eighty?" There I was waving my hand. "How about ninety?" That's when my competition disappeared. The woman with the phone was shaking her head and seemed to be trying to redial without any luck, then she shrugged, and seconds later, I was the painting's proud owner.

I called the auction house. The manager who answered the phone remembered me. "We've had a lot of people comment on your story. That was good publicity for us. Come back anytime."

"It was a fun assignment for me, too. And that's why I'm calling. I've had an offer for the art I purchased. Do you remember a phone bid for that particular painting? Apparently he saw me on TV with it that night."

"Do I ever," he said. "Boy, that guy was furious. He called back and wanted us to reopen the bidding, but I told him he was too late. Apparently he lost his cell signal, but that's not my fault."

"Well, the same man contacted me," I said. "But I couldn't make out his entire message; he must still be having phone problems. I'm wondering if you could look up his name for me. It sounded like David or Damon, but I couldn't hear the last name. He said his bid number was eleven."

There was a pause on his end of the line. "You know I can't give out contact information. That's confidential."

"I don't need that. I'd just like to confirm his name so I know who I'm dealing with before returning his call. And if I end up selling the art to him, I might even do a follow-up story and use the video from your auction house again."

He put me on hold while he went to get the file. When he came back, he told me the man's name was David Johnson.

CHAPTER 55

A lot of things weren't making sense. Why did David want the painting so badly? And since he did, why didn't he show up to bid in person? My instincts were kicking in, but I needed proof of his true identity.

Malik was just returning from a news assignment when I waved him into my office and shut the door. "Please, help me get the painting off the wall."

"Are you selling it?" he asked.

"Not exactly."

We counted to three and lifted the back wire over the nails and set the painting on the floor, facedown. "Now help me get the picture out of the frame."

"I'm supposed to be editing shots of flying trapeze lessons into a music video for the early newscast," he said.

"This will just take a minute," I responded.

Malik pulled out a pocketknife and pushed back a few nails. We removed the carved wood frame and propped the glass pane against my desk near the door. I had hoped to find some hidden document, key, or a stash of cash tucked underneath. So far nothing unusual.

"We need to examine the whole thing carefully." We both sat on the floor and I handed him the cardboard matting, while I ran my fingertips over the artwork, paying careful attention to the fish images.

"What are we looking for?" Malik asked.

"I'm not sure. Something that doesn't belong."

"Will we know it when we see it?"

"I'm not sure about that either."

Just then someone opened my office door, smashing the picture's glass pane. Jagged chunks fell against the painting, harpooning one of the fish, and tearing the artwork. I even felt a shard hit my wrist and saw pinpricks of blood on my skin. I jerked back as red spatter dripped on the painting.

"I think you just kissed two grand good-bye," Malik said.

"I am so sorry." Xiong stood in the doorway, twisting his hands. "I came to discuss the license plate computer records. I will help clean up the mess."

"Good, because I have to leave." Malik scrambled to his feet. "My editing deadline is approaching and I haven't even selected a song."

Xiong moved my trash can near the shattered glass and we started to pick up pieces. I'd have to get a vacuum cleaner later to finish up.

"Oh no, this is the picture from the news." Xiong was dismayed as he recognized the fish painting. "I feel much worse now. I must fix it."

"Don't bother. It's doomed."

He gestured to southeast Asia on the map. "Here is my family's journey. My parents were born in Cambodia. I was born in Thailand. We came to the US as refugees with nothing. I am now an American with a good job. So never give up. All will be well."

I explained that restoring the art was not top priority and about my hunch that the painting concealed some kind of secret message.

"Like a code?"

"Maybe. But I haven't found anything. This relates to the charlatan whose name you checked. David Johnson."

I peeled back the torn edge by one of the fish to see if there might be another layer below, but no luck. Now the art was even more damaged.

"Let me look." Xiong surveyed the canvas methodically, concentrating on Southeast Asia. "What are these letters and numbers?"

He was pointing to an island just south of his homeland in Thailand, where I noticed a line of tiny handwritten letters and digits under the name Singapore. They were difficult to read. "Are they the longitude and latitude?"

"No. That is incorrect."

"So what do we know about Singapore?" I asked. "Big in tourism, right?"

"I believe so," he said. "But I also know Singapore is an international financial center."

"And that means?"

"It is prominent in offshore banking."

That's when I realized the number might be disguising money. "Xiong, you're brilliant."

I reached in the junk drawer in my desk, looking for a magnifying glass I'd once used as a Sherlock Holmes prop on set. The handwriting was now legible, letters followed by numbers.

Malik stuck his head back in. "The assignment desk decided to hold my piece for the weekend. Any luck?"

I showed him what we'd found. "We only stumbled onto it because Xiong was mapping out his genealogy."

"Let's check Pakistan," Malik said. "That's where my father was born. It's a country of many mysteries."

Our eyes shifted west from southeast Asia, but neither of us noticed any handwriting within the Pakistani borders.

"Look to Dubai." Xiong pointed at a city on the Persian Gulf, and immediately I saw a similar number.

"How did you know to look there?" I asked.

"Dubai is also a world financial center that offers confidential banking services to moneyed clients," he said. "Considering the provenance of the artwork, it is certainly possible Jack Clemens might maintain international accounts."

We quickly checked all the cliché countries for hiding money and also found handwritten numbers near Switzerland and the Cayman Islands.

"I don't suppose any of us has any firsthand knowledge with offshore banking?" I looked from Malik to Xiong, but one shook his head and the other held up empty palms. "I know. We're all underpaid journalists."

Fortunately, I knew where to turn. I called Agent Jax and yet again left a message. "This is Riley Spartz from Channel 3. I might have something to trade regarding Operation *Dissimulo*."

CHAPTER 56

Jack Clemens was ghosting—living the life of a dead man. With the right connections, rising from the dead no longer required a miracle. If migrant workers could do it, so could he.

He had a limited window to escape the country before his ruse was discovered. He was running low on cash, down to his last ten grand. And credit cards left a paper trail he was trying to avoid.

Federal agents had raided his office and homes before Jack even realized they were building a fraud case against him. They took his files and computers, and while those records damned him for his crimes, they did not lead authorities to his entire fortune. While prosecuting him, one of the government's top forensic accountants had followed the money backward, finding an offshore account in Panama. They were convinced he had stashed more millions elsewhere—secret accounts or buried cash. But every time they pressed him, he had claimed to be broke.

His cut from his work with the identity-theft ring had been deposited in several other covert accounts. He knew better than to leave details on his computer, hide them in a safe deposit box, or even tattoo them on his body. He had been prepared to wait a long time behind bars before claiming—and spending—that money, until an opportunity presented itself for hiring out his prison sentence.

The fake Jack was supposed to die of cancer, naturally, in the penitentiary, and with his passing so would end any debt to society. Jack's own invisibility would be assured.

Riley Spartz was becoming a problem. But luckily, he was good at solving those. That was why he was on his way to her house.

CHAPTER 57

described David Johnson to Channel 3's best graphic artist and realized his physical characteristics—shaved head, beard, brown eyes, earring—might all have been altered. The sketch was ready when the FBI guy arrived at the station and was ushered into our conference room.

Agent Jax had great interest in the fish painting numbers and tried claiming the art as evidence.

"You had your chance," I said. "I bought it. I own it."

Miles also resisted, on legal grounds. "My client has been extremely cooperative. Unless you have a search warrant, the painting stays here."

He knew what a big hurdle law-enforcement agencies faced trying to get warrants against news organizations. All sorts of First Amendment issues would come into play. The FBI might eventually win, but not before embarrassing jokes about the feds' "catch-and-release" property seizure went public. And bottom line: Jack would hear about it.

"I might consider giving you the painting," I said, "should we arrive at an understanding."

We talked about the picture's path from Jack to the government to me. The artwork had come into federal custody when agents were interviewing Jack's family and friends to track down

hidden assets. An aunt had apparently agreed to hold on to the
fish painting while Jack was in prison. Then the feds came by,
throwing around scary words like "conspiracy" and "accom-
plice." So instead, she'd stepped aside, and the art had been
seized for auction.

"We need physical possession of it," Agent Jax insisted.

So we agreed to let him take custody, provided he keep us in
the investigation's progress. I didn't exactly trust him, but Malik
had already videotaped the fish painting from the inside out, taking special care with close-ups around Singapore, Switzerland,
the Cayman Islands, and Dubai. My cell phone held my own pictures of the key numbers. Xiong had reassembled the frame and
matting around the artwork as best he could, gluing some of the
damaged spots. The result was less mangled, at first glance, than
I'd expected.

Agent Jax had questions of his own: When do you think you'll
see this man again? Where does he live? What type of vehicle
does he drive?

I didn't have useful answers, except when he asked if I knew
of anything David Johnson had touched. "Something that might
leave usable fingerprints?"

Our lunch table would have been long wiped clean. The
door handle to the restaurant would be sullied with prints
from other customers. But then I remembered him briefly
holding my cell phone, and how he'd touched the screen to
magnify the painting. The picture would still have been too
small to read the account numbers, but I had no doubt that's
what he'd been attempting. I'd used my phone since then, but
there was always a chance a legible impression of him might
still exist.

"You can dust for prints," I said. "But I want to watch."

I didn't want the feds accessing my emails or contact numbers. My phone was my phone. My fingerprints were also mine,

but I agreed to let them compare and eliminate them from any others on the device. Ends up, they found a thumbprint that didn't belong to me. All we could do was wait as the print was run against the 450 million fingerprints in the FBI's criminal database.

CHAPTER 58

It was official. David Johnson was Jack Clemens. The print on my phone matched his arrest fingerprints.

Surveillance video from a street camera across from the restaurant yielded a face who resembled the sketch. I confirmed him as the man I knew as David Johnson.

Bryce and I were eager to broadcast the name and photo and launch a manhunt. But the feds wanted to keep quiet.

"He'll just go underground again with a different identity once he hears his cover's blown," Agent Jax said. "Our best chance of catching him is by letting him claim the fish painting."

"You mean using it for bait?" I asked, pleased at the pun.

I made the phone call. The cell number he had given me was turned off so my message went straight to voicemail.

"Sorry I wasn't able to get back to you, David. Call me to finalize our deal with the fish painting. Name a time and place. This time, I'll pick up the tab."

David had always phoned me at the station through our switchboard. He didn't have my direct desk line or cell phone number because I hadn't wanted him pestering me. I waited at my desk for the phone to ring, certain he'd want to be in touch as soon as possible. But when it did, it wasn't the caller I was expecting.

"The police were just here," a woman said, speaking fast. "And it didn't go so well. I'm hoping maybe you can help. I've been watching your stories on the news for years, but I never thought I'd be calling you."

"Who are you?" I asked.

"My husband was Jack Clemens's barber. And I fear he was the man killed in prison."

CHAPTER 59

As he waited outside Riley's house, Jack recalled Lloyd Martin making a call to his own former home and giving him one last trim around the ears, just a few days before he would surrender to federal authorities. They were both defeated men. One couldn't beat prison; the other couldn't beat cancer.

"This is good-bye," Lloyd said. "I'll be dead long before you get out. The worst part is leaving Gina stuck with all my debts."

Jack had been reading the *Week* newsmagazine just before Lloyd had arrived and remembered a brief mention about wealthy Chinese lawbreakers using substitutes to serve prison sentences. As he watched his and Lloyd's reflections in the mirror, he took a gamble. "Maybe there's a way you could leave her a nest egg."

Within minutes, Lloyd had decided to sell what was left of his life. He'd sworn off betting, but he liked these odds better than the guarantee of being both dead and broke in less than a year.

"We'll need new looks," he said, appraising their appearances with his barber's eye. "First me."

Lloyd unbound his graying ponytail, picked up a pair of scissors, and gave himself the same corporate haircut he'd been giving Jack for years. Then he applied the same shade of coloring that kept his client looking younger than his fifty-four years.

Side by side, with their arms around each other's shoulders, they might not have passed for twins, but with blue eyes and similar height and build, they looked enough like brothers that the caper might work.

"You next," Lloyd said, turning to his new dopplegänger. "Relax."

With a clipper, he trimmed Jack's hair close to his scalp. Adding shaving cream and producing a razor, Jack was soon bald. "Meet the new you." Lloyd instructed him to grow a beard and cover his blue eyes with brown contact lenses.

"Oh, one last thing." He put some alcohol on a cotton ball and picked up a needle.

Jack protected his ear with one hand. He might be ruthless regarding money, but he was a baby when it came to physical pain. "Do I really have to do this?"

"I'm afraid so," Lloyd said. "You need to leave your banking image behind. My best protection is looking like you. Your best protection is not looking like you."

So Lloyd had pierced Jack's ear.

Jack stopped fixating on that jolt of pain from the past and returned to the moment. He was fingering a small amethyst earring belonging to Riley Spartz. He'd taken it as a souvenir from the meager jewelry box in her bedroom and inserted it in his earlobe in place of his gold one for good luck.

He'd followed her home after their first meeting just because he could. The next day he'd driven by the small bungalow when he knew she was at work to scout out the Minneapolis neighborhood. Lake Nokomis was near, so there was enough foot traffic that he wouldn't attract suspicion if he parked a few blocks away. Now he had tired of negotiating and had decided to play art thief.

He never planned to physically steal the picture. It was far too cumbersome to carry, and too memorable if a witness happened to notice him. He merely wanted the information hidden in the map.

The break-in was easy. He kicked in the window of a back-porch door, shielded by a tall hedge. There was no alarm, and no dog.

But no painting either.

CHAPTER 60

The address Gina Martin had given me was a large and un-inspired apartment building in Eden Prairie, south of Minneapolis. It stood in the middle of a giant parking lot set back from the highway, surrounded by a retail complex with a grocery store, pharmacy, and gas station.

Malik came along. He hadn't wanted to, but I promised he could take a nap in the van while I met with Gina. He'd developed a talent of being able to sleep anytime, anyplace while working as a military photographer. As the father of two young children, it served him well.

"I'll phone you when it's time to bring the camera upstairs. I'll do a meet and greet first."

I buzzed Gina's unit from the lobby, but she was so slow to answer that I wondered whether she'd changed her mind. But the security door eventually unlocked, and I stepped onto the elevator to the fourth floor. Down the hall, her apartment door stood open.

I stuck my head in, and she urged me to come in and join her at the kitchen table where a teapot sat with two cups and saucers. A walker with tennis balls taped to the front legs stood nearby on a worn carpet. The place was a mess, but I pretended not to notice the open drawers, clothing draped across furniture, and books on the floor.

I immediately poured us each hot tea because she was less likely to ask me to leave if I was still sipping a cup.

Gina's hands trembled as she removed a picture from her wallet and showed me a man with shoulder-length hair. "This was my husband. Handsome, huh?"

"He doesn't look much like Inmate 16780-59."

"But it's Lloyd," she assured me, unfolding a newspaper with the mug shot of the fake Jack.

I had to admit, the man's eyes and nose looked similar in each photo. "So what was the deal he worked out to serve Jack's time?"

"I'm not exactly sure. I wasn't in on it."

"You didn't know he was in prison?" I asked.

"Not until the media started reporting that a man had been killed behind bars while posing as Jack Clemens."

"So where did you think your husband was?"

"That's complicated," she said.

Lloyd Martin had once run a high-end hair salon for men and women. He even made home and office calls to a few wealthy clients, including Jack.

"Jack was a good tipper," Gina said. "But Lloyd was more than his barber—they were also friends."

I had no problem believing that. My own experience taught me that it was easy to develop an intimate relationship with someone who touches you, even if just to trim your bangs each month. When physical boundaries come down, so does discretion. My own hairdresser knew secrets about me no one else did.

"When times were flush, Lloyd mortgaged us to the hilt to lease a building in a trendy neighborhood for his salon," she said. "To clear a profit, he needed his best clients to come in every six weeks for color, cut, style—the full works."

When the economy tanked, Gina lost her government communications job and no one else was hiring. She started shampooing customers' hair and training to do manicures. After their health insurance ran out, she developed Parkinson's disease. Her hands shook too much to work with customers, so she helped out by answering the phone.

"By then the recession was even worse," she said. "Lloyd's regulars stopped being regular, stretching out the time between appointments. Many stopped getting facials and buying designer shampoo products. Some moved to cheaper salons. One started dying her hair at home in the sink. Lloyd couldn't pay the rent."

He lost the lease. Their home went into foreclosure and bankruptcy was next. Desperate, Lloyd rented a chair in a franchise salon—the ultimate humiliation. He'd gone from cutting some of the best-known hair in Minneapolis to hoping for a walk-in cut from a college student or a mom with two kids. Bills piled up while he frequented casinos, hoping for a big score.

Their life hit bottom when he was diagnosed with inoperable colon cancer a couple of months ago. The doctors didn't mince the prognosis. He had one year at most. Lloyd might not have looked like a walking dead man, but he was.

Gina came home one day and found a briefcase with a note on the kitchen table. "It said he didn't want me to go through the agony of watching him die, and that I was not to look for him, or contact the cops. He was rejecting a long painful death and was going off to kill himself."

"Do you still have the note?" I asked.

"The police took it."

"So you called them when he disappeared?"

"No, they just showed up today. Someone else must have tipped them, maybe from his doctor's office. The police brought a search warrant and tore the place apart. That's why it looks so bad. They think I was in on the plan. I'm worried they'll come back and arrest me."

"Why do they think you were involved?"

She handed me the search warrant affidavit and I flipped to the back page where it listed the items seized:

1. Medical records
2. Photographs of Lloyd Martin
3. Suicide note signed Lloyd Martin
4. Bank account statements
5. Briefcase containing $75,000 cash

"Seems like a lot of cash to have around the house," I said.

She pointed to a corner closet where coats and shoes were in disarray. "They found the money Lloyd left behind with the note. Because his cancer was fatal, he wrote that he had qualified for an early payout from his life insurance. I was surprised because I thought he'd cashed out the policy long ago. I figured it must be gambling winnings he was saving up to help me after he passed away."

"So you kept quiet and kept his money while your husband went off to kill himself." She didn't come across as very sympathetic in her version of the story.

"I know it looks bad, but I'm a victim. That's why I want to get my story out first, before the police do. Now I figure the cash was his payoff for taking Jack's place in prison."

"Did Lloyd take anything with him? A car?"

"Just one thing was missing. He took a gun."

That certainly lent some authenticity to his suicide threat. "What kind?"

"A .38 caliber revolver."

"I figured by the time I got home and found the note," she continued, "it was already too late. I kept waiting for the police to come to my door and tell me he was dead. But I didn't expect it to happen like this."

I phoned Malik to bring the camera upstairs. As he set up, I wrote the news in my mind.

((RILEY CU))
CHANNEL 3 HAS LEARNED
THE IDENTITY OF THE
MAN IMPERSONATING JACK
CLEMENS IN PRISON.

I texted the line to Ozzie with a note saying I had tonight's
lead story.

CHAPTER 61

The air was cold inside my house and my living room had been ransacked, but not by cops executing any search warrant. The law would have come in the front door and left a receipt. I was fairly sure the intruder was gone, but I climbed back in my car, locked the doors, and called 911 to report a burglary.

"Could you please send an officer to do a walk-through with me?"

A squad was there within minutes. Nothing obvious appeared missing. The bathroom had been throughly searched—the contents of my medicine cabinet and vanity drawers strewn across the floor.

"Looking for prescription drugs, I'd guess," the officer said. "Did you have any painkillers?"

I shook my head. The pain of loneliness couldn't be stemmed by Vicodin or oxycodone.

The shelves in my study had been cleared, and even though the floor was carpeted, at least two of my vintage books, including Agatha Christie's *Thirteen at Dinner*, had chips in their spines. At least they weren't first editions.

"You're lucky they didn't completely trash the place." The officer started writing his break-in report. "Anything missing? Thieves like guns. Did you have any guns hidden behind the books?"

"No guns." My deceased husband, a state patrol officer, had owned a Glock. I'd kept it close for a while, but later decided I was safer without it handy.

One item was gone from my bedroom. "I keep a tablet computer by my bed. That seems to be missing."

"Easy to carry, easy to sell. That's routine." He had me sign some paperwork. "The TVs stayed behind, so that might mean the burglar was on foot."

The cop left to knock on the door of my neighbors on each side in case they'd seen anything, but I reckoned he was only going through the motions because I worked for a TV station. Unlike home invasions and armed robberies, residential burglaries hold no urgency in criminal investigations. I knew better than to expect them to dust for fingerprints and string any POLICE LINE tape.

My landlord arrived to board up the back door and see if I needed anything else. "I'll have someone over to replace the glass."

I knew he didn't want to lose me as a tenant. I paid my rent on time and didn't hold wild parties. My lease was month by month, and now that I no longer owned a dog, a backyard wasn't vital. Moving to a more secure building—maybe a downtown loft— sounded appealing. After all, I was a single woman living alone.

The doorbell rang while I was cleaning up. I thought the police officer might have learned something and come back. Instead, Nick Garnett stood outside. He no longer had a key, so I let him in.

"Heard you had some unwelcome company," he said. "How bad?"

I didn't ask how he knew about the break-in. He'd spent twenty years as a Minneapolis cop, most recently a homicide detective, and had contacts in every department. He'd probably hear if I got a speeding ticket. No doubt, a burglary at the home of a TV reporter would be buzzed around law-enforcement circles.

"Just a blip, Nick, compared to everything else I have going wrong," I said. "I just want to straighten this place and forget that some jerk violated my space."

"I'll help you pick things up. Where do you want to start?"

I didn't have time for him, and was about to tell him not to bother when I thought of a way he might be useful.

Offshore bank accounts weren't just a means for white-collar criminals to hide assets, or for drug dealers to launder money, or even for the top one percent earners to manage their wealth. Terrorist cells also used them for anonymous cash flow. So I was fairly certain that Garnett, who just left a job with Homeland Security, might have some insight about the mysterious numbers on the fish painting.

"You can help shelve books." I figured I might as well put him to work while picking his brain. My literary interests were varied, classics like *The Great Gatsby* by F. Scott Fitzgerald as well as epic sagas like Barbara Taylor Bradford's *A Woman of Substance*. "Let's try to keep them alphabetical."

Garnett handed me *In Cold Blood* and I made a mental note to reread Truman Capote's nonfiction novel and look for the fabricated scenes now raising controversy. I wasn't surprised by the allegations that Capote had fibbed—very few true-crime stories can't be improved with some fictionalization. Unfortunately, it was another example of a relationship between a journalist and a cop crumbling under scrutiny.

When he passed me Robert Ludlum's *The Bourne Identity*, one of the top spy novels of all time, I saw my chance to transition to some news research.

"This book uses a secret Swiss bank account as part of the plot," I said. "Do you know much about offshore banking?"

"Does your question involve Jason Bourne or Jack Clemens?" Garnett immediately knew I wasn't just making idle conversation or trying to start a book club.

"Jack Clemens."

He rolled his eyes. "Why don't you tell me the whole story."

We abandoned the books and moved to a leather couch where I showed him the photo of the fish painting on my phone. He called it ugly, but became hooked when I filled him in on the hidden ciphers in the artwork.

"Here's the one from Singapore, that started it." I showed him a close-up I'd taken. The letter-number combination was legible when I expanded my screen.

He explained that the letter code was an abbreviation for the name of the offshore bank, and that the number code was the actual account number.

"So the FBI has this information?" he asked.

"But that's not all." I told him about David Johnson's intense interest in purchasing the painting, and then revealed the true identity of my potential buyer.

Garnett was surprised, which pleased me. He was not an easy man to catch off guard.

"They're using the painting to lure Jack Clemens," I said.

That news disturbed him. "The painting's not the only bait, Riley. You are."

The wind howled through the plywood nailed over the shattered window. Garnett walked to the back of the house to examine the boarded door, then checked the locks on the front door and ground-floor windows. He didn't linger in the bedroom like he did the last time we were there alone, tangled together in blankets and bliss.

But if that night was on his mind, he didn't show it. "I'm worried your burglary might be a bit too convenient to be coincidental."

"But the painting wasn't even here."

"He wouldn't have known that. This might have been a . . . fishing expedition. And if it was him, that means he knows where you live."

"The feds have the art now. He'll never get it."

"Unless he has you."

I went back to the bookcase and methodically began filling the shelves, abandoning all alphabetical ambition. It was something to do while I processed his take on the events.

"Are you staying here tonight?" he asked.

I hadn't thought about that until just then. "No."

He didn't invite me to crash at his place. Even if he had, I would have declined. Let him wonder where I was sleeping, even though, at that moment, I had no idea myself.

CHAPTER 62

"Thanks, Nicole." I carried an overnight bag into her apartment. She lived near downtown, a few blocks north of the river. "It was either your couch or the green room. And it's hard to get a good night's sleep when the morning crew shows up at four AM."

"Sorry to hear about your house getting broken into," she said. "You're welcome to stay here as long as you need."

We unfolded a hide-a-bed, and she tossed me a pillow and blanket. I lay down and shut my eyes to test the mattress. Decent.

The door bell rang, prompting me to sit up. "That's the pizza," Nicole said. "No slumber party without pizza."

We each grabbed a slice from the cardboard box and settled in front of the TV. Nicole had been watching a crime drama featuring a child abduction storyline. Just as the show went to commercial on a cliff-hanger where we couldn't tell who was screaming, Scott popped up on the screen with a Channel 3 news update. There really wasn't anything fresh, but he read his lines smoothly and promised to be back at ten with more.

"I hate to say this," I said. "But he really has that read-with-authority anchor presence down. It'll be interesting to see if viewers connect."

"Just be careful around Scott. He may not show it on the air, but he's real upset."

"Why? What happened?" I asked.

"His line got cut from the movie."

"Really?"

"Scott doesn't want to cover the wedding anymore, but Bryce is making him because of all the exposure."

Speaking of which, a thirty-second promotion touting the wonders of Channel 3's new studio set came on at the end of the commercial break.

"I'm impressed how much airtime Bryce has managed to get for promoting the new set," I said. "Especially during network prime time."

"Bryce gets what Bryce wants," Nicole said. "And since Scott wants off the wedding beat, I'm putting together local reaction pieces to Rachel and Ricky exchanging vows at the mall."

"Better you than me."

She insisted it was actually fun. "There's a pack of girl fans who don't want Ricky to marry. We've got video of them waving a banner reading, RICKY, WAIT FOR ME!"

"Sounds more like fanatics than fans."

"True, but look at it from the perspective of teenage girls," Nicole said. "Once he gets married, that ends each of their individual dreams of marrying him."

"They can join forces with the same-sex marriage opponents to try to shut down the film," I said.

"Three heterosexual couples dropped out as extras because they didn't want to be wed in the same ceremony with gays and lesbians," she said. "But the waiting list had plenty others to choose from."

"There seem to be a lot of people with motives to stop this wedding."

"Add the happy couple's family to that tally. While interviewing them, I got the impression his mother was hoping for a more traditional—and private—ceremony. And her father is upset that he won't get to walk his little girl down the aisle."

We spent the next minutes debating whether the engagement and subsequent nuptials were a Hollywood ruse to get publicity for the movie and even boost the actors' film careers.

"Whether that's their intent or not, the wedding is getting attention in all the right places." Nicole showed me a *People* magazine article about how Hollywood couples have been finding love on the movie set for decades, from Elizabeth Taylor and Richard Burton to Brad Pitt and Angelina Jolie. "Just having their engagement picture next to those superstars has to elevate their own status."

I skimmed the article and saw a relationship expert quoted.

> When actors rehearse being in love, trying to convince an audience their emotions are authentic, they sometimes convince themselves it's the real thing.

"So what do you think, Nicole? Is it possible to find true love on the job or not?"

"I don't know. I have my doubts two people can fall in love so fast. They might be pulling a Kardashian."

"It's not falling in love that's hard," I reflected, "it's staying in love."

"Some people need a lesson in falling out of love." She pointed out a sidebar article on the next page with a picture of Rachel on a beach with another man. "This is Rachel's old boyfriend. He didn't take the news that she's found someone else too well."

He had a reputation as an emerging bad-boy comedian and was quoted as saying he was still certain the two of them would end up together. "Don't rule out me showing up and stealing the bride."

"Sounds a bit obsessive." But then I wondered if he and I weren't so very different. "Maybe I need some advice on getting over a past love."

"Which one?"

"Nick Garnett."

I had a rule against discussing my private life with work friends, Malik being the exception. But because Nicole was sharing her apartment with me, that made us more like sorority sisters. Since I didn't want to bounce this off Father Mountain, she was my best bet for a sympathetic confidante.

"I thought that relationship was over," she said.

"It is." Now we were coming to the part I hesitated saying out loud. "But I'm not sure I want it to be."

"I don't see how you have any choice, Riley. If one half of a couple says it's over, it's over."

"But on some level, I know he still cares for me. He dumped me and doesn't want to admit he was wrong."

Our relationship had been on, off, on again, off again. I needed to do something to break the pattern.

"Is it possible your pride is the problem?" Nicole asked. "He dumped you and you don't want to admit you were wrong? I'm just asking."

That wasn't the kind of gal pal advice that I wanted to hear, so I changed the subject. "So are you seeing anyone?"

"Are you kidding? With my crazy schedule?" Because Nicole was low on the seniority list, she often worked night and weekend shifts. "How would I meet anyone? Actually, how did you?"

"Well, I've been married once and engaged once, and I met them both on the job. So there's hope for you."

"And they were both cops," she said.

I nodded, thinking maybe that was another pattern that needed breaking. I vowed my next love would not wear a badge.

I slept poorly that night, telling myself it was because of a streetlight outside the window, but it was really because my heart was pining for Nick Garnett. I wondered if he wondered where I was sleeping.

CHAPTER 63

The next morning I called my realtor, the one who'd sold my old house before the real estate market collapsed, and told her I might be in a buying mood. "Security is important to me."

"There are lots of great deals still to be had," Jan Meyer said. "Our agency just listed one that sold for four million before the bubble burst. We'll be lucky to get half that now."

"Too rich for me. Too bad for the sucker who owned it."

"Actually, he's out of the picture." That's when she told me it was Jack Clemens's mansion and one of her coworkers was selling it for the court to recover money for the victims fund.

"How about a tour?" I asked, curious how Jack had lived day to day.

"Showings are really only for serious buyers."

"How about if I bring a camera and interview one of you about the house for the news? That's essentially free advertising for the listing."

I sold her with that line.

Xiong was as pleased as a geek can be when I arrived at the station. The license plate database Channel 3 had purchased from the city was up and running on his computer system.

"More than two million numbers," he said, anxious to demonstrate its tracking feature, a display of where and when specific vehicles were photographed by law-enforcement cameras. "What is your license plate number, Riley?"

I actually had no idea, and Xiong took the bus, so I fumbled in my wallet to find my auto insurance card. I set it by his keyboard and he typed it in, then showed me the results, arranged chronologically by most recent sightings. My car had been captured on camera thirteen times, mostly in downtown Minneapolis. He stroked a few more keys and it appeared over a geographic map.

"If we knew nothing else about you," he said, "we could deduce you lived or worked around here." He pointed to a two-square block area that included the station.

"Interesting," I said.

He seemed disappointed I wasn't more effusive, but the whole thing was a little anticlimatic, telling me something I already knew. I tried to muster some enthusiasm. "Let's watch for an opportunity to try it out on a news story."

I sold Bryce on touring Jack Clemens's mansion by promising him a news version of Lifestyles of the Rich and Famous Convicts.

Malik drove the van over a small bridge to Manitou Island, the most exclusive address in the town of White Bear Lake. Gates opened and we pulled into a sprawling modern estate on an acre of wooded grounds.

"Sweet," Malik said.

Jan disabled an elaborate security system I envied before taking us through the eight-thousand-square-foot house, which included a fitness room, an outdoor swimming pool, and a guesthouse.

"It must've been hard to trade all this for a prison cell," I said.

We interviewed Jan about the property. "Whoever buys this will be getting a bargain."

Without furniture, houses sometimes don't show well. But this place had special architectural touches, like fancy moldings, tile, and custom windows, that made it memorable. I was disappointed. Because Jack was such a crook, I had expected his place to be tacky, not tasteful.

Malik recorded wide-angle images of the stairway and arched ceilings while I lingered in Jack's home office, the scene of his financial crimes. According to the auctioneer, the fish painting had hung on one of these walls. We looked out over the frozen lake. The water level had dropped dramatically over the past few years, and the shoreline was ragged, extending far into where there had once been open water. That geographic shift, almost as much as the depressed real estate market, accounted for the lowball price.

We moved outside so Malik could get an exterior shot looking up from the shoreline, following Jan out the back door to the lake. But the minimal snowfall clearly revealed more dirt than grass.

"The landscaping's a little rough," I said.

Malik noticed some animal tracks amid holes in the ground. "Looks like something's been digging here. Badgers? Gophers? Raccoons?"

"That's where the feds were digging this fall," Jan said.

"Really" I asked. "For what?"

She shrugged. "They didn't say. I supposed they wanted to rule out buried treasure before the place went on the market."

"Any success?"

"If so, they didn't tell me."

I didn't tell her that what they'd been searching for had been in plain sight.

Malik shot close-ups of shovel marks while Jan and I talked about what price range of houses I might want to see. Just as I was telling her not to rule out downtown Minneapolis condos, I got an idea on how to deter intruders from my current rental home until I could relocate.

CHAPTER 64

David—I still couldn't think of him as Jack—had returned my call, leaving a message offering to meet me at five o'clock at Stella's, where our alliance had begun. "You bring the painting, I'll bring the cash."

The FBI guy wanted me there an hour early to get into position. Agent Jax was wearing a long-sleeved polo shirt instead of his usual dark suit, in an attempt to not look like a federal agent. He and a colleague carried the fish painting inside from a full-sized van and propped it against the wall by my table. One of them sat in a corner booth and the other near the front door, waiting for Jack Clemens.

Malik was undercover at the bar with a plate of fish tacos and a hidden camera waiting to record the action. I ordered oysters on the half shell and a glass of wine to pass the time—after all, the government was picking up the tab and my cameraman was driving.

The restaurant manager stopped by to admire my artwork and even offered to buy the painting for one of their walls. He had no idea his place was the backdrop of a federal sting operation.

"Sorry," I told him. "It's off the market." I hung my coat over the painting to avoid attracting other prospective buyers.

We waited while five o'clock came and went. Then I recognized a figure walk in the front door and head for the bar. It was Garnett. I switched chairs, but he spotted me anyway and walked over to my table with a glass.

"Is this seat taken?" he asked.

"Actually, it is," I said. "I'm meeting someone."

"That's fine." He sat down anyway. "I won't stay long."

I was surprised by his brazenness, but didn't want to tell him he was in the center of a sting operation.

"Do you remember the last time we were here?" he asked, taking a slow sip of his drink. "We didn't stay long then either."

I was pleased that he had fond memories of that night, but couldn't let him sabotage my assignment. Out of the corner of my eye, Agent Jax was pointing at his watch, signaling for me to get rid of Garnett.

But Nick was in no hurry, clicking his glass against mine playfully, almost like a peace offering. Smiling back, I noticed a text message appear on his cell phone, which was lying on the table. He placed his hand over it, but not before I read the name VELMA upside down.

"Maybe we should make a toast," he suggested. "How are you doing after that break-in the other night?"

"I'm doing rotten. And you need to leave."

"Really?" He didn't seem in the mood to move. "How about I wait till your friend gets here? You can introduce us." He leaned over and grinned at me. "Unless he really doesn't exist."

"How dare you. You want to talk about dates? Maybe we should talk about you and Velma."

"Me and Velma?" He tried acting like there was nothing going on. "What's to talk about?"

"Why don't you tell me. You're the one she's messaging."

"What if I told you we're just friends?"

I found that hard to believe, so I threw my wine in his face.

"Lucky for me it's white," he said.

I handed him a napkin, but no apology. I hoped Malik hadn't gotten that scene on video.

Garnett wiped his face, but didn't get up to leave. Instead, he leaned in close and murmured a soulful line from an obscure film. "We were a mess together. We were a beautiful mess."

"Maybe we still are."

"Is that all you have to say?"

I shook my head. "Ben Kingsley, *The Wackness*, 2008."

He nodded and walked away.

CHAPTER 65

An hour later, it was obvious I'd been stood up. I checked my voicemail and found no new calls from David saying sorry, he'd have to reschedule.

"Did you do anything to make him suspicious?" Agent Jax asked.

"I don't think so," I said. "I left him a message. He left me a message back. You heard it. He sounded normal."

"Well, something's gone wrong." It was clear he blamed me. "I'm not sure this working relationship is working out."

Bryce was also upset that we came back with zip. It was also clear he blamed me. Our deal with the feds was that we'd run an exclusive story following Jack's arrest. I soon learned that Bryce hadn't seemed to grasp that an arrest wasn't a sure thing and had left a big hole at the top of the late news, expecting to air our scoop.

The story was so hush-hush that not even the newscast producer knew what it was about, only that I'd be there late with the lead.

"Is there anything we can salvage from it?" he asked upon learning it was a bust.

I shook my head. "There's nothing we can report at this time."

He looked at Bryce, who also gave him a thumbs-down.

"We're an hour from air," the producer said. "What else do

we have to lead with? How about that funeral-home drug story you're working on? Can that go?"

He was talking about the marijuana-spiked-with-embalming-fluid piece I'd mentioned the day before during the news huddle. The head of the narcotics unit had confirmed it was a real problem.

"The package is written but not tracked or edited," I said. "It was being held for Sunday night."

"Forget Sunday," Bryce said. "Run it now as a voice-over tape."

Voice-over was the least creative way to tell a television story, usually reserved for short pieces or breaking news when time was tight.

"What about running the identity-theft victim story?" I asked. "It's edited and in the can." That would also get Lisa off my back. Each day she was calling to check when her story was going to run. I kept telling her soon, but I could sense she was getting discouraged.

"It's not sexy enough for a lead," Bryce said. "Don't forget we're still in a sweeps month."

"Right," the producer said. "The identity piece is also too long. It'd be a better in-depth piece for the second section."

I knew better than to argue. I sent them the drug script and hurried to the green room for makeup. I realized the production would be rough, but never anticipated how close I'd be to being fired in ten minutes.

CHAPTER 66

I was more nervous about this story than any I'd broadcast in years. Not about the facts: those were nailed. But with no time to record a voice package, I'd be reading at least two minutes of copy on the self-operated teleprompter nonstop. I had just slid off my shoes and taken a deep breath when Scott looked at me with sympathy.

"Do you want me to just run it for you, Riley? This is the lead story and I'd hate to see it messed up."

What a relief. "I was just thinking the same thing. Thanks, Scott. I owe you."

The Channel 3 music open ran and soon the floor director was cueing Scott to stand by, then counting him down.

((SCOTT CU))
GOOD EVENING EVERYONE.
TONIGHT WE LEAD WITH A
DANGEROUS DRUG THAT
SOUNDS SO GHOULISH YOU
WON'T BELIEVE PEOPLE
SMOKE IT.

((SCOTT/TWOSHOT))
RILEY SPARTZ HAS MORE IN
HER INVESTIGATIVE REPORT.

((RILEY, CU)
ON THE STREET, THE DRUG IS
CALLED "WET" . . . MARIJUANA
LACED WITH EMBALMING
FLUID . . . YES, THE SAME STUFF
USED TO PRESERVE DEAD
PEOPLE.

((RILEY NAT))
USERS CLAIM A LONG-
LASTING

Scott was moving the script like a snail, advancing each line at half the usual pace.

HIGH . . . BUT THE SIDE EFFECTS
CAN CAUSE . . .

As I fumbled for the hard copy on the news desk, he speeded up to twice the normal timing.

COMA, STROKE OR EXTREME
VIOLENCE.

I read faster and faster to try to keep up, but my words weren't matching the images as I reported on how funeral homes were being targeted by thieves looking for the drug. The producer was yelling in my earpiece and the story's power was diminished by my shaky on-air performance.

The camera cut to Scott, who apologized to viewers for "technical difficulties" and picked up the next story, reading effortlessly until we broke for commercial.

"What happened?" I asked him.

He shrugged, covering his microphone with one hand as he whispered, "Just remember, without a teleprompter, you're nothing."

The floor director rushed in to unclip my mic and usher me off the set in mortification. Bryce was standing near the control booth and ordered me to his office where he lectured me on my lack of professionalism.

"We're in a major market station, Riley. And you embarrassed us tonight. This is live television. If you can't handle your job duties, I'll find someone else who can."

Bryce had unfairly admonished me many previous times, threatening to fire me. But while he was a jerk most of the time, this was different. This time I deserved it.

Instead of going home to cry alone, I went back to Nicole's place. She'd been watching the news and hugged me as I came through the door.

"How bad was I?"

"Plenty bad. It was Scott, wasn't it?"

I nodded. "Yep."

She handed me a blanket and I curled up in the hide-a-bed with a pillow over my face. While that maneuver blocked the streetlights from the living room window, I was still too tense to sleep because the teleprompter fiasco kept replaying in my mind. First too slow, then too fast. My breathing followed the same erratic pattern until the last thing I remember thinking was that at least we didn't go black on air.

But maybe that would have been better.

CHAPTER 67

Nicole didn't have to be in to work until afternoon, but I was due in first thing. She toasted me a frozen waffle. I didn't bother with a plate or syrup, just ate it on the run as I dashed to the station after my restless night. After the waffle, the day went downhill.

The feds blindsided me with a news conference which I was sent to cover. They announced a $25,000 reward for information leading to the arrest of Jack Clemens, who was now officially on the FBI's most wanted list.

"We've learned he's believed to be traveling under the assumed name of David Nathan Johnson," Agent Jax said. "Here's a picture of what he looked like a couple days ago."

They handed out copies of the surveillance photo of the bald and bearded man I'd identified for them. They gave no shout-out to Channel 3, or to me. Malik was stunned, and I was afraid to go back to the station. My news director would probably be waiting outside the door to fire me. I tried to remember everything I could about David Johnson, delving for any clue to where he might go.

Bryce called my phone. He was plenty mad, but didn't order me to clean out my desk. "We'll talk about this fiasco later, Riley. Quick—post something about this reward and Clemens's new description on social media, and then prepare to report live for every newscast."

I was trying to remember how many characters Twitter allows, when I noticed the last thing I'd tweeted had been a "relatable," a photo of a car being towed from outside Stella's the night of the snowstorm.

My brain found a possible answer.

David had complained about his car being towed the night we had dinner. The timing and location led me to believe it might be the vehicle featured in my towing photo. I found the original picture on my cell phone, but the license plate wasn't visible. It was a silver Toyota Camry, among the most popular vehicles on the road.

I asked Malik to head over to the Fifth Police Precinct. "Wait outside. I might have an idea."

I could have called the feds and let them in on the puzzle, but after the debacle of the news conference just now I didn't trust them and was afraid of being accused of sending them on another fool's errand.

"I'm with Channel 3, and I'm looking for the parking ticket issued to this car for towing." I showed the photo to the desk sergeant. "I have the date and time, make, model, and color of the vehicle, as well as the location."

"Why do you even care?" she asked.

Knowing how lame my request sounded, I was prepared for her question. "I'd like to profile the owner about what it was like finding their car gone."

She rolled her eyes. "Just wait for it to snow again and stand out by the impound lot. You'll have your pick of folks to interview."

"Believe me, I agree, but my boss wants me to do it this way."

"It would be much easier if you had the plate number," she said.

"I know, but can you break down the citations by time or location?"

She messed around on her computer for a few minutes before

giving up. "I can give you a digital list of all the tickets issued that day, but you'll have to make sense of it yourself."

I wrote a check for the file, she gave me a receipt and emailed me the information in an attachment.

"Did you find what you were looking for?" Malik asked.

"I'm not sure."

Malik dropped me outside the newsroom door while he parked in the basement. I rushed over to Xiong's desk and found him hunched over his keyboard.

"Surprise," I told him. "We might be able to put your license plate program to the test."

I filled him in on the mechanics and forwarded the email to his account.

"You want these citations arranged chronologically?" he said.

"Yes," I said. "Then we'll take the ones from this ten-minute time period and look for any towed vehicles from this street and see if we find a silver Toyota Camry among them. That will give us a specific license plate."

"Whose car are we looking for?"

"Jack Clemens's, I hope."

CHAPTER 68

This vehicle fits all your criteria," Xiong said. "But it is registered to another party, not Jack Clemens."

"David Johnson?" I asked.

"No." He handed me a piece of paper with a different name, address, and phone number. "This data is a couple years old, so might be out of date."

It was worth a try. I dialed the phone number and a woman answered. "Hello, Mrs. Basch? I'm calling from Channel 3. Do you own a silver Toyota Camry?"

She informed me that her husband, Ed, had sold the vehicle on Craigslist List a month ago.

"Do you remember the buyer's name?"

She didn't, but thought her husband might. "He won't be home until late afternoon. The man who bought the car was supposed to change the title to his own name. Is there a problem?"

"No. The vehicle was towed during the storm, and I'm tracing its ownership for a potential story. Either the driver didn't turn in the paperwork or the state records haven't been updated yet. Did you by any chance see what the man looked like?"

She recalled him being bald.

That was all the confirmation I needed. I told Xiong to run the plate number through his license database. "I want to know where that car's been, and where it might be now."

I drove around a popular residential neighborhood near the University of Minnesota with Xiong, block by block, looking for a silver Camry with Jack's plate number. The area was a mix of frat houses, student apartments, and professional condos. The computer records showed the vehicle had been spotted in the vicinity six times during the last month. We hoped the pattern held. Once we found it, we'd let the cops stake it out.

But it would soon be dark, and with the traffic and stoplights, I decided we could make more progress on foot. So we pulled over and split the territory.

"Xiong, you head east, I'll go west while we still have some daylight."

I combed an apartment parking lot in case Jack lived there. No luck. So I set out down the street, checking cars in front of a grocery store. After all, everyone has to eat. Nothing. So I moved on past homes, schools, and parks, searching for silver cars. But none had the correct plate.

Twenty minutes later, Xiong called me. "I have finished my section and have not located the vehicle."

I sensed his disappointment. He really wanted to see his computer skills applied to news-gathering on the street. Instead, it was proving to be a bust.

"I'm almost done, too. No success. Let's meet back at my car and regroup."

I was walking down a narrow side street toward University Avenue when the silver Toyota we were looking for drove past me. The make and model caught my attention first, and then my eyes dropped to check the plate number. Turning around to double-check the license, a sense of déjà vu hit me. Apparently I wasn't the only one. The driver and I both stopped at the same time.

The vehicle backed up, the window rolled down, and a man wearing a blue-stocking cap called out to me.

CHAPTER 69

R iley Spartz," he said. "What a coincidence."

"David?" I faked ignorance of his true identity. "I didn't recognize you without your beard. What happened with our meeting? You didn't show."

"Get inside and we'll hold our meeting now."

"I can't. I have to head back to work. I'm parked just a couple blocks over. Do you live near here?"

I knew getting in a car with a fugitive was a poor idea. I had more to lose than he did. And once those doors closed, I'd be vulnerable to any sort of chilling abuse. I tried to keep things cordial. "Can we get together later?"

"I don't think so."

That's when he pointed the gun at me. It looked like a .38 caliber revolver. I thought about turning and running, but I remembered the hunting trophies that'd been sold at the auction and knew he was a crack shot. And at this range, even a lousy shot could kill me.

I mumbled something about there being a misunderstanding.

He leaned over to open the car door, not wavering in his aim straight at my chest. "Get in."

Even though I knew it was a mistake, I didn't see much choice. I was settling into the front seat when he immediately asked to see my cell phone. My guess was he didn't want me secretly pocket-dialing for help. I handed my cell in his direction, but he shook his head.

"Throw it outside, Riley."

That told me he didn't want anyone using the GPS coordinates in my phone to locate me and stage a rescue or, I worried, to find my body. So at gunpoint, I tossed my phone in the snow, wishing for a miracle as he put the vehicle in gear and the doors automatically locked with a foreboding click.

"Buckle up," he ordered. "I saw you with the feds last night. You were setting me up."

"I don't know what you're talking about, David."

"Stop calling me that. I've been watching the news. Everybody knows who I am now. Sure, I stood you up. But you stood me up, too. I waited by your house last night, but you didn't come home."

I didn't answer, but was glad I'd slept on Nicole's couch. I thought my best chance at survival was pretending we were pals. It's harder to pull a trigger on a friend than a foe. The sky was turning dusk, and I worried he might drive to some isolated corner.

"I'm not going to hurt you."

On one level—the part of my brain that didn't want to believe I was on the road to my own murder—found his words reassuring. But on another level—the common sense part of my brain—my instincts told me that dying while trying to escape might be a better death than whatever torture lay ahead.

Looking over to gauge his sincerity, and admire his ability to drive while holding a loaded gun, I noticed he was wearing a tan puffy coat, like the hooded figure from the post office surveillance footage. My bizarre journey was now full circle to the package of bloody teeth. My jaw ached, but I knew not to bring up Leon's name.

Jack Clemens wasn't just a white-collar criminal: he was a psychopath. And it's never good to tease an armed psychopath. So I lied and told him I trusted him.

"Take me to the fish painting," he said. "And then I'll let you go."

That's when I realized I was safe, temporarily. He wouldn't kill me until after he got the account numbers.

"I just need to look at the art," he continued. "You can keep the painting."

"Does this mean I don't get the two thousand dollars?" I was trying to keep the mood light.

"You should have sold it to me when you had the chance. Then we could have avoided all this drama."

Him needing the painting gave me power. I didn't have to just wait to see where he took me. I could pick our destination. But if I told him the FBI had the picture, he'd probably execute me on the spot. I could tell him the answer was on my cell phone. But once we retrieved that, he wouldn't need me anymore.

My home turf would give me the edge for our showdown.

"It's at my house," I said.

"It wasn't there the other day."

"So that was you, huh?" I acted surprised. "The painting was hanging in my office at the station, but I brought it home the other day."

"You better not be lying."

"I'm not," I lied.

He turned onto the freeway entrance and headed toward south Minneapolis in rush-hour traffic. Occasionally he needed both hands, and gripped the gun against the steering wheel. I considered trying to unlock the door and jump out, but figured a semitruck would probably flatten me.

I was tempted to make conversation, but under the circumstances reckoned the less I knew about any hidden money or plans to leave the country, the more likely I was to get out of this jam alive.

Traffic stalled ahead and we crept along slowly, making it easy for him to keep a bead on me with the firearm.

"Don't even think about trying to escape," he said. "We have a deal. The painting for your life."

That was hogwash. He couldn't risk me calling the cops. He had too much at stake. He'd have to kill me. He must have thought I was stupid, which made him stupider. And made me determined to outthink him.

I'd seen dumb guys often swayed by the fairer sex and decided to gamble. "You're an intelligent man." I paused to whisper his name slowly. "Jack. You outsmarted the feds in that prison switch. Maybe, wherever you're going, you should take me along. As a partner, not a hostage."

"You're not serious." He clearly wasn't buying my proposal.

"I have a passport. They'll be looking for a man traveling solo. Being a couple is a good disguise."

"You don't have to act like this. As long as I get what I want, I won't harm you. I'm not violent, just unscrupulous."

Because of the evidence of his puffy coat, I had no faith in his promise not to kill me. Also, the homicide of the fake Jack in prison had all the makings of a murder for hire. I didn't have any evidence, but I figured Jack had something to do with his impostor's death.

Jack was trying to keep me upbeat, all the better to catch me off guard when he made his final move. My jaw hurt, and I just hoped he didn't have a pair of pliers in his glove compartment.

"We could relax on a beach in some country that doesn't extradite to the United States," I suggested.

Jack ignored my offer.

"All I need to do is pack a bag, and we can be on the road," I said.

"I'll think about it." He didn't seem to trust me enough not to blurt out his identity to airport security.

"Or we could hole up at my place for a while."

We exited off the freeway, turning left. He didn't need any directions to find his way to my house. I wondered how long he'd been stalking me from the shadows after work.

Patience, I reminded myself. Within minutes, I would have the home court advantage. Even though it was nightfall, there was always a chance a neighbor might be outside. Or Jack might slip and fall on my icy sidewalk, accidentally discharging the gun into his chest and wasting himself—wishful thinking on my part.

He parked in the driveway by my garage, obviously not wanting to be seen at the front door. Anybody glancing out their window would assume from the taillights that I'd just gotten home from work. I was fine entering from the back. That would put us in the kitchen; a rack of knives was on the counter. The problem? A bullet moved faster than a blade.

Jack turned off the engine, tucked the key remote in his pocket, and held the gun steady. "I'm going to get out of the car. Then I'm going to open the door for you. We'll walk to the house together. You first. Me, on your heels."

A cold wind blew from the north. Under the moonlight, snow sparkled on the ground as I unlatched the gate to the fenced backyard. The sidewalk hadn't been shoveled, so I moved cautiously toward the rear house light, being careful where I stepped, trying to keep my balance.

Jack watched me sliding and followed behind me, seeking more secure footing. He cursed because he was wearing fancy loafers with smooth soles rather than winter boots with traction.

My stomach grew tense because in another ten steps or so we'd be at the back porch. Once inside, it wouldn't take long for him to discover there was no fish painting. Our deal would be void, and I'd learn firsthand whether he'd lied about not being a violent man.

I wasn't sure how the next few minutes might unfold. Jack stayed close, making it impossible for me to beat him—or a bullet—to the other side of the door. Instead of hurrying to my fate, I stalled.

"I'm looking for the house keys." I pretended to search

through my pockets before pulling them out. "I don't want you breaking the glass again or my landlord will raise my rent."

"Keep moving." He pressed the gun muzzle hard against my back and, despite my bluster, I felt like a soft target, defenseless against the whim of a madman.

CHAPTER 70

Three steps later, Jack howled as he went down. This was no routine slip and fall. His scream was so loud I was certain someone else would hear his pain and rush to lend assistance. But the surrounding houses were apparently well insulated or the inhabitants devoid of curiosity.

Jack clutched his foot in agony as he rolled in the snow, caught in a metal body-gripping trap.

When he collapsed, the gun flew from his hand and slid across the ice toward the garage. I rushed to retrieve it, and breathlessly pointed the barrel at him and cocked the trigger. Just that faint clicking sound put me in charge of our fate.

I didn't like guns. I had good reason. But I knew if I had to, I could blast my adversary. Let him worry about my marksmanship. So I faked being comfortable with the firearm.

"Freeze, Jack."

He wailed again, kicking his foot. "What is this thing?"

"It's for trapping vermin. Like you."

I'd set the trap near the back door, under a coating of snow, after being burglarized. Because the yard was fenced, and the season was winter, I didn't worry about stray dogs falling victim.

The outline of the trap under snow was just barely visible to me in the dark at the bottom of the porch steps. Jack hadn't had a clue he was walking into an ambush. Usually when journalists refer to trapping someone, it means catching them in a lie during an on-camera interview. This was even more satisfying.

I wanted to call 911, but my cell phone was miles away and I had no landline inside. A snow shovel was leaning near the back door of the house. Shoot. Shovel. Shut up. Even more than the gun, it reminded me that I was armed and dangerous.

"Don't move," I warned him. "I swear I'll shoot you."

Jack kept struggling to pry open the trap and free himself. But if Scott wasn't strong enough, Jack sure wasn't. As he thrashed about in the snow, he shrieked again, this time even louder. His hand was now stuck in the steel leghold trap.

I held the gun over my head and discharged a few rounds straight in the air, being careful not to empty the chamber, but hoping someone would call the police to report "shots fired."

Jack started yelling for help in a shrill voice, because he knew the gun still contained enough ammo to put him out of his misery like trappers do to wounded animals.

"Oh, stop being such a baby," I said. "It's not like I ripped your teeth out of your mouth. Did Leon cry like you? Answer me."

"What do you mean?" Jack was now curled up in a ball, an arm protecting his head, afraid I'd fire. "I didn't kill him."

"And what about your *ding zui*? Substitute criminal? How'd you pull that murder off?"

"I had nothing to do with that either. I'm innocent."

"Tell it to the cops. They should be here soon. You had motive, opportunity, and a puffy coat."

I fired another shot in the air, but otherwise forced myself to remain still. Help came much quicker than I had expected. Within a minute, I heard sirens and seconds later, flashing red lights surrounded my house. And finally, neighbors emerged from their homes and their suppers to see what was unfolding.

I set the handgun on the porch steps, far out of Jack's reach. "Back here," I called out, arms in the air so the cops wouldn't shoot me first and ask questions later.

A couple of officers in blue arrived to secure the scene. They were impressed when I introduced them to Jack Clemens as he continued to flail around amidst the snow and steel.

He was yelling something about wanting me charged with assault when Xiong raced up, hugging me tight.

When I hadn't showed up at the car, he called my cell phone. A stranger walking her terrier in the neighborhood answered, saying she heard it ringing on the ground. The only explanation Xiong could come up with for my disappearance was not that I'd found Jack's car, but that Jack had found me.

"I told the police I feared you had been abducted and gave them the license plate number," he said. "They put it in their camera search system as most wanted high priority."

Apparently a bridge camera had recorded the silver car getting off my freeway exit in real time. Xiong deduced we might be headed to my house and squads were dispatched about the same time Jack pulled into my driveway.

He whimpered as the cops removed the metal traps from his hand and foot. They slapped handcuffs on him even though his fingers had red sores across the knuckles. His ankle was swollen and bruised as he limped to the back of the squad car demanding to stop at the hospital for an X-ray.

CHAPTER 71

Jack continued to deny having anything to do with Leon Akume's murder. The police theorized he'd sent the package to a TV station for grisly kicks.

He had motive and opportunity for the homicide. He lacked an alibi. Yet authorities had no real evidence to pin the crime on him other than the puffy coat. And apparently hundreds of people were likely to have one just like it in their wardrobe.

Clearing the case wasn't important, because anyone at his court sentencing who could do fourth-grade math knew that if you added up his age and his new sentence, even just for the escape charges, Jack Clemens would never leave prison alive.

For now he was being housed in a rural county jail north of the Twin Cities until his ankle was healed enough to transport him to a maximum-security federal facility.

Della Sax, who had performed Leon's autopsy, removed his picture from her murder wall, even without an official conviction. "I need space for all the new ones being plotted."

We celebrated by sharing caramel cappuccinos and war stories in her office. "You were lucky, Riley. I'd hate to have your photo on my wall."

"I'd hate to be on your wall." I made her promise that if anything bad ever happened to me, she would never stop searching for my killer.

"Stop that kind of morbid talk," she said. "Any fun plans coming up?"

I smiled and laughed in anticipation.

"You can tell me," she said. "Date, perhaps?"

"Not exactly." I hadn't heard from Nick Garnett since throwing the drink in his face. And I didn't expect to.

Phil McCarthy had left a message saying that he was going to ask me out again after the legislative session was over. "It won't be a conflict of interest then."

I had nixed any hopes he had of a romantic relationship, leaving him a message back. "Reporter-source is all we'll ever be to each other."

I spared Della all those negative vibes. "Actually, I'm being celebrated as a hero tomorrow night."

The Minnesota Trappers Society was presenting me with their Lifetime Achievement Award at their annual banquet. I'd been added to the evening program because they wanted a celebrity face for how traps can keep society safe. I agreed to attend once I learned the menu offered a choice of chicken or beef, not possum or raccoon.

I'd already drafted my acceptance speech. *I might not be alive today, but for a body grip trap.* But the trappers didn't know that I was planning to urge support for the elevated restrictions to protect dogs from the deadly devices.

"Are your parents driving up from the farm to cheer?" she asked.

"Yes, they'll be spending the night at my place."

We'd be sitting with the president of the trapping organization and his wife, and I was supposed to bring three more guests to fill the table. That's when I realized my circle of friends was limited. Many were married with children, their evenings spent at basketball games and school plays. Chasing TV news took up too much of my time to find new ones. Toby was still in prison. Nicole and Malik were scheduled to work that night, but I convinced Bryce to let them cover the ceremony for the late news, and they were glad for the free dinner.

That left one seat. I thought about asking Phil, presenting it as lawmaker research, but figured my parents would read too much into that invitation. I couldn't risk my mom telling all her friends back home something crazy like we were engaged. Though there could be an upside: I figured spending an evening with my parents would dissuade Phil from ever asking me out again.

Lisa called just then to check on the status of her identity-theft story. It had been lost in the brouhaha following Jack's arrest. I told her my news director had assured me her piece was slotted for next week.

While we were chatting about our jobs, I mentioned my upcoming award. "Would you like to sit at my banquet table?"

"Really?" Lisa was thrilled to be included. She'd been in a better mood since Jack was back in custody and Akume's murder had been resolved. I offered to pick her up on my way.

Lisa and my mom got along fabulously at dinner. The wife of the trapping president was a little disconcerted because the two kept talking about funerals. I nudged Mom once when she went into too much detail regarding open versus closed caskets and how to ensure looking good for burial.

The Minnesota Trappers Society applauded as I described using traps in my backyard to snare Jack Clemens. Even though their members didn't agree with trapping restrictions, they were good sports and were even including a profile of me on their Who's Who in Minnesota Trappers website.

Their president unveiled a campaign encouraging more people to use traps for personal protection. Their slogan: SAFER THAN GUNS.

I was presented with a lovely silver medal reading Lifetime Achievement in Trapping. They fastened it on a chain around my neck, and I posed for pictures. Nicole had taken me shopping for a navy-colored sleeveless sheath dress and black stiletto heels, and managed to finally convince me that panty hose were passé—even during the winter.

The Trappers Society tried giving me a beaver fur coat, which I declined. "I'm sorry, this is much too extravagant."

Before I could stop her, my mother accepted it on my behalf. All the trappers in the room gave her a standing ovation as she modeled it around the banquet room.

CHAPTER 72

Mom and Lisa sat in the back of the car on the way home, laughing like gal pals. If Lisa hadn't been a third her age, I think my mom would have invited her to join her Red Hat Ladies Club.

Dad and I sat in the front, not saying anything.

I dropped Lisa off at her place and told her she could come to Channel 3 the night her story aired and watch it from the news control room.

"Meeting you, Riley, has been the best thing to happen to me in a long time."

I parked in front of my house because it was easier for my parents to get in that door with my dad's bad knee. My mom pulled the beaver coat tight around her, then spotted something shiny on the backseat.

"Riley, you dropped your trapping medal."

"No, I have it here." I held it up in all its glory.

"Then what's this?" She handed a necklace to me.

The sterling silver pendant on a neck chain showcased a woman's face with a halo around her head. I squinted to read the embossed words. Across the top, SAINT APOLLONIA; along the bottom, PRAY FOR US. On the back of the jewelry, Lisa Melby's name was engraved.

"Lisa must have dropped it." I stuck it in my pocket. "I'll give it back when I see her.

I got my parents settled for the night, and then looked at the pendant again. I was raised Catholic, but had never heard of this obscure saint until a couple weeks ago. Now, every time I turned around, she was waving a set of pliers at me. She might not be trying to pull my teeth, but she was jerking my chain.

Then I remembered what Father Mountain had said about not praying to saints for answers, but for helping in finding them. Might this be a clue? So I said a silent prayer to St. Apollonia, whose appeal was broader than I'd ever imagined. I'd since learned that artist Andy Warhol, the pope of pop, had printed colorful lithographs in her honor that have been displayed in museums around the world.

That Lisa would possess such a medallion still seemed odd based on our brief acquaintance. What did I actually know about her? Certainly, she had been a victim of identity theft. That much was corroborated, but I needed to dig further.

CHAPTER 73

My mom fixed blueberry pancakes for breakfast on my stove while we waited until after rush hour traffic cleared for my parents to climb into the pickup truck and head south to the farm.

Leon Akume's court file was in a stack of paperwork on my desk at the station. I phoned the court reporter with the case number and she verified that Lisa's testimony had not been transcribed.

"You're the first request. If you pay the fee, I can have it for you in a couple days."

"Any chance we could speed it up?" I asked.

"Part of the time and cost depends on how long the witness was on the stand."

From Lisa's description, it sounded like the prosecutor had wrapped her fast, so I figured the transcription wouldn't take too long or be too expensive. "Call me when it's ready. This is one of those ASAP situations."

She agreed to try to complete it by the end of the day.

Lisa's transcript was five pages of fresh ink on crisp paper. I skimmed through the boring parts about her swearing to tell the truth and the prosecutor establishing her background until she started talking about broken dreams.

LISA MELBY: It's not like when someone steals your car and you can fix a dent. My life is ruined, and my reputation can never be restored. I discover new roadblocks every time I apply for credit, an apartment, or a job. I have to convince strangers all over again that I'm not a deadbeat or even worse, a thief. This man deserves to go to prison for a long time for what he did, not just to me, but to so many others. I worked hard and took out loans to put myself through school to become a dentist. And now that will never happen.

Those words stopped me. I even went back to reread the line. In her interview with me, Lisa had claimed to be studying for a medical degree. Could the court reporter have transcribed it wrong? Could I have remembered it wrong? I checked the videotape and she definitely said "doctor." Could Lisa have simply misspoken?

I might have given her the benefit of doubt, except for two things: the pendant in my pocket exalting St. Apollonia and the manner in which Leon died.

My next call was to the registrar's office at the University of Minnesota and confirmed it: Lisa had been a dental student for her one semester there.

CHAPTER 74

The police were content to lump Akume's murder in with Jack Clemens's crimes, so I knew they would be no help.

Lisa wasn't at her apartment, nor was her car on her street. Outside the Rest in Peace Funeral Home, her vehicle was the only one in the parking lot. Lights were on in the back of the building, so I figured she must be cleaning. I pounded on the back door for more than a minute before she answered.

She was surprised to see me. "Riley, what are you doing here? Is the story running tonight?"

I assured her everything was fine. "You dropped something in my car. Let me in and I'll show you."

I expected Lisa to refuse, telling me it was against their policy to allow nonemployees in after closing. And that would make sense, considering the sensitive nature of their business, but she motioned for me to come inside and locked the bolt behind me. I followed her down the hall past the showroom of caskets.

"What going on?" she asked. "Is there a problem with the story?"

"That's what I'm here to find out."

I pulled the St. Apollonia pendant out of my jacket pocket and dangled it by its chain. "I think this belongs to you."

She didn't reach for it nor did she say anything.

"Your name is engraved on the back." I flipped it over, handing it to her. "It must be a special piece of jewelry."

"Thank you." She unhooked the clasp and hung it around her neck, tucking it inside her soft denim shirt.

"What's the significance, Lisa?"

"It was a gift."

That's when I told her I'd checked into her educational background. I didn't accuse her of lying, but I explained about the need to be accurate in any news story.

"Why did you tell me your dream was to be a doctor instead of a dentist?" I asked. "Do you think being a doctor sounded more glamorous for the cameras?"

"Definitely not. I've always wanted to be a dentist."

She turned away then, so I followed her down another hallway, past a coat rack where a tan puffy parka hung. We arrived in the embalming room with its eerie blue light. A ventilating system made a low hum. We were alone, but knowing a corpse might have laid there hours earlier was a little unnerving.

"You mentioned your St. Apollonia necklace was a gift," I said. "From who?"

"My grandma."

She explained that she'd first decided on a career as a dentist while watching the holiday classic *Rudolph the Red-Nosed Reindeer* with her grandmother. The impassioned speech by Herbie, the misfit elf who wanted to be a dentist, had settled her on that path.

"Remember the Abominable Snowman?" she asked.

"Who could forget? He was some villain."

"I loved the ending. The Abominable fingering his empty gums in bewilderment while Herbie waved the forceps in triumph. A mouthful of monster teeth piled at his feet as trophies."

Lisa was smiling with such glee I had no doubt where our conversation was going. "Yep." I tried mimicking her enthusiasm by giving her a thumbs-up. "The dentist saves the day. Well, I just wanted to make sure you got your necklace back." I wanted to leave, but she was closer to the door. I pretended to admire an anatomical wall chart of the circulatory and muscle systems of the body.

"I knew you would understand, Riley. We're on the same side. Good vanquishing evil. The world is a better place without him. He needed to be stopped."

I wasn't certain if she was talking about Leon or the Abominable, but seeing that puffy coat made me fear her. And her next words clarified everything.

"This is where it happened." She patted the steel embalming table. "I invited him over to smoke wet, but I made it so concentrated that he passed out. The first tooth was the hardest to extract."

She described the crunchy feel, followed by a satisfying yank, and spoke of her fascination watching dark blood oozing from the gap in his smile. "By the third one, I got my rhythm and decided to pull them all. I felt like a real dentist."

"Yet you lost your patient," I said. "Leon died, choking on his own blood. Did you mean to kill him?"

"No. I wanted him to wake up without teeth, just like the Abominable, but I didn't expect so much blood. The others I practiced on didn't bleed."

I remembered my autopsy discussion with Della about dead people not bleeding, and suspected Lisa was referring to corpses at the funeral home. "You pull teeth from the bodies here before they're buried?"

"Just a few to hone my technique. Some have dentures so there's nothing to work with. I just take back teeth, so their lips look natural during viewings. Dental schools train with cadavers. This way I can continue my education, like Herbie and the Abominable."

Looking back on our encounter, I realize I should have applauded Lisa for her determination and praised her for her ingenuity instead of asking questions. But that's the nature of being a journalist: asking provocative questions that sometimes backfire. Like my next one did.

"But deep down, wasn't the Abominable actually good? In the final scene he puts the star on top of Santa's Christmas tree."

Her expression told me I'd made a big mistake challenging her view of the holiday classic.

"I should just leave and let you finish cleaning, Lisa. Let's continue this another time when you're not so busy. I'll see you at Channel 3 for the story."

That's when she closed the door, shutting us inside the embalming room. "I thought we were friends, Riley, but maybe that pretty TV smile of yours can't be trusted after all."

She reached into a drawer for a shiny tool. I thought she was going to try to scare me by threatening to pull my teeth, but wasn't particularly alarmed until I saw Lisa was holding a scalpel, not pincers. I knew the kind of damage that sharp-bladed instrument could do to the living as well as the dead.

"Lisa, we're friends, remember?"

"Are you going to the police?"

"No, of course not. Are you?"

Playing dumb with her didn't work any better than it did with David Johnson. She knew I couldn't let her get away with murder. My options for escape were few.

"You've been through a lot, Lisa." I tried to talk her down. "Leon Akume may have stole your identity, but don't let him steal your soul."

She seemed to be considering my words. "It's easy for you. My life is ruined."

"That's not true, Lisa. And even if you believe that, do you want your afterlife ruined?" I urged her to pray to St. Apollonia for guidance.

Lisa fingered the medallion through her shirt and mumbled something under her breath that I could not understand. She took a step toward me. I took a step back. After all, she was the one armed with a scalpel; all I had was my wits. The blue light across her face distracted me so I didn't see her slash coming.

I screamed as the metal blade sliced the sleeve of my jacket. Everything happened so fast, I wasn't even sure if it hit my skin until the fabric turned red. I veered away as Lisa's next swipe cut the strap of my purse. The handbag fell from my shoulder, skidding across the floor.

I bumped against the embalming table, and it moved. Realizing the wheels must have been unlocked from cleaning the floor, I shoved it between me and Lisa. Like a battering ram, I pushed her against the wall. She grunted in surprise, doubled over.

So I raced for the door.

CHAPTER 75

I was confused by all the interior walls and clumsy in my new shoes. Mentally, I cursed Nicole for her fashion advice. I turned a corner, looking for the exit or somewhere to hole up, and found myself by the refrigeration unit. Two of the spaces were already occupied. It would be a cold day in hell before I'd crawl in there.

I heard Lisa coming down the hall, and realized I'd been dripping blood from the gash in my arm—a dead giveaway to my location. I waved red spatter on the refrigerator to fool Lisa into thinking I had hidden inside. The injury was not deep, and pulling my sleeve tight stopped the bleeding. I opened a door marked STORAGE.

The room was dark, so I brushed my hand across the wall for a light switch. I flipped it and was greeted by rows of closed caskets—like an aboveground cemetery.

The surplus inventory ranged from pine boxes to polished woods to stainless steel. Outside noises from the hallway sounded like was Lisa opening the refrigerator. Within minutes, she'd know I wasn't hiding in one of the body drawers. I had no doubt she'd keep looking until she found me.

My cell phone was in my purse, back in the embalming room. I was on my own.

I could think of only one ruse—and it was morbid. I switched off the lights and felt my way from casket to casket, blindly selecting one. I lifted the lid—which was heavier than I expected—and climbed inside. All the padding made the fit snug, but not uncomfortable. Because the room was already pitch-black, I didn't think closing the casket would bother me. But I was wrong. My panic didn't come from the lack of light, rather the fear of being trapped.

I'd never considered myself claustrophobic, but I'd never been shut inside a seven-foot by two-foot box—much less one with so much macabre symbolism. I could see why some people were paranoid about being buried alive.

My head rested on a pillow, the padded lid a mere six inches above my face. My breathing increased as I shuddered at the thought of suffocating. Rationally, I knew caskets must not be airtight, or bodies couldn't decompose. But there was no room for logic in my tight quarters. My hands pressed up to open the lid a crack. Even though my situation was grave, that small link to the outside seemed to calm me. So did deep, measured breaths. Even though the air smelled stuffy, my nose was drawn to the chasm.

My arms were starting to ache when I heard a door open.

Lisa was inside the storage room.

I closed the casket, hoping that when she flicked the light switch, she would see nothing amiss and simply leave. Instead, the floor creaked.

"Riley?" she whispered.

I held my breath, praying my casket would not be my final resting place. A tiny line of light was now visible across the middle, and I tried convincing myself that I was in a womb, not a tomb.

"Come out, come out. I know you're in here."

Maybe she did. Or perhaps she was just guessing. Running out of air, I braced myself to inhale softly, quietly, through my mouth. Even though it was dark, I shut my eyes. When I did,

Nick Garnett came to mind. I didn't have time to think of what that meant because a thumping noise caught my attention.

Lisa was opening the caskets, one by one. "Eeny, meeny, miny, moe."

It was like she was playing a shell game and I was the pea. Was she fantasizing about plunging her scalpel through my heart like a vampire hunter? Disposing of my body would be easy. Lisa could just bury me underneath a paying customer, and I'd be one more missing woman whose body was never found. Perhaps I could become their patron saint.

"Come on out, Riley. You know I would never hurt you."

You already have, I thought to myself.

I estimated there were a few dozen caskets in the room. Soon, Lisa would come to mine. I weighed whether I was more vulnerable waiting for her to uncover me, or if I would fare better by jumping up as if rising from the grave. But what then? I felt around for some sort of weapon. Nothing, not even car keys— they were also in my purse. I kicked loose a high heel, and an idea came to me. One hand stretched downward while my foot nudged the shoe closer until my fingers clutched the leather toe.

"Knock, knock." Lisa was tapping on the top of my casket.

The hollow sound echoed; my body tensed. I wondered if she could hear my heart beating like the deranged narrator in Edgar Allan Poe's short story.

She asked, "Who's there?" while flinging open the lid. My eyes blinked at the sudden light, but she seemed equally shocked I was actually inside. Her face was close to mine, her arms extended high, holding onto the cover.

I punched her face with the heel of my shoe. She shrieked and tried slamming the lid shut while I fought to sit up. Our ruckus tipped the casket forward off of its stand, crashing both of us to the floor where I was sandwiched between Lisa and the casket.

She seemed dazed, so I wriggled free and left. But not before she pleaded, "Stay with me, Riley. I'll turn myself in. I promise."

• • •

Two cars were parked in the lot, Lisa's and mine. Without keys I couldn't drive off; without a phone I couldn't reach help. I jogged south toward downtown Minneapolis in bare feet on snowy concrete trying to put distance between me and the Rest in Peace Funeral Home. Other storefront businesses appeared closed. This was a neighborhood that shut down at night. I waved at a transit bus but couldn't reach the stop in time.

My feet were cold, but at least I wasn't six feet under.

My biggest fear was that a hearse would pull over to offer me a ride, and Lisa would be behind the wheel. A block of pubs were ahead in the next half mile, and surely someone there, despite my disheveled appearance, would believe my story and phone the police.

CHAPTER 76

All the local television stations led their morning newscasts with the overnight fire at the Rest in Peace Funeral Home. Three bodies were discovered, but only one—a woman—was actually killed in the blaze. The other two were corpses under refrigeration awaiting burial.

Authorities suspected arson.

Della, the medical examiner, sat across me with a file folder labeled LISA MELBY. "I'll keep it simple. Suicide."

"I shouldn't have left her," I said.

"If you hadn't, *your* picture might be on my murder wall right now. She proved herself capable of violence against herself as well as others."

"Can you tell me anything more about her death?"

"This case was rough. Are you sure you want the full account? Some things you can't unknow."

"Tell me." Maybe the viewers wouldn't need all the gory details, but I did.

Della shuffled through the papers before looking up at me with melancholy eyes. "Lisa Melby climbed into a casket, doused herself with embalming fluid, and lit a match. Think self-cremation."

I'd been right. Lisa was crazy.

"If there was a note, it went up in flames with her," Della continued, "but we found this around her neck."

She handed me the pendant—once silver, now blackened. Even though damaged, I could still feel the texture of the outline of St. Apollonia.

In her demented state, Lisa must have convinced herself she was emulating the martyr. But she was mistaken. There was no honor in her death, only tragedy. While she had escaped being judged here on earth, I prayed another judge might be merciful.

CHAPTER 77

Despite the discord in the newsroom, or maybe because of it, Bryce insisted that the Mall of America wedding coverage proceed as planned. "Viewers need some upbeat news. There's been too much blood on our air."

That meant Scott would have to broadcast live on location for the ceremony even though he'd lost his exuberance for the story as well as his line in the film. Nicole was assigned to wait outside with a photographer and report on any same-sex marriage protests.

As long as I didn't have to cover the event, I didn't care.

With our news hole filled with bridal fluff, there was no pressure on me to chase down real stories, so I retreated to my office pretending to organize my files regarding Lisa, Akume, and Jack so they could be sent down to the station basement for storage.

What I was really doing was reliving the drama of the last forty-eight hours and despising myself for not having prevented Lisa's death.

I used to think the key to my success as a journalist was seeing the world clearly a couple of seconds faster than everyone else. That was enough to give me an edge on the street and on the screen. But clearly, I was mistaken about my talent. As proof, Lisa's death scene played out, over and over, in slow motion whenever I shut my eyes. I wished I could shut my ears because I kept imagining her screams after she ignited herself.

Della was right. As much as you might want to, there are some things you can't unknow.

This was my worst Valentine's Day ever. Head on my desk, I hungered for the sleep that would not come to my bed. The sound of a ringing phone took me out of my lethargy. It was Ozzie. "I'm in Bryce's office. He wants you here immediately."

I didn't hesitate, figuring news must be breaking. Both men were upset, and Ozzie looked pale. Miles, our attorney, was right behind me, having also been summoned.

"Shut the door," Bryce said.

"I just got an anonymous call that there's a bomb at the Mall of America," Ozzie said. "Couldn't tell if it was a man or a woman. The phone number was blocked."

"I think we have to assume it's related to the wedding," I said. "There's plenty of people who have reasons to want it stopped. Could be a jilted lover. Or someone opposed to even the idea of gay marriage being portrayed in a film."

"We need to contact the police immediately," Miles said. "This is their problem, not ours."

"You mean dial 9-1-1?" Ozzie asked.

"Let me try someone faster." I called Garnett's cell phone. "The director of mall security." He'd be busy, and I wasn't even sure he'd answer after our last encounter at Stella's. Perhaps he'd be curious when he saw my number. Pick up. Pick up. I begged silently. Please, Nick.

And he did, even sounding sympathetic. "I realize you're probably a mess right now, Riley, after that funeral home business, but seriously, this isn't a good time to talk. I'll call you later. I promise."

"The timing is worse than you think." I quickly briefed him on the threat situation and explained that I was putting him on speaker with my boss and the station lawyer.

"We get numerous bomb threats," Garnett said. "That's why we constantly make rounds with explosive-sniffing dogs and watch for suspicious packages. Our K-9 team hasn't signaled any alerts. And we can't close down the mall every time someone makes a wild phone call, or we'd never be open for business."

"So you don't consider this a credible threat?" I asked.

"We will certainly share your information with Bloomington Police, but we're already at our highest level of security because of the wedding film, and without any specifics, we're not inclined to change our mode of operation."

There were other things I wanted to ask him and other things he probably wanted to say, but we both kept our conversation professional because of the other parties listening. He thanked me and I thanked him, while fearing it was a formality on both ends.

"So, air or not air?" Bryce asked.

I didn't want responsibility for the decision, so I kept quiet and let the station management hash it out.

"I vote no air," said Ozzie. "If the bomb is a hoax, we look stupid. If there is an explosion, we can say we informed authorities, and took our cues from them."

"We have fulfilled our duty as citizens," Miles said. "You decide whether we have a duty to viewers."

"All right, no air," Bryce said. "But, Riley, I want you to head out to the mall in case something happens."

"You want me there if the place gets bombed? Am I that disposable?"

"We've already decided this is a long shot," he said. "If we thought the threat was legitimate, we'd air it. I think the caller is trying to use us to cause a panic, but I'd feel better with another set of eyes on the ground."

"Should we tell Scott and Nicole?" Ozzie asked.

"No," said Bryce. "I don't want them distracted from their assignments."

"But shouldn't we let them know there's a chance of danger?" I asked.

"You heard the man," he answered. "Not credible."

I knew it was nothing personal; we were all replaceable under Bryce's business model. But that still didn't make me feel any better heading to the Mall of America. Under orders to get there pronto, and knowing the mall parking ramp would be full, I hailed a cab from the hotel across the street and handed the driver a fifty-dollar bill.

CHAPTER 78

Explosive-sniffing dogs and their K-9 trainers paced around the mall rotunda, sticking their noses in wedding gowns to rule out a bomb being smuggled by a bride. From my point of view overhead, it was a comical sight.

I couldn't get through the security line or close to the action without a filming pass or special media credentials for the wedding. I had to be content with sticking my head around the shoulders of other onlookers on the third-floor balcony.

The film crew was positioning the extras below in a sea of black and white. I didn't see Rachel or Ricky, but figured they'd be escorted in by bodyguards at the last minute. An elderly couple was admonishing me to stop pushing, when I recognized someone below who stuck out because he wasn't complying with the tuxedo dress code.

He jerked his head around, like he was afraid someone was watching him. His hand was in a briefcase as if hiding something. Just the kind of behavior mall security staff might deem suspicious and worthy of a security interview. And then I realized the bomb call contained a clue.

I tried to keep an eye on him, but he disappeared into a crowd waiting near the elevator.

I called Garnett, just in case my hunch was right, but this time he didn't answer his phone. With so many people calling, taking photos and sending text messages at the same time, I wasn't sure my call was even going through. Sometimes during stadium concerts or sporting events, the cell network gets jammed by all the activity.

Down the hall, the Chapel of Love was open for business, and a rack of designer wedding gowns beckoned me with an idea of how to get past mall security and into the filming perimeter.

White was the new camouflage.

My own wedding dress had been short, cheap, and polyester, bought on the fly in Vegas for a whirlwind ceremony now too painful to remember. I'd never had the princess wedding most little girls dream about, but this was not the time to search for the perfect gown.

I dashed toward the dresses on display at the bridal shop. All were floor length with unique features and challenges. I disregarded a mermaid-shaped one because it looked too tight to run fast. Another had a long train that might get caught on an escalator. Fear of a wardrobe malfunction made me rule out strapless designs.

A saleswoman offered me professional assistance. "What season is your wedding?"

"I need a dress now," I told her. "Today. Right this very minute. No time for alterations or questions." I handed her my credit card to prove I was serious. "Something that will fit well enough."

She sized me up. "How about this?" She held out a scoop-necked design with a silver belt and black floral beading in diagonal rows throughout the skirt.

"Too distinctive," I said. "I need all white. With easy movement."

"This might work." The dress had a tight bodice with a wide ball gown.

I was about to say fine, when I noticed the back had a corset closure. "That'll take too long to put on. I want a plain zipper."

She pulled out a halter top with an A-line skirt. "The sweetheart neckline is flattering on most figures."

"Where's the changing room?"

My clothes fell to the floor as I disrobed. I reached behind to unhook my bra. Stripped down to a pair of nude panties, I stepped into the silky disguise, and struggled to fasten the back.

The woman knocked softly. "Need any help in there?"

I opened the door and turned around. "Zip me."

Fifteen seconds later, I looked beautiful, except for my frizzy hair. I wished my mom could see me. I considered texting her a photo, but time was too precious. I was on a mission.

"Just ring me up," I told the saleswoman as she was explaining the store's no-return policy regarding wedding gowns. "Oh, and I'll also take this garter."

I slipped a wide vintage lace one over my thigh, making sure it was snug enough to hold my cell phone in place since my dress had no pockets. It did have a built-in brassiere with enough give to hide my wallet. I'd seen what could happen when identification went missing.

The clerk tried to up-sell me a bridal headpiece and I was about to decline when an idea hit. "Anything that might cover my face?"

She reached for a floral lace hair comb and tucked my locks behind my ears. "This one has a face veil attached."

The French netting covered my eyes and nose, but didn't obscure my vision. It actually looked quite romantic.

"How about shoes?" The clerk suggested some white strappy heels with rhinestones.

"Nope. These will have to do." I raised my skirt to show off a pair of worn brown loafers. The four-figure price on my credit

card receipt astounded me, but I signed anyway before racing
out the door.

The saleswoman followed, shouting after me. "Miss, you forgot your clothes!"

"Keep them," I yelled back.

CHAPTER 79

I had lost sight of my target while shopping for my dress. I moved from one escalator to another to reach the ground floor, apologizing as I cut in front of people who were holding shopping bags and small children. My costume worked, getting me past security and into the mall rotunda without warranting a second glance.

I was one bride among a hundred.

Then we heard some music coming from the indoor amusement park, but not any wedding song I recognized. Everybody watched as a young man in sweatpants and a T-shirt danced to a rap tune, arms waving in the air, his shoulders spasming to the beat. Ten seconds later, a dozen bystanders joined in, moving across benches and fences, legs kicking and hips swaying. One even jumped on the table of a coffee shop and spun around.

"It's the Harlem Shake!" a groom shouted.

I had heard this Internet dance craze was sweeping schools, workplaces, and sports arenas. The giant wedding party started hip-hopping rhythmically while spectators cheered. I prayed Bryce wasn't watching, or he'd make us tape a Channel 3 version on the new set to post online to be relatable to younger viewers.

The crowd parted as Rachel and Ricky made a grand entrance to the rap beat. While they mimicked the dancers, I saw the man I'd been pursuing and moved toward him, still suspicious.

I wasn't sure if the timing of the music was spontaneous or choreographed, but it provided the distraction the man needed to pull something from his pocket and fling it onto the ground. A loud noise followed.

I tackled Scott before he could get far, but already smoke was billowing in the air. My dress ripped as we wrestled on the floor of the mall rotunda. He held the advantage of not having to roll around in a full skirt or worry about a wardrobe snafu, yet I managed to keep him from fleeing by holding on tight to his necktie until security staff separated us.

The smoke was actually fog and slowly dissipated as the source was identified as dry ice in a travel mug filled with hot water. Most of the crowd seemed unfazed by the commotion, figuring it was special effects from the film.

Scott recognized me when the veil netting fell off my head, and he tried to smack me in the nose. But this was one of those moments when I *did* see life faster and was able to dodge the brunt of the blow. His swing was enough to get him led away in handcuffs. By then the security camera operators downstairs had replayed the surveillance video and verified that Channel 3's news anchor was behind the threatening incident.

Nick Garnett had heard about the commotion and arrived on the scene. He was more surprised than Scott to see me dressed to wed. "Hello, Riley. You look lovely." He politely ignored the stains and tear in my dress, although he did slip me a handkerchief and mention that my arm was bleeding.

"So how did you wind up in the middle of this mess?" he asked.

"Remember the bomb call?" I dabbed the blood from my scalpel wound. "Ozzie said it rang up as a 'blocked' number. That means the caller phoned the assignment desk direct, rather than being transferred through the Channel 3 switchboard. Not too many folks other than station employees or media contacts have that number. When I noticed Scott acting odd, it fell together."

"Heckuva job, Riley."

"Are you being sarcastic or sincere?"

"I meant it."

For a second, his eyes seemed to hint at something much more personal. Then the wedding march began to play with a slow crescendo. The ceremony was about to begin. All around us, brides and grooms smiled, held hands, and awaited their big moment.

I tried to retreat from the wedding mob, but Nick startled me by raising my hand to his lips and kissing my fingers. "That's not all I meant. Riley Spartz, will you do me the honor of becoming my wife?"

"What? Hush, Nick. No jokes. These people are about to get married. Stunt or not, to them it's real."

"I know. And I want it to be our wedding, too. I'm tired of brooding over why we're not together. Let's end the drama right here right now and not let this moment pass us by."

I looked around to see if anyone was listening to us, but all attention was on the minister and Rachel and Ricky.

"Nick, we can't just horn in on this ceremony and exchange vows on thirty seconds' notice. Weddings need more than love to be legal. They need rings. And witnesses. And marriage licenses."

"Rings can come later. And there's plenty of witnesses around. Plus, I have our marriage license right here."

He pulled his wallet from his pants pocket and removed a folded piece of paper—the license we filled out months ago at the courthouse after we first became engaged.

"It's good for six months, so it's still valid anywhere in Minnesota," he said. "When this song ends, one hundred couples will promise to have and to hold each other. I want us to make it one hundred and one. I hate to take the romance out of this moment, and the anticipation out of our nuptials, but you only have about ten seconds to accept my proposal and say 'I do.'"

I was so touched that he had carried our marriage license

with him all this time that I couldn't speak, but I realized few people get a second chance at a once in a lifetime spontaneous moment.

"Please, Riley." He held my shoulders and gazed into my eyes. "I'll say anything you want. I'll do anything you say. Just as long as you tell me yes."

"Just shut up, Nick. You had me at 'hello.'"

He smiled like this was the happiest day of his life and replied, "Renée Zellweger, *Jerry Maguire*, 1996."

"And, Nick, unlike *Annie Hall*, they do live happily ever after."

The music stopped and we joined the crowd of eager lovers, pledging to love and cherish each other for better or for worse. And when the judge instructed the grooms to kiss their brides, he locked his lips against mine while rose petals fell from above.

I closed my eyes to protect the moment, and when I opened them, Velma was standing beside us, also wearing a white dress. The last thing my wedding day needed was a cat fight. Still, I was about to tell her to back off and find her own man, when she confused me by congratulating us.

"Same to you and Ellen," Garnett said.

"Thanks," she answered. "We're just glad to be able to get married like everyone else."

That's when I noticed Velma was holding hands with another woman—the security guard from the protest. I glanced back and forth between them and realized the only romance between Velma and Garnett had been in my jealous mind.

I embraced my husband and whispered in his ear. "Honey, I'm so sorry for doubting you."

As our bodies pressed close, he kissed my neck and my cell phone started buzzing on my thigh underneath my gown. We both felt the unwelcome interruption. Nick knelt and laughed as he hiked up my dress, removed my garter, and handed me the phone. The call had come from the Channel 3 newsroom, along with a voicemail message.

"Somehow I don't think they're calling to congratulate me," I said. "Now that Scott's in custody, Bryce probably wants me to do a live shot from the mall."

"That's not a call you need to return." Nick hit the off button on my phone and put it in his suit pocket. "You're on your honeymoon. I'll drive. You pick what direction."

"I need to stop at home and pack some clothes first."

"You won't be needing any clothes."

But there was a bonus to getting married in the nation's largest shopping mall. I ducked into a lingerie shop to buy something special for my wedding night, anyway.

EPILOGUE

We cropped our wedding photo from one of the Mall of America's surveillance cameras. Hands clasped, facing each other, it was a grainy but real moment frozen in time.

The crowd thinned out after the ceremony, and Nick was carrying me over an imaginary threshold when I heard my name being yelled from the second-level balcony over the rotunda.

It was my parents.

"Riley, wait for us!" Mom rushed to the glass elevator while Dad limped behind her, and within a couple minutes they were plastering us with hugs and kisses.

"The whole thing was just beautiful." My mom wiped tears from her face on the sleeve of the beaver fur coat. "I knew you wouldn't get married without me."

The only one disappointed at being left out was Father Mountain. Apparently, I'd once promised him he could perform my next wedding ceremony. Instead, he later blessed our union.

The film *We Do* opened on all fourteen screens at the Mall of America movie theater. Garnett and I attended the premiere with the other wedding couples, including Velma and Ellen. The film was panned by critics. Rachel and Ricky filed for divorce one month later.

• • •

Anchor Scott Ramus was charged with making terrorist threats, incitement to riot, and creating a public disturbance at the Mall of America. Defense attorney Benny Walsh won an acquittal by arguing his client was temporarily insane. The station invoked an "unsuitability" clause in his contract to fire him anyway.

He wasn't the only member of the Channel 3 News family to be sent packing.

Ends up, the reason that so many promotions for the new set were airing on Channel 3 was that Bryce was running them over commercials for the network's own prime-time entertainment shows. The network owned the station, so it fired Bryce, ending his dream of becoming my boss's boss's boss.

The Minnesota Legislature privatized the license-plate tracking data during their session, but did not restrict placement of body grip traps.

Even though I was eligible for the $25,000 reward for information leading to the capture and arrest of Jack Clemens, I waived the money, choosing to donate it to the crime victims fund instead.

That was nothing compared to the millions federal authorities were able to seize from Jack's offshore bank accounts, now that they had the numbers.

The fish painting hangs in Stella's restaurant. And every once in a while Garnett and I dine at the table next to it. On our anniversary, he told me that the moment he knew he couldn't live without me was the moment I threw my wine in his face.

• • •

When police searched Lisa's apartment they found a tooth in her desk drawer that matched Leon Akume's. That piece of evidence cleared Jack Clemens of having anything to do with the man's murder. Without that, all they had had was my word about her confession. Even the puffy coat had been burned in the fire.

As for Lloyd Martin's death behind bars while posing as Jack Clemens, the former barber's fingernails had scraped enough of his attacker's DNA to identify him from the felon database. But that inmate refused to talk, so no one else—in prison or out—was implicated in the protection scheme. Not even Scarface.

Jack's ankle healed enough that he was scheduled to be transported to serve time in a maximum security prison. A guard directed him to strip down and bend over, then handed him an orange jumpsuit that was much too big, a dingy T-shirt, threadbare boxers, and a pair of socks that wouldn't stay up.

After an hour in a holding cell, Jack heard voices and the sound of chains rattling. Soon he was shackled, handcuffs attached to a chain around his waist and leg irons digging into the soft skin of his ankles.

He was no longer Jack Clemens, rather a living metaphor of Jacob Marley. *I wear the chain I forged in life. I made it link by link, yard by yard. It is a ponderous chain.*

With baby steps, Inmate 16780-59 followed others down the hall and onto the prison bus. His final destination was Leavenworth, Kansas—five hundred miles away. But there was no telling how many days the journey would take. Long before they stopped for the night, the bus was already reeking.

ACKNOWLEDGMENTS

Thanks always to my editor, Emily Bestler, for keeping me on course; to assistant editor Megan Reid, for bringing fresh eyes to my series. Their editorial suggestions made *Delivering Death* better.

But a book needs many hands to bring it to readers, so my gratitude extends to all who helped with the publication: Kate Cetrulo, Mellony Torres, Hillary Tisman, Isolde Sauer, Toby Yuen, Fausto Bozza, and Kyle Kabel.

To my agent Susan Ginsburg, of Writer's House, for staying calm when I am not; to her witty assistant, Stacy Testa.

I've been able to live much of my TV news research, but have needed help with other elements of life and death. Thanks to all the law-and-order folks in Minnesota who shared insight into white-collar crime and identity theft: Doug Kelley and Josiah Lamb (Kelley, Wolters & Scott, PA), Pat Henry (Minnesota Financial Crime Task Force), and John Ristad (Ramsey County Attorney's Office); for allowing me a behind-the-scenes tour of the Mall of America: Major Doug Reynolds, top security dude, and Dan Jasper, public relations honcho; for teaching me about trapping, Jason Abraham of the Minnesota Department of Natural Resources; once again, to Vernon Geberth, author of *Practical Homicide Investigation*; and to Dr. D. P. (Doug) Lyle, author of *Forensic for Dummies* and *Forensics: A Guide for Writers;* and to Taelor Johnson at Mueller Lake Mortuary for aiding my research by letting me lie inside a closed casket and, most important, for letting me out again, so I could finish writing this book.

To my crack reading team—Kevyn Burger, Trish Van Pilsum, and Caroline Lowe—by which I mean skilled, not addicted, for laughing and crying with me over the years.

And now for the obligatory list of relatives who like seeing their names in print: Ruth Kramer; Mike Kramer; Bonnie and Roy Brang; Teresa, Galen with Rachel Neuzil; Richard and Oti Kramer; Mary Kramer; Steve and Mary Kay Kramer, along with Matthew and Elizabeth; Kathy and Jim Loecher with Adriana and Zach; Christina Kramer; Jerry and Elaine Kramer; Mae Klug and all who love her; George and Shirley Kimball; George Kimball, Shen Fei with Shi Shenyu; Nick Kimball and Gannet Tseggai with Helena; Jenny and Kile Nadeau with Daniel; Jessica and Richie Miehe with Lucy and Pearl; Becca and Seth Engberg with their baby girl; David and Alyssa Nadeau; Mary and Dave Benson with Davin; Steve Kimball and Susan Jenkins with Craig and Shaela; James Kimball; Paul Kimball; and numerous far-flung cousins and other kin.

Besides fans, every author needs a family, and I am lucky to have Andrew and Alex Kimball, sons who love to read, in my corner, along with little Barlow Kimball and his parents, Katie and Jake, and out west, Joey and David Kimdon with Aria and Arbor.

But my best fan is my soul mate, Joe.